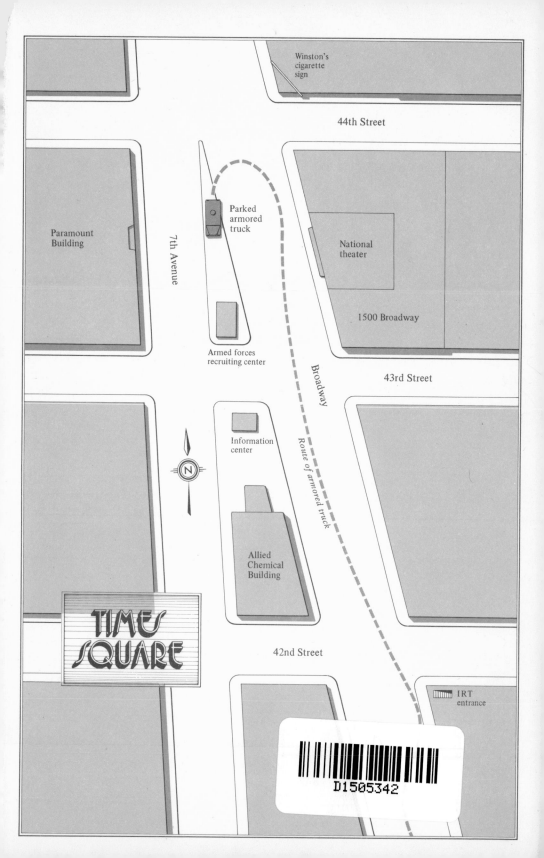

The Kidnapping of the President

CHARLES TEMPLETON

The Kidnapping of the President

A NOVEL

McClelland and Stewart Limited

0-7710-8458-7

The Canadian Publishers
McClelland and Stewart Limited
25 Hollinger Road, Toronto

Printed and bound in Canada

By Charles Templeton

Jesus

The Kidnapping of the President

"Presidents can never be protected from every potential threat. The Secret Service's difficulty in meeting its protective responsibility varies with the activities and the nature of the occupant of the Office of the Presidency and his willingness to conform to plans for his safety."

> Excerpt from the Warren Commission Report
> on the assassination of
> President John F. Kennedy

"The Secret Service agent on protective duty lives on the brink of disaster. His job borders on the impossible."

> Rufus W. Youngblood
> Special Agent in Charge of the
> White House Detail (Retired)
> United States Secret Service

At exactly five A.M. on the Monday prior to *"the first Tuesday after the first Monday in November,"* the date of the off-year Congressional elections, 23 teams of police officers in the New York City area —acting on information supplied by the United States Secret Service —entered the domiciles of and arrested 19 suspects on a variety of charges ranging from suspicion of seditious activity to possession of an unlicensed firearm.

In the course of the arrests, three handguns and a scope-mounted .38 calibre rifle were seized. In a boarding house on Bedford Avenue in Brooklyn, a suspect fired three shots at the arresting officers, wounding one of them slightly. The suspect escaped. In all, four of the men on the Secret Service list were not apprehended.

The suspects were removed to nearby police stations and held without bail. Instructions from the Secret Service were to release them at ten A.M. by which time it was anticipated that the political rally in Herald Square would be finished and the President en route to the second engagement of his final day of campaigning.

As it happened, none of the suspects were released until the following morning.

Part One

Chapter One

The house was set back two hundred feet from the gravel road behind a sagging snow fence against which leaves had piled in drifts. Unbroken by porches or wings, its two stories reared from the crumbling concrete of an unfinished basement and peaked in a steeply pitched slate roof surmounted by two rusted lightning rods. The faded red brick was eroded, the wood trim was blistered and peeling. Beyond the house, a barn, moored to the back door by a footpath, appeared to be afloat on a sea of undulating weeds. It had never been painted, but forty years had put their sheen on the weathered boards and they gleamed bleakly in the half-light of a waning moon.

At the rear of the house a door opened and a silhouette loomed on the pool of light flooding from the doorway. A man emerged and descended a short set of stairs. Walking slowly — each foot placed deliberately before the other, hands held before him — he followed the footpath to the barn, hooked the toe of a shoe under one of the two great doors, pulled it open and slipped inside.

Within the barn, at its center, starkly lit by a naked 500-watt bulb, was an armored truck of the type commonly seen on the streets of most North American cities: its color dove-gray, its utilitarian shape conceding nothing to streamlining. On its sides was the familiar insignia BRINK'S and superimposed on a broad white band the words SECURITY SINCE 1859.

Walking as circumspectly as though he were on a tightrope, holding with both hands a rectangular bottle filled with a clear liquid, the man crossed to the truck and entered it. On the floor in a rear corner of the van there was an unpainted wooden box, its hinged top open. He kneeled before it and carefully fitted the bottle into an insulated receptacle suspended on all sides by small metal springs. In an adjoining compartment, neatly arranged and clamped to the floor, were a timing mechanism, a blasting cap and a dozen sticks of dynamite. The bottle secured, he made a final check, lowered the lid and fastened it tightly with two wing nuts.

Moving to the driver's seat, he started the motor. When it was running smoothly, he depressed the clutch and shifted through the gears. Checking against a printed list propped on the dashboard, he operated the windshield wipers, the ventilating and heating systems, the electric doorlocks, the headlights and the directional signals. Satisfied, he turned off the motor and flipped a switch on an amplifier mounted under the instrument panel. In a moment there was a hiss from a speaker. He picked up a microphone and blew into it. A brief roar filled the barn.

He turned off the amplifier, stepped from the truck and slowly circled it, kneeling with a gauge at each wheel to measure the tire pressure. That done, he went to a nearby table, picked up a gun belt, and strapped it about his waist. He pulled the gun from the holster, spun the cylinder, and to his surprise saw that his hands were trembling.

Roberto Saldivar Moreno was surprised because he had been certain his emotions were entirely under control. There was no reason to be nervous: Had he not come to this moment as the result of ten months of meticulous planning and an unremitting commitment to the task? Every contingency had been isolated and considered. He was ready; the enemy was not. The plan could fail, and of course, the stakes were enormous, but for lesser goals and with infinitely less preparation he had taken far greater risks. Beyond that, Roberto Moreno believed with the zealot's certainty that he had been borne to this moment on the tide of an historic imperative and could not fail.

And, granted the events of his life, there was a certain inevitability in his being at this particular place on this particular day. From his teens — in emulation of his idol, Ché Guevara — he had lived as a dedicated revolutionary in a half dozen Latin American countries and had been chosen for the mission on which he was now embarked because, of all the members of *El Mano Verde,* he was unquestionably the best qualified. His English was perfect — a result of his years as a tourist guide in his native Antigua, Guatemala — his voice was soft and his manner was gentle, yielding no hint of the contained rage yeasting beneath the surface. He was a tall man, and the light gray uniform he was wearing — identical in every detail to that worn by Brink's guards — did not hide the fact that he was heavily muscled and fit. A relative unknown among Latin American leftists, he had never been either a leader or an official in any of the guerrilla groups he had served with and had never been arrested or jailed, and while the United States Central Intelligence Agency had a file on him, it was thin and in need of updating.

The only evidence of his Latin extraction was, perhaps, the glossy black hair that emerged from beneath his officer's cap to form carefully crafted sideburns. His skin was fair, and although he had shaved within the hour, the hint of a heavy beard was visible. The most notable feature of his face was his eyes: Set too closely together under heavy black eyebrows, they were a gem-hard emerald green, a genetic bequest from his Irish maternal grandmother. A small pale scar curved upward from one corner of his mouth suggesting a mirthless smile even when his face was in repose. When each day he shaved, it was a reminder of the police truncheon that had fractured his cheekbone and broken off six teeth. The scar was pale now and almost invisible; when he was angry it flamed red.

He picked up four canvas money sacks from the table, reached through the open door of the truck and placed them on the floor. As he did so, the barn door opened and what appeared to be a short, dumpy Brink's guard entered, carrying in his arms a folded gray blanket on which rested a pliofilm-wrapped loaf of bread, a sealed two-quart jar of water and a metal chamberpot. Closer scrutiny revealed that the guard was a woman. Her shoulder-length blond hair had been coiled under a dark brown male wig, a thick gunfighter-style mustache was affixed to her upper lip, and under the ill-fitting uniform she was wearing a woolen suit with a culotte skirt.

Linda Rodriguez was not pleased with the lumpy figure she presented. At thirty-one she was a full-bodied woman who drew pleasure from the knowledge that her figure was superior to what it had been at eighteen. Unlike Moreno she was tanned, and her coloring set off the blackness of her eyes and the strong white teeth

11

now barely visible behind the mustache. As with Moreno, her normal appearance belied her role. Though she was a convinced leftist, was trained in karate and was an extraordinary marksman with a light rifle or pistol, she had been chosen for the assignment only because the plan required a man-woman team and she was the best qualified of the three who had volunteered.

She went directly to the truck and placed the things she was carrying on the floor behind the driver's seat. As she emerged, Moreno was replacing the radiator cap.

"Is everything all right?" she asked. Her voice was a trifle strained.

"Seems to be," he said. "She should have had a road test, though. She's an old clunker." He slammed down the hood and checked that it was securely latched. "House closed up?"

"Yes."

"How's the time?"

"A minute past six."

"Time to go."

He climbed into the driver's seat and started the motor. As he turned on the headlights, Linda touched a switch and extinguished the lights in the barn. She swung open both doors, and when the truck had passed through, closed and padlocked them, threw the key into the weeds and climbed into the passenger seat. Moreno let out the clutch and plowed through the waist-high weeds. Pausing at the road, he turned left and slowly accelerated, heading south toward the Palisades Interstate Parkway and New York City, some thirty-seven miles distant.

A fine, misting rain had begun to fall.

Adam Northfield Scott, the President of the United States, was not pleased with his appearance. He was sufficiently aware of the political importance of the way he looked for the wan visage looking back at him from the mirror in the Lincoln bedroom to give him some concern. Two years earlier, when he was campaigning for the Presidency, one of the Washington columnists — Lisagor? Reston? — had written that the craggy handsomeness of his face was worth a million female votes, and while this did not impress him, for he was not a vain man, he was pragmatist enough to realize that his physical appearance was a sizable political asset.

The face in the mirror was that of a man in his late fifties. He was in fact fifty-two but, tanned and rested, his enormous vitality normally shucked off a half dozen years. At the moment he was neither tanned nor rested and was conscious of the accumulated tension across his shoulders and at the base of his skull; familiar signs of fatigue still there despite the twenty lengths of the White House pool he had just completed.

Adam Scott had first come to national attention during his initial bid for a seat in the Senate, his ascendancy owing as much to timing as to talent. A relatively obscure dark horse with only six years' experience in the House, he had achieved an astounding upset, ousting the man who had held the seat for twenty-four years and whose grasp on the apparatus of power in the state was commonly believed beyond loosing. In the course of the campaign, Adam — using the investigative skills he had learned in his years as a journalist — had uncovered a mare's-nest of bribery, kickbacks and criminal alliances but, for all that, was trailing in the polls. The event that thrust him to victory happened two days before the election. As he was walking home from his campaign headquarters in the early evening, a man stepped from behind a construction-site hoarding and fired two shots at him. The first missed. The second struck a rib, ricocheted, ripped a ragged hole through a lung and lodged in his left shoulder. He was in hospital under sedation, his condition critical, when he was declared elected. When three weeks later the gunman was arrested and was found to be a hired killer, the media reacted almost as to a cue. The story was exploited to the limit. The nation, hungry for a hero, saw in Adam the incarnation of courage and integrity it had been yearning for, and within months he had become the darling of the journalists and the odds-on favorite to capture his party's Presidential nomination. He won the nomination (after a fight) and the election (by a landslide) but it was a personal victory and he failed to carry the party with him to a majority in either the Senate or the House.

In an effort to correct this imbalance, he had been junketing about the country for the past six weeks, campaigning with a zeal unprecedented in off-year elections. With the vote tomorrow, the last bases would be touched today with rallies in New York City, Boston and Philadelphia, and he felt a slight lift in his spirits at the realization that tomorrow night, as soon as the results were clear, he would be on his way to a ten-day respite in the Caribbean sun.

There was a gentle knock on the door. He called out, "Come," and Jim Rankin, his Press Secretary, poked his head through the door.

"Good morning, sir," he said. "Dave Christopher's here."

"Send him in."

Dave Christopher was the senior Washington correspondent for the *New York Times*. The early morning appointment had been agreed to because no reporters would be allowed aboard the Presidential jet on the three-city tour and because Adam would not otherwise be able to find the time before leaving on his vacation. When making the request, Christopher had been apologetic but insistent: He was doing a piece for the *Times* magazine on the fifteenth anniversary of John Kennedy's death on November 22nd and had an inflexible deadline.

As the reporter entered the bedroom — slightly taken aback that the President was dressed only in shorts — Adam told him that he'd have to settle for an interview on the run, took a shirt from a drawer and began to dress. Christopher began with a series of questions about Kennedy's political legacy and then turned to the assassination.

"I don't think I know your view on the conspiracy theory," he said.

"You mean, do I think it was a complex plot?"

"Were there more people involved than Oswald?"

"I don't think so. No."

"Why not?"

Adam inserted a cufflink. "Mostly because I've seen no hard evidence to support it."

"A lot of people find it impossible to believe that Oswald could have done it by himself."

"I don't know why. Most assassination attempts have been made by individuals."

"That's true. Is there a reason?"

Adam headed for the bathroom and stood before the mirror knotting his tie. Christopher followed and leaned against the doorframe. "I think it's because you have to be some kind of nut to try. It's precisely because he *is* irrational that the assassin dismisses the risk. A group would have enough sense to realize that, while it's not difficult to have a go at the President, it's impossible to get away with it. Look at the record . . . they never do."

"But the man who shot you wasn't acting as an individual. Couldn't it have been the same with Oswald?"

"You're comparing apples and oranges. I wasn't the President and the two instances are in no way similar. I was alone on the street, I had no bodyguards . . . it was easy. But it isn't with the President. I doubt that you could find a professional gunman who'd even consider it; he'd know he hadn't one chance in a million of getting away with it."

Christopher studied him as he adjusted the knot. "You're certainly objective about it. Doesn't the risk worry you?"

Adam passed him, heading for the closet. "Of course it does." He emerged, removing a pair of trousers from a hanger and tossing the hanger on the bed. "There's a risk, of course; there's also a risk in crossing the street."

"If you'll allow me," Christopher said, smiling, "*now* who's comparing apples and oranges?"

Adam zipped his trousers. "Touché."

"I got the impression, chatting with the Secret Service people earlier, that they take a very dim view of your indifference to security: your insistence on using an open car, for instance, and appearing at outdoor rallies like today's in New York City. They tell me that under such conditions it's simply impossible for them to guarantee your safety."

Adam slipped into his jacket. "To paraphrase: The Secret Service was made for the President and not the President for the Secret Service."

"But in a climate like today's, aren't you inviting trouble?"

Adam shrugged.

There was a silence while Christopher made some notes. He looked up. "Will you permit a personal question?" he asked.

"Depends."

"Would you describe yourself as a courageous man?"

Adam didn't answer for a moment. He had moved to an escritoire and was putting papers in an attaché case.

"I won't pursue it if you'd rather not," Christopher said.

"No, that's okay. Courageous? — I don't think so. When I think about the danger it scares the hell out of me. But the fact is, I don't really have an option. It's part of the job, and if I permitted myself to worry about the possibility of being killed, I wouldn't get it done. So I dismiss the risk."

"That's what you said a would-be assassin does."

Adam grinned. "And I said he was nuts — right?" He snapped the attaché case closed. "Maybe that's one of the qualifications for the job."

There was a tap on the door and Joan Scott entered. She was a handsome woman whose patrician features and conservatively elegant clothes communicated good breeding.

"You and your open cars," she said, patting her coiffure. "I've got more lacquer on me than a Chinese chest." She went to Adam and planted a kiss on his cheek.

"Dave Christopher. *New York Times*," Adam said.

"Oh," said Joan, turning. "Sorry. I didn't see you."

"Speaking of open cars," Adam said, "that's what Mr. Christopher's been talking about. And about Jack Kennedy."

"Oh. . . . "

"How do *you* feel about it, Mrs. Scott?"

"About Jack Kennedy?"

"About Dallas. . . . The whole thing."

"It's a subject I never discuss."

"I mean . . . "

"I mean *never*."

Christopher flushed. "Sorry."

He asked a few more questions of Adam while folding his copypaper and putting it in a jacket pocket. After a few pleasantries he let himself out. When the door was closed, Joan said, "I hope I wasn't too short with him."

"You said it all, love," Adam said, smiling.

He reached into the closet for a topcoat and put it on. Joan watched him affectionately. "You look a bit tired," she said.

"A bit tired, the lady says. I may well go down in history as the first President of the United States to expire in office of an advanced case of bloodshot eyes and sagging jowls."

"That's not *all* that's sagging," Joan said archly. Adam sucked in his stomach. "That, too," she laughed.

"Lies. All lies," Adam said, taking her arm with an exaggerated firmness. They left the bedroom, descended the staircase and left the White House by a rear door, picking up four Secret Service agents as they emerged.

"Four of you today?" the President asked.

"Mr. Regan's orders, sir. Double coverage today."

The Presidential helicopter, Marine One, was ready, squatting on its pad. A sergeant snapped a salute and gave Joan a hand up the stairs. Adam followed.

"New York, New York. It's a wonderful town," he sang gloomily.

As Joan fastened her seatbelt, the rotors began to spin and the usual apprehension drew her stomach muscles taut. She was wishing that the man from the *Times* hadn't raised the subject of John Kennedy and Dallas, especially after her conversation yesterday with Gerry Regan. But as the helicopter lifted from the lawn and swept off above the treetops, she deliberately thrust the thought from her mind, as she had done so many times. There was nothing she could do anyway; the plans for the day were already fixed.

Earlier that morning, in another part of Washington, the telephone on the night table had jangled. It had rung three times before the sleeper was able to get his bearings and locate it in the darkness.

"Good morning, Mr. Regan," a cheery voice said. "It's the answering service with your wake-up call. It's 4:30."

Gerry Regan, Special Agent in Charge of the White House Detail, United States Secret Service, mumbled a thank you, swung his feet over the edge of the bed and sat groggily trying to will himself awake. Then he staggered through the darkness to the bathroom and turned on the shower.

As the water washed away the sleep, a sudden acute awareness replaced it. God, but he had been a fool! He had surely put his job in jeopardy. How idiotic even to have contemplated enlisting Joan Scott as an ally. How mad it all seemed this morning when yesterday it had seemed so right. There could be no defending his lapse in judgment apart from the fact that his usual good sense had been warped by the depth of his fatigue.

And his exhaustion was profound. For the past six weeks he had been traveling with and seeking to protect the President as he zigzagged across the nation — fifteen states, twenty-one cities — in a sustained flurry of speechmaking and mainstreeting unique in off-year elections. The last eight days especially had had the quality of a nightmare. A dozen times he had been almost paralyzed by sudden fear when, despite all the forethought that had gone into the security screen with which he surrounded the President, a tiny gap or a gaping breach had suddenly opened.

When the President was campaigning, Gerry Regan lived with fear. It was a fear that overarched his days, stole his sleep and invaded his dreams; the unremitting dread that at any minute, without warning, an attempt might be made on the President's life. Four American Presidents had been shot; others had been shot at. So had other political figures. Regan's concern was intensified by the realization of his impotence; the knowledge that it was impossible to prepare for every contingency. No matter how careful the planning, no matter how assiduously suspects were rounded up in advance, no matter how swift the reflexes or how courageous the men surrounding the President, there was no way of guaranteeing that somewhere in that shoving, shouting, excited mob there was not some madman with hate in his head and a weapon in his hand, a weapon that could be drawn and fired in seconds. Robert Kennedy was a reminder of that; so was George Wallace. Worse was the awareness that the assassin need not even draw near: He could put an eye to a scope, tense a forefinger and deal death from a distance. Only senior people in the Washington Field Office of the Secret Service knew exactly how many attempts had been made on the President's life and how frequently a deadly plan had been aborted by swift, silent action, unobserved by press and public.

But Gerry Regan knew, and toweling himself after the shower, he was contemplating the day's schedule. It would be the most dangerous day of the campaign; especially during the outdoor rally in Herald Square. God, how he hated New York City! How do you so much as begin to provide security in an environment where a thousand windows and dozens of vantage points overlook any given spot? How do you guard against the actions of the warped, sick and messianic fools who have gravitated to the great city in the thousands? How do you predict the convolutions of the sick minds that pencil-scrawl their unreasoning hate on the soiled pages of the letters forwarded daily from the White House? And how do you protect a President who, in the face of history and despite the importunities of the agency established by government to protect him, insists on campaigning in an open car and walking into the midst of crowds of half-hysterical men and women?

It was yesterday's batch of hate mail that had precipitated his approach to Mrs. Scott. Awash with weariness, he had been catching up on long-neglected administrative paperwork at his desk at home when the doorbell chimed. Seventeen bounded down the stairs; it might be a boyfriend. It wasn't. A shout from the hallway: "Dad, it's the courier."

He pushed wearily to his feet, signed for the sealed manilla envelope and dragged back to his desk, slitting the heavy paper with the side of his hand. Within was the usual bundled packet of threatening letters addressed to the White House. He counted them: fourteen. Fewer than usual — but then it was a Sunday. He sifted through them, separating those with eastern postmarks, and began to read.

The second letter set off alarms. Most hate mail was of a kind that experience had taught him could be disregarded: Usually the handwriting was illegible. More often than not the text was hand-printed, with heavy underscorings, frequently in various colored inks. There was often a newspaper clipping enclosed, with statements by the President underlined and with question marks or obscene comments scribbled in the margins.

But this one was different. It was typed with stenographic skill. It was postmarked New York, N.Y., was addressed to The Fascist President of the United States and included a pasted-down newspaper photo of President Scott with a gaping bullet hole drawn on his brow and red ink blood flooding down his face. The text revealed an educated mind and a smoldering, Vesuvian hate. There were two other worrisome letters in the batch, both postmarked New York City.

Regan sat for a few minutes, staring off, his eyes unfocused. Then he picked up the telephone and called the White House. On identifying himself, he was immediately put through to Mrs. Scott. Without hesitation she agreed to see him within the hour.

The moment he sat down opposite her and began to outline his reasons for seeking the appointment, he knew he had made a mistake. She was sympathetic and attentive, but noncommittal. And when he suggested that their conversation be held in confidence, she was direct and candid.

"I can understand the concern you feel, Mr. Regan," she said. "I share it. But I'm sure you must realize that I can't promise to interfere in matters related to my husband's responsibilities, nor can I covenant to keep our conversation from him."

Afterwards, he cursed himself for a fool, fretted through the evening, contemplated calling the Director to tell him what he had done — deciding finally that one precipitate action was enough for

19

one day — and was unable to get to sleep until after three. Awakened at 4:30, he boarded the helicopter at 5:15 at Andrews field and an hour and a half later was in the Secret Service Command car en route from LaGuardia to Manhattan.

Ethan Roberts, Vice-President of the United States, had slept even less; indeed, he had not been to bed. But as he strode down the flagstone path from the front door of his massive Georgian-American fieldstone house to the waiting limousine, there was nothing in his face or bearing to reveal that he had reached the watershed of his life and was facing a crisis that seemed likely to force his withdrawal from politics.

And politics was life to Ethan Roberts. He was in every sense — as he had often been described in the press — a "political animal." He loved the process and the apparatus with intensity. It was not that he was a limited man — he was a student of American history, a lover of ballet and an amateur watercolor painter — but from his youth he had never had any major ambition other than to be in politics and had spent twenty-six of his forty-eight years in one or another elective office: City Councilman at twenty-two; youngest member of the House of Representatives at thirty; junior and then senior Senator from his home state, and now Vice-President of the United States. The events had almost duplicated the schedule he had set for himself early in his twenties. Only three steps remained: a second term as Vice-President, the nomination, and then the Presidency.

But now, with the prize in sight, all his hopes seemed about to abort. Last night, that possibility had driven him to his study to pace and ponder, and at midnight, to slip away from the Secret Service agent assigned to guard him to walk the streets of the capital alone in a tumult of indecision. At three, his mind made up, he had returned home to work out the strategy involved and then to shower and shave and pack for the day's trip.

The Secret Service man, who was also his chauffeur — resentful that he had been given the slip — stood scowling at the door of the limousine, holding it open. Within the car Ethan could see his Appointments Secretary, an attaché case on his lap. The agent had informed him grumpily of Ethan's early-morning disappearance and of the light and activity in the study through the night, and it was troubling him, for he liked Ethan and liked his job.

"Good morning, sir," he said with only slightly more than his normal cordiality.

Ethan made no acknowledgment other than to nod, dropped his considerable bulk into the seat and plumped his briefcase down between them. The door was closed and the car pulled away smoothly, heading for National airport.

"Would you like to go over the day's schedule?" his secretary asked, a file open on his lap.

"We'll do it on the plane."

At one point, Ethan had considered canceling the trip. It was a Joe-job assignment, typical of the peripheral activity he accepted without resentment as part of the Vice-Presidency. Lansing, Des Moines and Indianapolis — duty calls; the party had little hope of a breakthrough in any of the areas. Nonetheless, he had decided to go. Not only because he was a disciplined and conscientious man but — he smiled grimly — because it was possible that today would be his final political act, his "last hurrah."

But he would not resign without a fight — he had made *that* decision in the early-morning hours. He would meet again with Adam and argue his case. Ethan Roberts was capable of seeing himself objectively. He knew he was essentially an honorable man who yet had a major contribution to make to his country. He was able to say that of himself without egotism or self-delusion, and he would say it to the President just that flatly. His failure did not result from venality. If he was guilty of anything, it was bad judgment. Surely, for that, life need not end.

John Rodemacher, head of Security Services for the R. H. Macy and Company's department stores, paid the toll at the eastern exit of the Holland tunnel, made a left turn, caught the light at Sixth Avenue and headed north. He normally drove this route a few minutes before eight and was surprised at the density of the traffic. Where in hell were all these idiots going at this ungodly hour? A better question was; what the hell was *he* doing here at six in the morning? He knew the answer to that one, but asking it of himself tempered his irritability.

Maneuvering mindlessly in the flow of traffic, he commiserated with himself over the annoyances that had roused him from his bed two hours earlier than usual. Every year, he fumed, it gets tougher to get good men. Schmuks and goof-offs you can get in carload lots

— they like the idea of the uniform, standing around looking like a cop and giving the broads the eye — but give most of them a couple of weeks, and one day they don't show and you're up shit-creek. Like today — like today of *all* days! — with the President making a speech in the Square and the store opening an hour earlier because there'll be ten, maybe twenty, thousand people there. . . .

And, by God, there was no way he wasn't going to tear a strip off that new girl. He'd personally handed her the memo reassigning eight guys from the other stores because of the rally and hadn't learned until after eleven last night that she hadn't notified them. Jesus, what a scramble! — right through until 1:30. Two solid hours on the phone trying to reach them and still coming up three short. What do those guys do nights — shack up where they can't be reached? So okay, he'd make do. He'd have to do a shift himself, and the coverage would be thinner than he liked when there was a big crowd in the store, but what the hell!

Lucky he'd thought of Charlie Jackson or he'd be four short. The old guy must be seventy-five and was getting a little soft in the head, but he'd worked twenty-five years in security before they retired him, so he'd know the ropes. He'd post him where he couldn't get in trouble and where he could take a load off his feet if he had to — at the side entrance on 35th. It was right next to the loading bays and hardly anybody used it but employees. Right, he'd put him there.

But wait till he got his hands on that girl!

In his spacious but spartan Washington apartment, C. Herbert Morris, Director of the United States Secret Service, cracked two brown eggs, slid the contents into the aluminum bowls of the egg-poacher, replaced the cover and turned the heat indicator to Warm. Then he inserted two slices of Hovis bread in the slots of a toaster, removed the butter from the refrigerator and went to the bathroom to shave. He had followed the same routine for a dozen years and knew that when he returned to the kitchen, shaved and toileted, the eggs would be at exactly the consistency he preferred, the toast would be crisp and cooling and the butter would have softened sufficiently for easy spreading.

Herbert — no one called him Herb — Morris had not taken a day off in all his twenty-two years with the Service, but he was considering it this morning. Another man in his position and with his authority would have made the decision in an instant, but not he. In a city where dedicated civil servants were not uncommon, the Director of the Secret Service stood apart — the incarnation of inflexible rectitude, a throwback to the flinty perfectionism of J. Edgar Hoover.

Now, scraping the razor over his jutting chin, he was examining the ramifications of his absence from the office. Characteristically, he was not considering taking the day off to indulge himself in something frivolous, but rather to drive alone in his aging but immaculate 1970 Mercedes to the foothills of the Alleghenies to do some bird watching. With any luck he might bring his life-list to a neatly rounded two hundred, and that possibility exerted a strong pull on him. However, his mind demanded a satisfactory rationale before it would approve a departure from the norm. It came: He would use the solitude to complete his thinking on the departmental reorganization he had had to postpone because of the elections.

That settled it: With the President and most of the Cabinet out of town and with most of the Service's personnel occupied with security matters, it would be a quiet day in Washington. He would take the day off.

Chapter Two

As Gerry Regan settled into his seat and the limousine left LaGuardia and headed for Manhattan, the driver passed him a lengthy telex from the Protective Research Section. The United States Secret Service has many departments and is itself a part of the Department of the Treasury, having been established in 1865 to safeguard the currency of the United States and to investigate such crimes as counterfeiting, forgery and the uttering of government checks. It did not become responsible for the protection of the President until almost four decades later. The Protective Research Section is charged with maintaining dossiers on the thousands of men and women who, for a variety of reasons, are judged to be potential threats to occupants of the White House and other senior political and diplomatic figures.

Gerry Regan's eyes ran with practiced speed over the names and condensed biographies on the telex: men and women in the New York City and surrounding area who were judged to be potentially dangerous. Most had criminal records or had appended to their biographies evidence of mental illness, treated or diagnosed. Coded annotations informed him that some had already been taken into custody and were being held until the Herald Square rally was completed.

The list was a tragic litany of human sickness and criminality. It ranged from addled cranks to homicidal maniacs, some of whom, having served a prison term, had been turned back to society, the warp in their minds untouched or further convoluted. Included were: paranoids who felt threatened by some malevolence for which they held the President responsible, political radicals who felt themselves called to be the saviors of mankind through the overthrow of the government, ethnics who had committed themselves to avenge real or imagined evils perpetrated against their homeland, even pranksters who "for kicks" might move against the President simply to demonstrate that it could be done.

Regan folded the telex and stuffed it in a briefcase. He wondered why he had troubled to read it; anything that could be done in advance to apprehend a potential assassin had already been done. The task now was to counter by planning and vigilance any hostile action by "a person or persons unknown" — someone who, if he was going to make his move today, would already have set his plan in operation.

Fumes from the engine were seeping into the cab of the armored truck. Moreno reached out to lower a window and then remembered that they were fixed. He touched the ventilation switch; there was a whir and a rush of air being exhausted. The morning was chill. A fine rain hung suspended and the incoming air was raw. He flipped the switch on the heater. Nothing. He jiggled it and cursed.

Linda went into the van of the truck and returned with the blanket. She cocooned it about her body, shrugging it high on her shoulders. Moreno glanced at her and shook his head.

"What's the matter?"

"You're supposed to be a man."

She tugged the blanket from her shoulders, tucked it around her hips and legs and wedged herself against the wall.

Moreno returned to his thoughts. The monotony of the Parkway, the drumming of the tires on the concrete and the pulsebeat of the broken line separating the traffic lanes had thrust his mind back to the past. He had been reliving his early years as a guerrilla: the seamy beginnings, the years of wandering, the months in hiding, the unending organizing of workers, the clandestine meetings, the plottings, the bombings, the bloody confrontations with police . . . the whole apprenticeship.

Remembering. . . .

Remembering the spartan life in the thin atmosphere of the mountain camp where they had done their preparation. Remembering that morning when, alone, he had run to the summit in a deliberate test of his will. Stumbling, falling but never slackening, fighting his way upward until it seemed his heart would burst and his tendons tear loose. Then, the summit conquered, collapsing, faint with fatigue but exulting in the hardness of his naked back against the sharp stones, in the spareness of his heaving belly and in the sweat drenching his body and stinging his eyes.

Remembering. . . .

Remembering that midnight at the camp that had been their home for five months. The hand in the darkness shaking him awake. The awkwardness of dressing in the darkness; it had been a year since he had worn a jacket and a tie. Then, when he and Linda were ready and the American money was in his wallet and the forged passports were in the luggage, a round of handshaking and the shielded beam of a flashlight jiggling a pool of light at their feet as they stumbled down the precipitous path to the waiting car.

In an open field at the base of the mountain, in the shadow of a great tree, they could see a Piper Apache. As they ran toward it, there was the whine of a starter, a metallic coughing and the engine burst into an erratic roar. Three hours and fifteen minutes later, following the valleys and flying so low the gray volcanic peaks sometimes reared a thousand feet above them — hedgehopping without running-lights when they approached borders — the pilot dropped down on an abandoned tanbark runway bulldozed out of the jungle of the Tortugas. Within minutes they had transferred to a Cessna 220 of Guatemalan registration. At Guatemala City they boarded CP Air's Flight 397 and passed through Customs and Immigration in Toronto with fewer questions than they had rehearsed and only a perfunctory flipping of the pages of their forged passports. Two hours later they were in a taxi approaching the Rainbow Bridge at Niagara Falls.

When the plan had been finalized, entry into the United States had been scheduled for Good Friday. The wisdom of that decision was now evident; each of the six lanes leading to the United States Immigration channels was backed up for fifty yards. The official hardly troubled to listen to their responses.

"Citizen of what country?" he asked, peering at their luggage on the front seat.

"Canada."

"Where do you live?"

"St. Catharines."

"And you, ma'am?"

"Same."

"What is the purpose of your visit?"

"We're going to spend the holiday with friends in Buffalo."

"Are you bringing in any gifts, any liquor or tobacco?"

Before Moreno could answer, the officer had slapped the top of the cab and the driver pulled away. After all the months of preparation, Stage One had been an anticlimax.

Moreno's hearing, sensitive to the operation of machinery, had detected a change in the sound of the truck; an almost inaudible overriding whine in the transmission. *Madre de Dios,* he thought, if that should go out on me now! To divert his thoughts he checked off the landmarks as they flowed past: the Texaco station . . . . . the Palisades Motel . . . . . Bernie's Bigger Burger . . . . . Howard Johnson's . . . . . He held up a wrist to catch the lights of an oncoming truck. 6:45. Right on time.

Suddenly, from beneath the truck, a report like a rifle shot and an erratic grinding. Fear exploded in his chest and there was a taste of acid in his mouth. He eased to the right-hand lane and braked. A speeding car swerved around them and sped by, its horn growling a diminishing protest. He depressed the clutch and jerked the gearshift into neutral. The grinding stopped. He gunned the engine, double-clutched and rammed back into high. Again, the tortured howl from beneath the floor. He shoved in the clutch and coasted. When the speedometer had backed off to twenty miles an hour, he shifted into second. There was a jerk and a descending whine, but the grinding was gone. Slowly he accelerated. The motor roared and the meshed gears wailed in a muted scream.

Linda was sitting upright, infected by Moreno's tension. "Are we all right?" she asked.

"We've stripped one of the gears. I'll have to go the rest of the way in second. We'll be behind schedule," he said grimly, "but I've allowed for that."

An exit sign whipped by. "Tappan," he said with satisfaction. "Twenty miles. Now if she doesn't get too hot. . . . "

For the first time since she was a girl, Linda's hand went involuntarily into her purse and rummaged around, feeling for a rosary that hadn't been there since she was sixteen.

The Secret Service Briefing Manual for a Presidential visit to an area within the continental United States is in the form of a burgundy-red loose-leaf binder, its pages segmented into categories by multicolored tab-indexed dividers. Prepared by Gerry Regan, the Manual has two principal sections: one printed, the other consisting of photocopies of typewritten or diagrammed sheets.

The printed materials — which undergo only slight annual revisions — deal with such fundamentals as the coordination of the various law enforcement agencies in an area, the structure and levels of authority in combined operations and such matters as crowd control during motorcades and at indoor and outdoor public meetings. So detailed are the instructions that they include a section on the materials to be used in constructing a speakers' stand for the President, specifying such minutiae as the space required for his notes, the wattage of the reading lamp and the maximum height to which broadcasters may elevate their microphones.

The typewritten materials, the larger of the two sections, differ from city to city and deal with the variables in any given local situation.

The Manuals are produced and distributed by the Secret Service in carefully controlled quantities (each is numbered and must be returned after the President's visit is concluded) to such law enforcement bodies as may be involved: usually the Federal Bureau of Investigation and the state and local police. On occasion, in circumstances where it is judged expedient, a copy goes to the Central Intelligence Agency, despite the fact the CIA has no authority within the boundaries of the United States. Sometimes State Militia and the National Guard are included.

On this particular Monday morning, copies of the Manual lay open amid a clutter of plastic coffee containers, overflowing ashtrays and pads of ruled foolscap on the boardroom table at the field office of the Secret Service at 90 Church Street in lower Manhattan. Ranged around the table were six men: Gerry Regan and his Deputy, Special Agent Jim McCurdy; Winston Harmony, Regional Director for New York state, Federal Bureau of Investigation; Etienne Favreau, Commissioner, New York Police Department; Homer Midruff, Superintendent, New York State Police; and as an observer, Gil Purdom of the New York City office, Central Intelligence Agency.

Regan had just completed a rundown clarifying areas of specific and overlapping responsibility and had begun to detail the President's itinerary, when there was a tap at the door. A secretary entered and began to circle the table, depositing steaming containers of coffee and clearing away the garbage from the previous round. Regan was silent until she had completed her task. As the door closed behind her, he resumed.

"As you know from our previous briefing, Air Force One lands at LaGuardia at eight hundred hours. Please note on your revised Time Schedule that we have scratched the plan to use a chopper from LaGuardia to the East River heliport — a request from Mrs. Scott; she doesn't like them. Instead, the President and Mrs. Scott will proceed by closed limousine via the Grand Central Parkway to the Brooklyn-Queens Expressway and through the Queens Midtown tunnel to the point designated on your route map as the Transfer Area at the western exit of the tunnel. Arrival time there, give or take possibly ten minutes because of traffic variables, is 8:25. At that point, the Presidential party will transfer from the closed limousine to an open car." He paused to light a cigarette.

"Mr. Scott has requested that there be no cavalcade of cars," he continued. "He wants things kept simple. The Presidential limousine will be preceded by only two vehicles: first, a New York Police Department cruiser, flasher-light in operation, and following one hundred feet behind, our lead car. Mr. McCurdy here will be in the lead car with a driver and four Secret Service agents. The President's limousine will follow one hundred feet behind, and it will in turn be followed by a second Secret Service car with a driver and four agents.

"The motorcade, if I may call it that, will depart the Transfer Area at 8:35, proceed south on Second Avenue and west on 34th Street at approximately seven miles an hour."

He paused, took a deep drag on his cigarette and turned a page. "Now, if you'll look at your map on the following page...." There was a rustling of paper. "As you can see, the area around Herald Square had been blocked off at 32nd Street on the south, Seventh Avenue on the west, Fifth Avenue on the east and 36th Street on the north. President Scott's limousine is scheduled to arrive at the Sixth Avenue intersection at 8:40. Flanked by eight agents, it will proceed to the area marked on your map with a red star at the southeasternmost point of the park — the spot normally used as a taxi stand. The President and Mrs. Scott will be met there by Mayor

O'Donahue and his wife who will escort him to the platform, the ladies following."

He looked up from the page. "I might add that although it doesn't show on your map, it is probable that the President will make a detour from the planned route to the platform. He has, I regret to say, a thing about shaking hands with the public — to 'press the flesh,' as Lyndon Johnson used to call it. I've tried many times, as diplomatically as I can, to get him to abandon the practice but . . . " He shrugged. "After all he's the President."

There was a round of dutiful chuckles from the men at the table, each of whom dealt regularly with politicians. Special Agent McCurdy did not join in; he had heard the comment many times and it did not amuse him.

Jim McCurdy was a direct and uncomplicated man who found it impossible to understand or sympathize with Adam Scott's refusal to minimize the possibility of an attempt on his life by ending his custom of public handshaking. It was an old-fashioned political technique of questionable effectiveness — McCurdy was certain it had never changed a vote — and was fraught with peril. History could be summoned to demonstrate that to move among the people was to court danger. William McKinley was shot while shaking hands in a reception line at the Temple of Music in Buffalo, James Garfield while walking through the concourse of the Baltimore and Potomac Railroad station in Washington. Governor George Wallace, safe behind a bulletproof speakers' stand, was wounded and crippled when he left it and went into the crowd during a rally at a Laurel, Maryland, shopping plaza. Senator Robert Kennedy had been mingling with campaign workers in the ballroom of the Ambassador Hotel in Los Angeles and was leaving when he was cut down by a bullet in the head. The risk in any public appearance, especially at an outdoor rally, was clearly apparent. Franklin Roosevelt was in the rear seat of an open car at Bayfront Park in Miami, Florida, when five shots were fired from among the crowd by an assassin, and Chicago's mayor, Anton Cermak, fell at his side. Theodore Roosevelt was saved from death while getting into his car in front of a Milwaukee hotel only because a bullet aimed at his heart was stopped by a folded fifty-page manuscript in his breast pocket.

To fly in the face of all this seemed to Jim McCurdy simple obduracy; not courage but foolhardiness. He was not concerned that Adam Scott's apparent indifference to danger endangered him, too. Nor was he troubled by the risks fundamental to his job. He accepted without trepidation the fact that it was his sworn duty to preserve the President from harm even if in doing so his own life might be forfeited; failing to grasp that his commitment to his job was of a kind with the President's. What offended and angered him was Adam Scott's repeated rejection of the counsel of the men delegated to protect him. As he heard the familiar reference to the President's custom of shaking hands with the public he felt resentment stir.

Regan had finished his rundown. He paused, checked his watch and looked around the table. "It's 6:45, gentlemen," he said. "Unless there's something one of you would like to raise, I think we'd all better get to work. I don't anticipate any problems; we're expecting a pretty routine operation."

The misting rain had ended. The sun, which had risen at 6:29, was now well above the horizon but the clouds lay in low sullen layers and the morning was gray save for a roseate tint to the southeast. The flow of traffic on the Parkway had thickened and the limping pace of the truck was an irritant to drivers approaching from behind and out of sorts at the beginning of another workweek. Some blew their horns and flashed their lights, and when they were able to insert themselves into the flow of faster-moving cars in the left lane, roared past and down the highway, casting their spume against the truck's windshield.

A battered and mud-encrusted Plymouth station wagon fretted behind the truck for a mile or two unable to pass, its horn hooting an increasing displeasure. When finally there was a slot in the traffic flow, it wheeled past the truck, cut sharply in front and slowed to ten miles an hour. Moreno swerved, jammed on the brakes to avoid collision, flashed his lights, pressed on the horn and hissed a series of venomous curses. His face had gone pale. His eyes were slits, but the livid scar at the corner of his mouth gave the impression that he was smiling. When the station wagon continued to block them, he accelerated and nudged it with his bumper.

"Roberto!" Linda said sharply.

He bumped the station wagon again. The truck swerved at the impact and he fought the wheel.

"You'll kill us!" she screamed.

31

His entire body seemed to sag, almost as though deflated. He eased off the accelerator. The Plymouth sped away. Moreno, his face gleaming with perspiration, slowly increased the truck's speed until it returned to thirty miles an hour. After a while he mumbled, "Sorry."

"He's a fool. You shouldn't let him bother you."

"I'd like to meet that fool on another day."

Watching him, Linda could see that he was fighting to contain his anger. Twice in the five months they had lived together she had seen him, with little provocation, explode in such sudden fury. Once, when something about the food displeased him, he had swept his own plate and then all the dishes from the table. And again, when a neighbor's dog became a daily visitor, whining and sniffing at the barn door when he was inside working on the truck. He had gone to the house and taken a piece of meat from the refrigerator. He called the dog to him softly and broke its jaw with a vicious kick of his heavy boot. The savageness of his anger frightened Linda. In recent weeks the memory of it had nagged her, worried her that it might be a point of vulnerability in the carefully fashioned plan.

If the argument is to be made that a man is the victim of his childhood, Roberto Moreno would serve its advocates well. He was born of an Irish sometime prostitute and a widowed radio repairman in Antigua, Guatemala. At the time of his birth it was impossible to authenticate that he was in fact the son of the man who subsequently raised him, there being no one to assert it but his mother and her assertions being suspect because they were so patently self-serving. Realizing that she was pregnant, she had reviewed the not-too-lengthy list of her regular clients and had decided that the one most likely responsible — and more important, the one most likely to be responsive — was the radio repairman, Manuel Moreno.

Manuel Moreno had been widowed after ten years of married purgatory. When his wife died as a result of food poisoning — a fate he regarded as only just since she had ballooned from 120 to 220 pounds in the ten years of their marriage — Manuel, being a religious man, had performed all the duties required of him by the priest with one exception: he failed to make a full confession. He did not divulge that on the night of his wife's death he had locked the doors, closed the shutters, drunk an entire bottle of tequila and lain abed giggling foolishly until he fell asleep.

Three years later, a solitary and lonely man, confronted by the skinny Doreen and charged with being the father of her unborn child — and what was he going to do about it? — Manuel drew the teeth of her cranked-up umbrage by accepting the responsibility without demurrer, pledging to support her during her pregnancy and to take the child when it was born. He made only one condition: that she forego in the interim further cohabitation with other males. Nonplused by his immediate assent, Doreen wept awhile and then made the required promise. And she did, in fact, restrict her nocturnal activities to not more than one or two paying customers a week. Manuel was aware of her duplicity but he had evolved a philosophy of life that expected duplicity so he was untroubled by it.

When the baby was born he took it from the hospital to his home, the living room of which housed the radio repair shop, and for the remainder of his life wondered whether the boy actually was his. He died when Roberto was seventeen, cheated of the knowledge that the lad was undoubtedly his — his genes not yet having created the mirror-image of the father that the son became. Roberto was cheated, too. In his youth he was never sure who he was, for Manuel was if nothing else, garrulous, and often when drunk would curse the boy as a bastard and throw him out of the house. And at such times he would shout of "your mother, the whore."

So the seedbed was prepared and hate rooted early in it; hatred of his father and mother, and eventually of the whole of society.

Manuel had withdrawn him from school at the age of thirteen and had taught him the rudiments of electronics. At fifteen he began to attend evening classes at the *Escuela Electrónica de Guatemala* and, on weekends and summer evenings, to guide tourists through the earthquake-riven ruins of the city. Schooling denied, he escaped early into books and became an omnivorous reader. Introduced by a friend to a popularization of the writings of Karl Marx, he knew immediately he had found his spiritual home. Before he was seventeen he was a passionate communist, finding that its rage against the capitalist society and the bourgeois leaders who ran it provided an outlet for his own. When his father died, he immediately sold the house and business and began what became a lifelong career as a militant revolutionary, moving from place to place, rejoicing in confrontation and finding an almost orgasmic pleasure in violent protest.

As like attracts like, he had been drawn to the budding guerrilla movement, *El Mano Verde*, immediately after receiving a letter from an old friend, Alejandro Vallejo, at whose side he had fought in the battle of the Bay of Pigs. The letter was unsigned but bore the code-word Cormorant, and told in cryptic language of the formation of the new underground revolutionary movement. Within three months he had joined it. Six months later he was elected a member of the Central Committee. Now, almost a year later, he was hugging the wheel of an armored truck driving on a rain-slicked parkway leading to New York City and fighting to overcome a tumultuous rage.

In the seat beside him, Linda had decided to divert him. She spoke quietly, "Roberto. . . . "

There was no response.

Undeterred, she said, "I know what I'm going to do our first evening home."

A grunt.

"I shall go to the *Cafe Hispano* and have a great plate of *chiles rellenos*."

"Yes."

"Some *tacos con chorizo*. . . . "

"Yes."

"*Con salsa caliente*."

He swallowed the sudden flow of saliva and smiled. She saw it and smiled too.

"No *guacamole?*" he grinned.

"*Si, guacamole*."

"Yes," he said, nodding. "We'll do that. Maybe tomorrow night we'll do that."

Herald Square was stirring from its nightly somnolence as Gerry Regan and Jim McCurdy ascended the stairs to the platform and stood scanning the area where the rally would be held. The clock on the façade of Macy's department store read 7:18. The threat of rain had passed. The sun was probing at the overcast and managing sometimes to sift slanted shafts of saffron light onto the upper faces of the taller buildings. Bored police officers paced before the barricades blocking the side streets where they intersected the Square. A New York City Parks and Cultural Affairs Department truck had been backed into the area reserved for the President's limousine, and two city employees, with practiced lethargy, were carrying and setting up battered metal folding chairs in the area to the right of the platform. Curled in the fetal position and blanketed with rumpled newspapers, a wino lay asleep on one of the permanent park benches within ten feet of where the men were working but undisturbed by their noise.

New York City had always depressed Jim McCurdy. He saw it as the ultimate extension of everything that was wrong with cities. Even though the commuting stole an hour from his day and the fuel filched dollars from his income, he lived thirty miles from downtown Washington in a one-time farmhouse on four acres of nondescript land. Washington he could grudgingly approve — its broad avenues and graceful buildings and the generous green spaces made it tolerable — but he could see no virtues in New York City. Studying Herald Square, his jaundiced eye focused on the debris drifted in the streets, the sooted faces of the buildings, the obtrusive ugliness of the signboards and the pitiful rows of dusty, stunted trees lining each side of the Park.

"Sure isn't much to look at this time of day, is she?" he said, making conversation.

"What is?" said Regan grumpily.

McCurdy slowly pivoted on a heel, looking about. "Know what this city reminds me of, mornings? It makes me think of a cheesy nightclub the morning after, when the naked bulbs are on and the cleaning women are sweeping up the crap from the night before."

Regan made no response. His thoughts were on the day ahead and he was striving to thrust from his mind the irrational sense of foreboding that had settled on him during the ride from LaGuardia into the city. It was a not unfamiliar feeling — over the years he had learned that it arose from abnormal stress and a messed-up metabolism and had no relationship to reality — but that did not dispel the dark trepidation that some dire something was about to happen.

McCurdy broke in on his rumination. "Shouldn't the rooftops be manned by now? I don't see any bodies."

"They're still running the check on all windows overlooking the Square. They'll be up there by 7:30."

There was another silence, each man immersed in his thoughts. Regan broke it. "Jim," he said, "a question: Forget what you know. If you were someone out to get the President, how would you go about it?"

McCurdy flashed a glance at him, frowning, sensitive from long exposure to Regan's moods. "You mean here?"

"Here."

"I can think of a dozen ways. Especially here."

"Why especially here?"

"Ger . . . That's a funny question — from you."

"Why especially here?"

"Well . . . to begin with, conditions couldn't be worse. There's no control. There's going to be, what? — fifteen, twenty, thousand people out there. The President'll be here on the platform, out in the open, above the crowd, a sitting duck. . . . I mean, I can think of a dozen ways."

"So can I. That's the goddamn problem."

"Cheer up, fella. That's because we know what we know. Anybody else. . . . " He shrugged a shoulder.

Regan grunted and headed for the stairs. "I've got to do a communications rundown and you've got to get out to LaGuardia. See you."

He ran swiftly down the stairs and headed for the Command car which was parked, facing east, at the center of the intersection at 34th Street. As he approached, the driver leaped out and opened the door for him.

"Lovely mornin', sir," he said.

"Is it?" Regan said and stepped into the car. For Presidential public appearances the Secret Service prayed for foul weather.

President Scott had moved from his private suite at the rear of Air Force One to the stateroom forward, leaving Joan immersed in a book she had dug from her handbag. He had spent fifteen minutes working his way through a pile of official documents requiring his signature and was now absently tracing with a forefinger the convolutions of the graining on the teak table before him while reviewing in his mind the frenetic schedule of the past ten days. Had the effort made any impact? When the vote was in, would there be any evident benefit from all the sound and fury? Was it worth the gray visage that had looked back at him from the mirror?

Adam was aware of the theory commonly held by political scientists that, once an election is called, campaigning is of little consequence. The campaign, so the thesis goes, is a traditional and flamboyant but essentially pointless charade played out mainly for the principals and the press. The crowds throng, of course, and cheer and applaud on cue — the charisma of the Presidency, the applied skills of professional organizers and the loyalty of the party faithful guarantee that — but the question remains: Does the complex apparatus of contemporary political razzmatazz — the banners, the bunting, the buttons, the handshakes and the carefully fabricated speeches with their skillful skewering of opponents and fulsome praise of friends — alter more than a few intentions behind the drawn curtains of the voting machines?

The efficacy of campaigning is, however, fervently believed in by politicians, and it was mostly because of the importunities of his political advisors and the urging of a variety of candidates up for re-election, many of them longtime friends, that Adam had thrust himself with characteristic vigor into the campaign.

American Presidents have tended either to relish or resent the "political" aspects of the office. Richard Nixon, John Kennedy, Harry Truman and Franklin Roosevelt were avid partisans and revelled in it. Others, men like Dwight Eisenhower and Herbert Hoover, were uncomfortable in the purely political role, assuming it reluctantly and tending to neglect it or delegate its prerogatives. Despite his years in the Congress and the White House, Adam Scott's attitude was ambivalent: he respected the office and enjoyed the exercise of power but had no stomach for the machinations in the so-called "smoke-filled back rooms" and little zeal for the intense partisanship of the campaign trail.

In the first thirty-seven years of his life, there was little to suggest that he would enter politics; even less that he would one day be President. Indeed, until his marriage, most of his friends — had the question been put to them — would have listed him among those least likely, despite the fact that American Presidents have been drawn from an astonishing diversity of backgrounds, many of them highly unlikely: Lyndon Johnson was a schoolteacher, Andrew Johnson a tailor, Harry Truman a haberdasher, Woodrow Wilson a university dean, Herbert Hoover a surveyor and Chester Arthur a socialite known to his contemporaries as a "New York Dandy."

Born of parents who were both artists — his father was a portraitist who specialized in flattering delineations of tycoons and his mother fashioned collages of everything from bus transfers to bottle caps — Adam lived a neglected but not unhappy childhood in the loveliness of Princeton, New Jersey. A high school dropout, he lied his way into the army at seventeen where he was given a pen rather than a sword. He was attached to the armed forces newspaper, the *Stars and Stripes*, and did a series of battlefield sketches which, while not attracting the international attention of Bill Mauldin's GI Joe, were hailed in some quarters as evoking more vividly than photography the desolation of modern war.

Honorably discharged at nineteen, he returned to Princeton and holed up in an attic room in his parents' Lawrenceville Street home, producing in a burst of industry sustained over fourteen months, twenty-six paintings based on his battlefield sketches. The Arlington Gallery in Philadelphia, as a favor to his mother, mounted a one-man show for him and beat the drum to the limit of a limited budget. The show was a disaster: He sold only six paintings, and those to friends, and the reviews in the press read like obituaries. He threw a "Going Out of Business" beach party, handed out wieners, buns, marshmallows and beer, and fed the fire with the twenty unsold paintings. It was fuzzily agreed that, while the burning oils and canvas did little to enhance the flavor of the food, they did no harm to the beer.

Six weeks later, the wounds to his ego apparently healed, he walked into the *Philadelphia Inquirer* and got a job, first as a courtroom artist and later as a reporter. There followed four years of heavy drinking and frequent fornicating, during which period his hell-raising became a Press Club legend and he gave every indication of becoming one of that anything but rare breed of working newspaperman, the good reporter who is also a drunk.

In the great tradition of American success stories it was a woman who "settled him down." Her name was Joan Carlyle and theirs was what is usually described as an unlikely match. She was a Mainline socialite and a Bryn Mawr graduate; born, raised and living in the opulent Philadelphia suburb of Bala Cynwyd. They met when her family's stables burned down and Adam was dispatched to cover the story. A half dozen dates later, Joan said yes, she would marry him, and left her parents' home to move into his three-room apartment, managing over the next six months to renovate it and him without evident strain.

Eleven years later, Lee Harvey Oswald's rifle and Jack Ruby's revolver put Adam in politics. At that time senior Washington correspondent for the *Inquirer*, he was in Dallas to cover the President's visit. He was not especially a John Kennedy admirer but was shaken to his roots by what seemed to be the pointless and prodigal waste of a vital young man only beginning to explore his potential. That, and the unseemly negation of justice in the gunning down of the assassin by the owner of a sleazy nightclub, worked their way deeply into his mind. It was believed by some of his closest friends, and by Joan, that Adam came to feel the death of John Kennedy required that someone move directly into the political field as a kind of surrogate. Nine months later he announced his candidacy for Assemblyman in the 5th District in Philadelphia.

Gerry Regan, in the back seat of the Secret Service Command car, was reviewing his notes and opening his second pack of cigarettes that morning. Men and women, many carrying or tugging children, flowed and eddied past the perimeter of the police barricades within which the car was parked, all moving toward the area facing the platform from which the President would speak. He estimated that as many as five thousand had already gathered and others were emerging in growing clusters from the subway exits or from streets leading to the Square.

A platform had been erected immediately to the south of the towering bronze memorial to the founder of the *New York Herald* and his son and namesake, James Gordon Bennett. The platform — a prefabricated structure designed to be swiftly erected and even more swiftly removed — was forty feet square, bordered by a wooden railing and reached by a stair unit attached to the southeast corner. It stood seven feet above the concrete; not simply to elevate a speaker to a height from which he could be seen from the farthest reaches of the Square but, equally important, to permit security forces to stand erect while working beneath it.

At the moment, the red, white and blue bunting festooning the sides hid from public view four Secret Service agents from the New York City Field Office who were busy laying out and checking an assortment of equipment. Stacked about them in orderly fashion were six cartons of tear gas canisters, six large-bore guns for lobbing them, two dozen gas masks, a Browning submachine gun complete with ten dozen clips, and four Springfield .308 semi-automatic rifles — three standard, one equipped with a scope-sight. Off to one side were open cartons brimming with first-aid supplies, inhalator equipment, a half dozen stretchers and a pile of folded woolen blankets.

On the platform, toward the rear, twenty-four chairs were arranged in two shallow arcs. They were gradually being occupied by an assortment of politicians, among whom there was one woman and three blacks. The platform was backed by a row of flags, the Stars and Stripes rippling and undulating as the morning breezes caught and lifted them. Immediately in front of the speakers' stand was an enormous beribboned basket crammed with fresh cut flowers, almost covering the forest of mike stands with their proliferation of emblazoned microphones.

The area immediately in front of the platform was empty. A strip of brilliant red carpet stretched from the foot of the stairs to the spot where the President's car would stop. A Parks Department workman entered and began taking small self-conscious runs with a carpet sweeper at various bits of debris. The crowd cheered and gave him a patter of applause.

Along both sides of the open area, the permanent park benches had been supplemented with numbered folding chairs, most of which were already filled with an assortment of officials and their wives. On the west, backed by a five-foot-high wrought-iron fence, the chairs ranged south to the extremity of the Park. In the area opposite, normally used as a taxi stand, a line of gray police barricades jogged to the east to form a slot designed to receive the President's limousine.*

The crowd was lively but patient. Lapels and hats were studded with sloganeering buttons. Signs stapled to sticks rode erratically overhead. There were small flurries of applause and occasional abortive cheers as local office holders or candidates mounted the platform and were recognized.

Gerry Regan's Command car was a black custom-built 1974 Lincoln, so adapted that it had become a complex mobile communications center. Two antennae sprouted from the trunk deck. A

*See map on the endpapers.

flared speaker horn was mounted on the forward edge of the roof immediately in front of a standard red flasher-light and a siren. Within, there were two communications consoles: an elaborate one with dozens of switches, three miniature television monitors and a small telephone switchboard — before which Agent Bill Lindstrom sat — and a relatively simple one, built into the wall beside Gerry Regan's seat. Up front, a Secret Service agent in plainclothes sat behind the wheel.

With relaxed skill, Lindstrom was running a systems check.

"Command to Section Eight. How do you read me? Over."

"Section Eight. I read you loud and clear. Over."

"Command to Section Nine. How do you read me? Over."

"Section Nine. I read you loud and clear. Over."

As Lindstrom continued, Regan put aside the Briefing Manual and glanced at the clock on the console before him. 7:48. The President's plane would be beginning its approach to LaGuardia.

"You finished?" he asked Lindstrom.

"All clear, sir."

"Get me McGillvray at LaGuardia, please."

Lindstrom threw a switch. "Command to LAG."

Almost immediately the response came, crackling with interference: "McGillvray here."

Regan picked up a small brown microphone and depressed a button on its side. "Mac, Regan. Anything?"

"No sir. Everything's on schedule. They're experiencing a little turbulence on the approach, but nothing really. Visibility three miles. Touchdown in approx three minutes."

"Very good. Command out."

Lindstrom said, "Telephone, sir. Line One."

Regan pushed a button and picked up his phone. "Regan here," he said.

"Mr. Regan. Russ Mowatt, FBI, New York City. Picked up suspect, John Svoboda, writer of hate letter, at 7:18 this morning at 322 West 45th Street. Suspect armed with .25 calibre Beretta pistol. Now in custody at the 14th Precinct station. Any further instructions?"

"No. That's fine," Gerry said. "Appreciate your cooperation. Thanks."

He hung up the phone. "Well," he muttered to himself, "at least that's one less to worry about."

Chapter Three

I'll have to stop and get water," Moreno said. The astringent smell of hot radiator coolant filled the cab of the armored truck. The motor was venting steam and rattling from pre-ignition. In the rear-view mirror, Moreno could see a contrail pluming behind them and swiftly dissipating in the wake of the truck's passage. He knew that if he did not soon slow and cool the motor, it would seize, or a bearing would burn out, or the radiator hose would rupture. But, if on the Henry Hudson Parkway he pulled over and stopped, he would inevitably draw the attention of a police cruiser, and that he must avoid.

A sign ahead: the 125th Street exit. He expelled a breath he hadn't realized he was holding. *"Bueno,"* he whispered.

He slanted onto the ramp and drew up to a stop sign. Off to his left, a block away, he could see a shabby service station with a single gasoline pump. As he approached and turned in he saw an incredible clutter of disemboweled trucks and cars clustered about a dilapidated garage, leaving scarcely enough room for passage. He eased past the gas pump and nosed up to a 1970 Ford, wheelless and resting on wooden blocks, its front end driven in and its windshield a ragged cobweb of bulged glass. He disengaged the gears but left the motor running, pressing the accelerator pedal lightly. In the rear-view mirror he could see a mechanic approaching. To Linda he said urgently, "Keep the gas pedal down a bit . . . about like this."

She nodded and slipped behind the wheel. Moreno stepped out of the truck, slammed the door behind him and turned a key in the lock.

The mechanic was a skinny, string-sinewed man of about forty.

His pants and T-shirt were heavy with a mixture of dust, sweat and grease. His hair was matted and there was a three-day grizzle of beard on his jaw. A sour and uncivil man, he lived alone in a filthy room at the back of the garage and had managed over the past dozen years to alienate most of his customers and to run his once prosperous business into near bankruptcy. He walked to the front of the truck and stood, hands on hips, looking at it.

"Good morning," Moreno said.

"You got a problem."

"That's for sure. I'll let her cool a bit and then put in some water."

Steam was venting from every aperture in the hood and gushing from beneath the motor. Moreno walked to the front of the truck and raised the hood. The hot vapor, issuing from beneath the radiator cap and whipped by the fan, swirled around him. He was in a tumult of concern and anger; concern that the problem with the truck might make him late, even force him to abort the plan, and angry with an unreasoning fury at the man who had sold him the truck.

"Got a water can?" he asked.

The mechanic looked at him: "Want me to cool 'er down for you?"

"That's okay. I'll take care of it."

"Need any gas?"

"No, thanks."

"You're gonna need some oil."

"No, just water."

The man looked at him sourly and spat on the ground. "No oil, no gas, no service. . . . Right?"

Moreno sensed that the man was edgy. He made his voice friendly. "Thank you, but we get all that at the company pump."

"You just get your parkin' here. Right?"

Moreno looked at him. The man was obviously spoiling for an argument. A mean bastard, he thought. "Sorry to bother you," he said. "I'll only be a couple of minutes."

"And in the meantime, block my gas pump."

"Oh, come on, man," Moreno said, bridling. "I'm not blocking your pump."

"Don't tell me, I'm tellin' you. This is a service station. You wanna park, go to a parkin' lot."

Moreno fought the anger engorging his throat. "For Christ's sake," he said evenly, "I'll be out of here in a minute. . . . "

"Oh no you won't! You'll get your ass the hell out of here now!"

Moreno had first seen the police cruiser in his peripheral vision as it passed the service station proceeding west. He saw it make a slow U-turn and head back.

"You don't want me to touch your fuckin' truck," the mechanic ranted, warming to his theme. "You don't want no gas. You don't want no oil. You block my fuckin' pump. . . . "

He turned, interrupted by the crunch of gravel under tires as the police car drew up. Two uniformed officers, with the exaggerated saunter policemen often affect, got out of the car and walked toward them. Moreno bent over the engine. The pressure of the steam was subsiding. Deliberately he put his hand to the radiator cap as though to turn it, and quickly jerked it away, putting his fingers in his mouth.

"I wouldn't try that with my bare hand," one of the officers said.

Moreno looked up at him. He was an enormous black man, inches over six feet and well over two hundred and fifty pounds. The other was a smaller, white man. He was lean, had a sallow, acne-scarred complexion and wore his hat far back on his head over longish hair. He began to circle the truck, examining it.

"Better use a cloth or something," the black officer said. "You can give yourself a nasty burn."

"That's for sure," Moreno said, examining his fingers.

The officer was looking at him closely. "You a new man?" he asked.

"A new man?"

"I mean, I haven't seen you around."

Careful, Moreno warned himself. Avoid specifics. He bent over the engine again so that his face was down and he could not be betrayed by an involuntary expression. "No," he said. "We don't work this area. The engine got to running hot and I had to pull off the Parkway."

"You know Schultzie and Tom Morgan?"

"Who ?"

"Schultzie and Morgan . . . the Brink's guys on this route."

He shook his head. "Don't think so," he said, pretending to examine the hose where it joined the block. "They'd work out of the Murray Street terminal."

44

From beneath the peak of his cap Moreno was watching the younger officer as he paced slowly around the truck. As he reached the door on the passenger side, he paused, rose on his toes, shaded his eyes with a hand and peered through the window. Moreno tensed. Surely he would see through Linda's disguise. Surely if he spoke to her, her woman's voice would betray them. He could see that Linda was bent over, that her face was turned away from the officer and that her head was moving as she simulated a struggle with some unseen mechanical problem. He would have to distract the man, and quickly.

"What's your partner's name?" he asked the black officer.

"Him . . . ? Al Hubbard."

"Didn't he used to work for Brink's?" he asked, and without waiting for a reply, called out, "Hey, Al . . . !"

The officer turned toward him. "Didn't you used to work as a guard?" Moreno said.

"Huh . . . ?"

Moreno gestured to indicate that he couldn't hear over the sound of the motor.

"Didn't you used to work for Brink's?" he asked, as the officer approached.

"Not me."

"You look like a guy I used to see around Head Office."

"Not me. I looked into it but the pay was lousy. And handlin' all that dough . . . !" He laughed and left the sentence dangling.

Now that the officer had been diverted, Moreno wanted to end the conversation. He said to the mechanic, "You got a can of water?"

The mechanic glowered but did not move.

The black officer turned to him. "You heard the man, Archie. Water." No reaction. "What's the matter, Arch?" the policeman taunted, "steal the can and don't want me to see it?"

. Archie went off reluctantly. "Old Arch'd steal your gas cap while he's filling your tank," the officer said.

"How much you carrying?" the younger officer said.

"Close to fifty thousand," Moreno said offhandedly.

Archie returned with a battered water can. The officer grinned. "If I was you, Brink's, I wouldn't let ol' Arch here within fifty feet of the truck. He'd poison his mother for fifty thou, wouldn't you, Arch?"

Archie banged the can down, sending a gout of water looping to the ground. There was a rotting piece of fabric beneath the wrecked Ford. Moreno picked it up, and covering the radiator cap with it gave a quick twist and stepped back. A geyser of steam mushroomed upward and then diminished. He picked up the can and poured water into the radiator in short and then longer flows. The vapor became an occasional wisp and the rattle of the pre-ignition crackled and ceased. He replaced the cap and banged down the hood.

"She'll be okay now," he said. "Thanks."

The policemen made a perfunctory touching of their caps and walked to the cruiser. Moreno turned the key in the door and climbed into the truck. As Linda slipped out of the driver's seat he replaced her. In a moment they were moving again.

He glanced at his watch. It was six minutes to eight.

A light blinked on the panel in front of Lindstrom. He threw a switch, talked briefly and then turned to Regan.

"Melvin Hamilton. Says he's with the CIA. Line One."

Gerry picked up the phone. "Regan here."

"Mr. Regan, my name is Melvin Hamilton. I'm with the Central Intelligence Agency in Washington. I supervise our Central and South American operation. Gil Purdom told me I could reach you at this number."

"Right."

"We've had a report from one of our people in the field that I thought I should pass on. I'm afraid it's a pretty nebulous thing."

"That's okay. I get lots of those."

"Yes, of course. At any rate, the word is that there's a plot afoot to kidnap President Scott."

"To *what?*"

"To kidnap the President. According to our source, the people involved are a small group of left-wing radicals. Guerrilla types. The story we get is that they've trained some kind of team for the job."

"Anything on when, or where?"

"Afraid not. We don't have much to go on. We know they call themselves *El Mano Verde* but not much else."

"Let me ask if *you* take the report seriously?"

"Only partly. As I said, it's all pretty sketchy. However, it might be wise to bear in mind that although political kidnapping is relatively rare in the States it's common in Latin America. Our press doesn't give it much play, but it happens all the time."

"Yes, I know. Anything else?"

"No. . . . Except that I've sent out a request to all our people for any additional information they can turn up. If I get anything I'll pass it along."

"Thank you. Appreciate the call."

It is probable that at the time no more than two dozen people in all of North America had ever heard of *El Mano Verde*. It is almost certain that the names of the score of urban revolutionaries who formed the core of the organization were known to no more than a handful of men in Washington, all of them connected with the Central Intelligence Agency, and they knew them only in other connections. It is unlikely that even they would have credited the possibility that from such an insignificant group could emerge a plan to kidnap the President of the United States. Surely none of them would have believed for a minute that such a plot would have any hope of success.

In the late fifties and early sixties, throughout Latin America, there was a breaking away from established leftist organizations and the emergence of dozens of new revolutionary groups. Most had brief lives, dying as swiftly as they had begun, sometimes as the result of government suppression, more often because of internal dissension.

El Mano Verde came late to the scene, arising in 1974 from the wreckage of earlier revolutionary organizations. Its leaders took as their model the *Tupamaros*, the Uruguayan urban guerrillas. To obtain funds, the *Tupamaros* had robbed banks. To create attention and communicate with the masses they had seized radio stations and bombed government buildings. And they were among the first to employ kidnapping either to wrest concessions from the government or to replenish their treasury.

These facts were well known to Alejandro Garcia Vallejo, the leader of *El Mano Verde* and himself a one-time *Tupamaro*. A former university professor, Vallejo had been reduced to teaching in an impoverished technical institute because of earlier communist activities. He had publicly broken with his former comrades and was commonly believed to have put his revolutionary days behind him, but two years earlier, in company with a mixed bag of Trotskyists, Communist Party dissenters and student radicals — in all no more than two dozen — he had created a new underground guerrilla movement dedicated to agrarian reform and consequently named *El Mano Verde*, The Green Hand.

The movement was surprisingly successful. Within a year neither the government nor the press could ignore it. Farmers and sugar-cane cutters began to look to it for leadership, and an increasing number of recruits joined. But success created problems, the most pressing being a lack of money, and it was to discuss the resolution of this need that Alejandro Vallejo had summoned the Central Committee to a weekend conference at a mountain retreat owned by a member of the party.

On the Sunday, all other fund-raising proposals having been rejected, Vallejo introduced the subject of a kidnapping for ransom. He proposed that ideally their hostage be a senior executive of an American-owned multinational company, his argument being that even if the government forbade the payment of the ransom, the company would almost certainly take independent action. The suggestion that instead they kidnap the President of the United States was dropped into the conversation almost casually, late in the afternoon, and came from Phillipe Gomez.

"The President of the United States?" Vallejo said, his voice laden with incredulity.

"And why not?" said Gomez ingenuously.

"There are a thousand reasons why not."

But a suggestion by Phillipe Cesar Gomez could not be dismissed lightly. A passionate and militant Trotskyist, he had been active as a revolutionary in Latin America for forty years. A caustically brilliant intellectual who tended to scorn others' opinions, he was disliked by most of the Central Committee but was tolerated because of the quality of his mind. Now, he peered over half-spectacles at Vallejo.

"What ransom would you get for your *Yanqui* businessman?" he asked.

"A million dollars. Maybe more. It's been done."

It had indeed. Kidnapping was a common political action in

Central and South America and sums of money as high as fourteen million dollars had been paid as ransom.

"And what would you get for the President of the United States?" Gomez asked.

"It's a ridiculous question."

"Why?"

"Phillipe! — You're talking about the most carefully guarded man in the world. The most sophisticated security screen it is possible to devise has been erected around him. It simply is not possible."

"So, it's impossible. But humor an old man and play a little game with me; if it *were* possible, what would be paid for his release?"

"It's a foolish game."

"A foolish game, but how much?"

Vallejo shrugged.

"Would you agree the sum could be twenty-five million dollars? Fifty million, perhaps?"

"I would agree, but . . . "

"Would not the only limit be how much gold you could carry with you when you left?"

The discussion ended there but the subject clung like a cocklebur to Vallejo's mind. When the Committee assembled the following morning he returned to it.

"Yesterday, Comrade Phillipe proposed that we consider kidnapping the President of the United States," he began. "I cut off the discussion rather peremptorily but have since been giving the matter some thought." He turned to Gomez. "Before I go into that, however, I must ask you, Phillipe, if you were serious?"

"I am never anything but serious."

"Then you believe it's possible?"

"If I hadn't, I wouldn't have brought it up."

"Then let me ask you to contemplate some of the problems. The first, of course, is getting near him. You can't reach him in the White House. Away from it, he's never alone. He travels in an armored limousine or in military air transport. He's surrounded by armed men, highly trained and prepared to die to protect him. To so much as lay a hand on him would be to invite death."

He paused to take a sip of coffee. Phillipe seemed occupied in getting his spectacles entirely clean.

"Nonetheless," Vallejo continued, "let me beg all those questions and assume that you have seized him and are holding him hostage. Now, with all the power of the United States arrayed against you, with more than 200 million people looking for you — every member of the armed forces, every policeman, every journalist . . . even every child on your trail — how could you possibly remain hidden, much less emerge from hiding, collect the ransom and escape with it? And do you realize, Comrade Phillipe, what fifty million dollars in gold weighs? — at least twelve tons. Twelve *tons*! To think you could get it out of the country and yourself with it is madness."

There was a silence in the room. Vallejo looked hard at Gomez who, having put on his glasses, was fussily adjusting them on the bridge of his nose.

"Don't you agree, Phillipe?"

"I certainly do. To attempt what you've just described would be madness indeed."

"I don't follow. . . . "

"I am saying simply that, as you just visualized it, it could never be done. But it *can* be done. What you would need to achieve would be to make the *Yanquis* so concerned about their President they would do anything to get you the money and to help you escape."

The sarcasm was heavy in Vallejo's voice. "And just how does one accomplish that?"

"I have been giving it thought," Phillipe Gomez said quietly.

Over the next hour he outlined a plan he had been formulating for almost a year. The seventeen men and two women in the room listened without comment, entranced by the audacity of the older man's concept, by the reasonableness of his argument and by the unorthodox daring of his approach. There were weaknesses in the plan and he confessed them readily, but when the session ended and they broke for lunch, each member of the group had come to believe the project feasible.

Among those who listened, his concentration so intense that at times it interfered with his breathing, was Roberto Saldivar Moreno, newly appointed to the Committee.

Gerry Regan hung up the telephone after the conversation with the

CIA man and sat quietly, his brow drawn down in concentration. Kidnapping! — he hadn't given serious thought to that possibility since his early months in the job. When he had first been appointed to head the White House Detail, he had reviewed the files amassed by his predecessors and in doing so had examined two on kidnapping. The first bore the legend KIDNAP THREATS — *The President* and consisted of a number of standardized report-forms listing apprehended threats during the years from when Lyndon Johnson was the incumbent. Few seemed of consequence. Most were obviously the products of deranged minds and were naively simple in conception. None had actually been attempted.

The second file, KIDNAP THREATS — *Presidents' families*, did arouse his concern. A fat folder, it contained a surprisingly large number of reports of plots to kidnap for ransom various members of the Presidents' families. Regan spent many hours reviewing the file, weighing the details against the security measures operative at the time, and as a consequence altered them radically.

But he was not worried about the possibility of the President himself being abducted. No sane man, he was certain, would contemplate it, and even if a rational and clever man did, such are the circumstances under which the President ventures into public that Regan judged the odds against success to be astronomical.

What did exercise him was the likelihood of an assassination attempt. The possibility had obtained since the Republic was formed, of course, but the swiftly proliferating and now almost pervasive violence in the nation had made that jeopardy palpable and had led Regan to urge that all public appearances by the President take place only under conditions that could be controlled.

Ten months after he assumed responsibility for the President's security, he had submitted a memorandum to the Director outlining what he believed those controls should be. He had urged that: the President never undertake surface travel except in a bulletproof car; schedules specifying the route to be travelled and the times of arrival and departure be kept secret; appearances by the President at public meetings be reduced to a minimum and no outdoor rallies be held; when the President attended indoor meetings, he enter the building by a route designed to keep him from direct contact with the public; and — precedent having been established at Lyndon Johnson's Inauguration — on any public appearance by the President, the podium be surrounded by bulletproof glass.

He had summarized the memorandum, which included thirty-five recommendations — even one designed to improve the method used to check the President's food for poison — with a strongly worded argument that, because of the swiftly increasing climate of violence in the nation and the easy availability of every type of firearm, Presidential appearances be made only on broadcast or closed-circuit television.

The Director had discussed the memorandum with him, had reminded him of the repeated attempts of his predecessors to achieve similar objectives and had made a number of suggestions. The revised document had been referred to the President through proper channels — namely the Secretary of the Treasury and the President's Executive Assistant — and had been returned ten days later. Attached to it was a For-Your-Eyes-Only note in the Secretary's handwriting. It read: "Himself asked, 'What's Gerry trying to do? — talk himself out of a job?' "

Moreno knew why the transmission of the armored truck had fouled him up: It was because everything had been going too smoothly. It was the heart of his philosophy that there is a balancing of events in life. If days are sunny and things are going well, watch out. When everything is coming up roses, have a care for the thorns.

He could — and, in conversation, often did — string out dozens of maxims to buttress his thesis: It's a long road that has no turning; a calm follows the storm; every cloud has a silver lining; when you're down a well you can see the stars in the daytime. . . . He used to quote them to himself when he was discouraged and they often buoyed up his spirits.

The coin had another side, of course, and he accepted it, too. It sustained his belief in the revolution. Was it not true that the mighty would be brought down and the proud humbled? The oppressor would surely be overturned; life balances out.

He took a perverse satisfaction in the fact that the gear had stripped. Better to get your bad luck out of the way early in the day. Pausing for the light at West End Avenue and 75th Street, he checked his watch. 8:07. He was running twenty-two minutes late. But that was all right, Herald Square was now only two miles away.

The light turned green.

Adam Scott was listening with only a part of his mind as Jim Rankin, his Press Secretary, briefed him on the morning schedule. He had just read a report summarizing the professional and the party's own public opinion polls, which were not encouraging.

"Our ETA at LaGuardia is eight o'clock," Rankin was saying. "You and Mrs. Scott will go directly from the plane to the limousine which will be parked to the left at the foot of the mobile stairs. Photographers will be permitted, but no spectators, for security reasons. It has been requested that you and Mrs. Scott do not pause at the top of the stairs; the photographers can get their shots at ground level. . . . "

> *The pollsters, Adam was thinking — the goddamn pollsters! The trouble with politics is that it's being taken over by the pollsters, the admen and the sociologists, with their integrated graphs, their demographic breakdowns, their socio-economic groupings and their everlasting computer readouts. They know nothing of and care less for "the gut-feeling factor" in politics. He wondered if the polls didn't determine attitudes as much as they reported them.*

"We have scheduled entrance to the Transfer Area at the Midtown tunnel at 8:25," Rankin droned on. "As you have requested, you and Mrs. Scott will change at that point from the closed to the open limousine. . . . "

> *"As you have requested," he thought. You're damn right he had requested. If the security boys had their way they'd encapsulate me in bulletproof plastic, or send in a double, or have me make every speech on closed-circuit television from a locked vault. His insistence on using an open car was not an act of bravado. He was fully aware of the dangers — Heaven knew, Regan had filled him in on that! It was simply that, years ago, he had faced the question and settled it in his mind. Nor was it that he was a fatalist. He didn't buy that nonsense that if you were going to get it you were going to get it. It had to do with meeting your obligations. If you accept the office you accept the risk. The Commander in Chief has the power to order troops into danger; he does not have the right to order himself out. Having accepted jeopardy as part of the job, he dismissed it. When the possibility that he might be killed thrust itself into his thoughts, he would say to himself, "The coward dies a thousand deaths, the brave man dies but once," and deliberately will to think of other things. . . .*

" . . . bringing us to Herald Square at approximately 8:40," Jim Rankin was saying. "The time has been chosen to take advantage of maximum street crowds — clerks, office workers, early shoppers. When you and Mrs. Scott step from the car, you will be greeted by Mayor O'Donahue and his wife. The local candidates will have assembled on the platform. There are fact-sheets at the beginning of your speech on all the candidates in case you wish to make particular reference to any of them. The important names are listed at the top. . . . "

Fact-sheets on the candidates. . . . You could bet Gus Badoglio would be high on the list and prominent on the platform — front row center if he could finagle it. He wouldn't need a fact-sheet on Gus! — patronage kickback artist, election-rigger, Mafia contact. . . . Jesus! — he thought, it's the bedfellows, the bedfellows . . . !

Rankin passed him a leather folder. "Here's the New York speech. You may want to run over it. Text runs about fifteen minutes."

He opened the folder and began to scan the speech. It was triple-spaced on light-blue paper. The typed characters were a full half-inch high so he could read them without glasses. He'd better do a runthrough and make any necessary changes. He looked up at Rankin who had remained by his seat. "Is there something else?"

He could see the Press Secretary was ill at ease. "No, sir," Rankin said. "Nothing except . . . "

"Except what?" He was surprised at how testy he sounded; he really *did* need that vacation.

"Mr. Regan asked me to request that for the Herald Square rally you forego shaking hands with the crowd. He'd prefer that you go directly to the platform after the greeting by the mayor. He suggests that, if you wish to shake hands, there'll be a group of VIPs seated to your left as you walk to the platform, and . . . "

Adam interrupted. "Those VIPs . . . They're all party people?"

"Yes."

"Then it's not unreasonable to presume that we already have their votes?"

Rankin contained his irritation. "Sir," he said, "Gerry has a tough job. I gather there have been some threats. He's particularly worried about . . . "

Adam ended the discussion by pulling a pen from his pocket

and beginning to work on the speech. Rankin turned away, saying something under his breath.

There was an amplified click and a voice came from the speaker system: "We shall be arriving at LaGuardia airport in approximately ten minutes. The tower advises that we may encounter moderate turbulence during the approach. Please fasten your seat belts."

Like a great ungainly bird, Herbert Morris was perched unmoving on a boulder deep in a deciduous wood in southwestern Virginia. He had not breathed for the past thirty seconds. No more than two minutes ago he had picked his way through the dense underbrush and settled on the great rock. There was no breeze, the leaves were motionless, the silence was total.

Without warning there was a flash of black and white, a flicker of red, and a large bird swept through the forest, swooped upward and landed on the trunk of a tree not fifty feet away. What he could see of the bird — it was almost obscured by intervening leaves and branches — told him that it was a woodpecker, possibly sixteen inches in length, larger than any he had ever seen. What was exciting him was the remote possibility that it was an ivory-billed woodpecker, a bird on the verge of extinction. There had been occasional reports, many of them questionable, of sightings on a line from the deep forests of southeastern Texas to northwest Florida and up into South Carolina, but so far as he knew, it had never been reported in Virginia.

He could discern part of the brilliant red crest and the black-and-white markings on head and throat, but in the poor light not clearly enough to determine whether the bill was whitish or yellowed, or whether a line of black surmounted the red crest. There were only two possibilities: a woodpecker so large could only be the ivory-billed or the pileated.

Moving slowly, he reached for the binoculars hanging at his chest. The bird drummed loudly, and then with diminishing speed and vigor. Not diagnostic: could be the pileated — he had heard and observed them many times. Then, suddenly, the bird called — a single high-pitched note. He almost leaped from the boulder. It *couldn't* be the pileated — their call always came in series. As he raised the binoculars, there was a sound off in the forest. Startled, the bird leaped into the air, turned and flew directly above him and away. There could be no question . . . the black body, the white underside of the great wings and, yes! — a black band at the center from wingtip to wingtip.

Herbert Morris could hear the rapid beating of his heart. Whatever else happens today, he thought, nothing could equal this.

Chapter Four

Patrolman Antonio Spellman Longo, badge number 13-724, twenty-one years old, four months a member of New York's Finest, paced slowly back and forth along the length of a police barricade blocking 35th Street at Seventh Avenue. At the moment he was drawing some small satisfaction from the fact that he had finally mastered the ability to twirl the two-foot-long riot stick he had been issued in such a manner that the dark-brown hickory completed two full revolutions on its leather thong and returned with a satisfying slap to his palm. Otherwise, he was filled with a sullen anger.

Patrolman Longo had been married Saturday afternoon to his fiancée of four years, Rosalie Lombardi, and despite a longstanding promise from the night desk sergeant that he would be relieved of duty until Wednesday, he had been telephoned on his honeymoon at two in the morning and ordered to report in.

"I'm sorry, Tony," the sergeant said, after Tony had reached across his bride's body to pick up the phone from the night table. "I got no choice."

"Whadda ya mean, you got no choice?" Tony said, despair in his voice.

"Like I told ya; the President's comin' in and I'm short of bodies."

"Sarge, look . . . you can't do this to me."

"Tony, didn't I say I was sorry? Three a the guys called in sick. What am I gonna do?"

"So *I* called in sick. Okay?"

"Tony, if I could, I would. You know that."

"I'm sick. Look, I'm tellin' ya, I'm sick!"

"Tony . . . I feel like a prick. You know that. I'm just doin' my job."

"There's no way?" Tony asked tonelessly.

"Like I said, I'm just doin' my job."

"What time?"

"What time what?"

"I mean what time at the station?"

"Six-thirty."

"Six-thirty!"

"A special briefin' by the Secret Service guys." A silence. "I'll put in for double time for ya."

"Thanks," Tony said. "Thanks a bunch."

So, at three in the morning, in the overstated sumptuousness of a 45-dollar-a-day room in a resort hotel in the Poconos, Tony and his bride found themselves dressing and packing. Rosalie hadn't said a word since he put down the phone and explained. From time to time she sniffed or dabbed at her eyes with a knuckle. Every few minutes she blew her nose into a moist tissue she stored in her cleavage. When in the elevator, for all her fishing she couldn't retrieve it, Tony passed her his handkerchief.

The night clerk looked at them closely when Tony tossed the key on the desk and said, "Checkin' out." Was the room not satisfactory? "It's okay," Tony said, and paid the bill in silence. The night clerk phoned for a cab and Tony and Rosalie stood enshrouded in mute misery for twenty minutes waiting for its arrival. Behind the mail-slots, the night clerk and the switchboard operator extracted ten minutes of ribald fun from the incident; it helped to pass the night.

The honeymooners arrived back in Queens at 5:15, and because Tony didn't have the key to their new apartment — he had planned to pick it up Tuesday night — he dropped Rosalie off at her parents' home, rousing the household in the doing, and as a consequence having to answer a series of questions. Then to his parents' home to get his uniform.

Now, at 8:17, he looked at his watch and weighed the risk involved in leaving his post for a minute and ducking into the pay phone across the street to call Rosalie. A Brink's truck, whining in second gear, made a turn and nosed up to the barricade.

He waved the driver away: "Move it out. Street's closed."

Moreno beckoned to him and he sauntered over. Although

Moreno was shouting through an open gunport, Tony could hardly hear him for the sound of the motor and the flow of traffic on the Avenue.

"I've got a delivery for Macy's," Moreno shouted.

"Sorry, buddy. Street's closed."

"Officer," Moreno shouted, "that doesn't mean Brink's."

"My orders are, *nobody* gets through."

Moreno could see by Tony's uniform and tell by his manner that he was a rookie. He decided to come on strong. He opened the door a crack.

"Goddamn it, man," he roared, "I've got fifty thousand bucks in here for Macy's! If I don't get it to them there's going to be hell to pay!"

Tony was beginning to feel uncertainty. Brink's and Macy's and fifty thousand bucks. . . . Jesus!

"This is a one-way street," he said. "You can't go in this way anyways."

"I sure as hell can't come in from Herald Square!"

Tony's mind was muddled by indecision and it was reflected in his face. Moreno decided to take a chance. "Where's the guy who's usually on this beat?" he asked, feigning a weary impatience.

"I don't know. I don't know whose beat this is."

"Can you find him?"

"How'm I gonna find him? I don't know who he is."

"*He'd* tell you I've got to get through, dammit!"

Tony looked off down the street as though miraculously to find some guidance there. Moreno could see his uncertainty. He opened the door further, lowered his voice and said earnestly, "Officer, listen to me. I've got fifty thousand bucks here for delivery to Macy's. If I don't get through they won't be able to do business today and you'll get shit. For God's sake, man, use your head . . . this is *Brink's*!"

Confronted with God and Brink's and Mammon, Tony's residue of resistance crumbled. He shrugged, crossed to one end of the barricade, walked it aside and waved the truck through. Moreno put the gearshift in low and moved slowly into the street. As the truck passed, Tony kicked the rear tire.

The most formidable problem faced by *El Mano Verde* in the formulation of the kidnap plan had been the obtaining of an armored truck. The scheme had foundered at that point until, in a sudden flash of recall, Alejandro Vallejo remembered a conversation with an expatriate French Canadian, Jacques Villeneuve, in Havana in the summer of 1972.

Villeneuve had been a member of a cell in the *Front de Libération du Québec* a leftist guerrilla movement, whose members in 1970 had been given a safe-conduct to Cuba by the Canadian government in return for the release of their hostage, the then British Trade Commissioner, James Cross. In the course of their conversation at poolside at the former Havana Hilton, Villeneuve had been reminiscing about his days as a revolutionary in Montreal and had recounted how the FLQ had planned to use an armored truck in a bank robbery. "What better cover could you want?" he laughed.

Now, remembering, Vallejo traced him with a long-distance call and reminded him of the conversation. "The truck," he asked, "what happened to it?"

"Didn't I tell you . . . ? We didn't get it. We had to call the whole thing off."

"Was it a Brink's truck?"

"No, but it was exactly the same. It was owned by either the *Banque Canadienne Nationale* or the Montreal Trust; I forget which."

"What happened to it?"

"They stopped hauling their own money and put it up for sale. That's when we tried to buy it. A guy named Jacoby bought it. Converted it into a camper. . . . "

"A camper?"

"For going hunting and fishing. . . . We tried to buy it off him, but no luck."

"Any idea where it might be now?"

"Now? I don't know. . . . It's so long ago. I heard that Jacoby moved to the States."

Vallejo's heartbeat increased. "Jacques," he said, "try to remember. . . . Any details you can. It's important."

For all the persistence of Vallejo's questioning, Villeneuve could recall no further details but did promise to check with the other exiled members of the cell and call back. Three days later he reported that one of the others had kept his notes from the time, that the man's name was Peter Jacoby and that he had moved to Patchogue, New York. Within weeks of his arrival in the United States, Moreno went to Grand Central station, found a Long Island telephone book and rang up the only Jacoby in Patchogue. Yes, he still had the truck and, yes, he would be willing to sell it.

Jacoby lived in a small white clapboard cottage, the front yard brimming with a variety of flowers. The living room walls were dominated by reproductions of paintings of fish being taken, framed photographs of Jacoby and friends standing by downed big game, and by an enormous tarpon mounted over the fireplace.

"So you're interested in the truck?" Jacoby said, puffing on a blackened pipe. "I'd better tell you right off, she hasn't been kept up."

"That's okay," Moreno said. "I'm pretty handy as a mechanic."

"What are you planning to use her for?"

"Same as you. As a house-trailer . . . a camper."

"I'm curious about how you heard about her. She hasn't been out of the garage for at least a year."

"Fellow mentioned it to me at a service station in town. I was asking different places where I could pick up a camper cheap."

"At the Gulf station?"

Moreno had taken out a cigarette, and as a diversion, had been feigning a search in his pockets for a match. Now he said, "Got a light?"

Jacoby jumped up from his chair. "Of course," he said. "Excuse me." He took a butane lighter from his pocket and after lowering the flame lit the cigarette. Before he could return to the subject, Moreno interjected that he had to be back in the city early and could he have a look at the truck.

Jacoby led him through the back yard to a double garage. Within, there was a 1974 Chevrolet Impala, and bulking large beside it, covered with an accumulation of dust, the armored truck. It looked very little like an armored truck. It had been painted moss green and bore the name *Lay-Zee-Daze* on the rear. A roof-rack, designed to transport a canoe and a small punt, had been added, and the spare wheel was affixed to an exterior wall. Within the truck, four metal bedsprings were hinged to the walls. The interior was covered with a flowered wallpaper and the floor was vinyl-tiled. Limp curtains hung at the windows and a small chemical toilet squatted in a rear corner.

Jacoby opened the garage doors for ventilation, took a heavy brass key from his pocket, opened the truck door and climbed in. He inserted another key in the ignition and after two attempts the motor roared to life.

"She runs pretty good," Jacoby shouted over the sound. "I turn her over for a few minutes every week or so to keep the battery up."

He turned off the motor and climbed down. Moreno got in and examined the interior, carefully masking the elation swelling within him. "Hard on gas?" he asked.

"Afraid so. She's a heavy bugger. Actually, it's not too good an idea using her as a camper."

Moreno asked a number of questions and then, finally, "How much do you want for her?"

Jacoby pursed his lips. "A thousand?"

Moreno shook his head. "I could get a second-hand house-trailer for that."

They reached a compromise at seven hundred dollars on the understanding that Jacoby provide license plates and an up-to-date registration in his own name — Moreno said he would make the transfer of ownership back home. He took delivery of the truck late the following afternoon and drove it in the darkness to the barn back of the farmhouse he had rented.

It took seven weeks to the day to restore the truck. The most difficult task was matching the gray exterior color and duplicating the band of lettering that extended along each side and bore the Brink's insignia. Using a camera with a telephoto lens, he shot three rolls of 35-millimeter color film of Brink's trucks moving in and out of the company headquarters at 66 Murray Street in Manhattan, projected the slides and matched the color. When he was finished it satisfied even his perfectionist's eye.

At Electronics Unlimited on East 48th Street he purchased a Fire-Lite, Series-50 heat detector, an Adamco Number-12 vibration sensor, some contact switches and a hundred feet of wire, and installed the devices on the ceiling of the truck. The wiring rigged and the alterations completed, he finished the job by lining the interior of the van with quarter-inch mahogany plywood, painting it a matching gray and sanding until it simulated the steel-plate lining of a Brink's truck.

As the truck moved slowly eastward along 35th Street, it became the focus of attention for Secret Service agent Marvin Rosenberg, one of five agents posted across the street from and to the north of Macy's. The unit was under the command of Special Agent Murray Thorsen and for the day's operation had been categorized Section Ten.

Thorsen had posted himself on the rooftop at the southeast corner of the Johnson building, thirteen stories up, and had ranged the others along the parapet so that they looked down on the intersection of 35th Street and Broadway. Rosenberg was an exception; he was alone on the roof at 131 West 35th, two stories higher, with responsibility for covering the entrance to the street from Seventh Avenue. He was twenty-two, a college graduate in criminology and a recent recruit to the Service. As were the others, he was equipped with binoculars, a transceiver and an AR-15 rifle. The rifles had been placed within easy reach, leaning against the parapet out of sight — Regan forbade any unnecessary show of weapons.

Agent Rosenberg had watched with increasing interest the conversation between Officer Longo and Moreno. When the policeman swung the barricade aside and passed the truck through, Rosenberg leaned forward and studied it through his binoculars. After a moment he picked up his transceiver.

"Station-A to Thorsen. Station-A to Thorsen."

Thorsen brought his transceiver to his lips and punched a button. "Thorsen here."

"Brink's truck entering from Seventh."

"Read you. Stand by."

Thorsen lifted the binoculars hanging from his neck and focused them on the street below. He followed the truck as it moved slowly past two sets of loading bays and drew up to the curb, coming to a stop opposite a narrow doorway over which there was a small and grubby sign reading Entrance to Macy's.

He could see nothing unusual about the truck and would have dismissed it had it not been for an almost inaudible hissing that rose to his ears with the roar of the motor, and a plume of steam venting from beneath the hood. He put the transceiver to his lips.

"Rosie. . . . You still there?"

"Station-A standing by." Rosenberg did not approve of the casual familiarity with which Thorsen was running his section.

"The truck. . . . How's she look to you?"

"Like a regular Brink's truck on a delivery."

"She's running hot. Otherwise everything looks kosher."

Rosenberg winced. "What's your briefing-sheet show about a Brink's delivery?"

"Stand by."

Thorsen reached into a hip pocket and pulled out a loose-leaf, plastic-bound notebook. He riffled through the pages swiftly and then repeated the action more slowly.

"Rosie?"

"Station-A."

"I don't show a Brink's truck."

"Nothing?"

"Nothing. But that doesn't mean anything. The advance people could've not bothered to list it. Wouldn't be the first time."

Rosenberg squinted against the sun, peering down into the street. "Why doesn't the guard get out?"

"Probably getting the money together. I'll give her another look."

Thorsen leaned his elbows on the parapet to steady his arms and raised the binoculars to his eyes. Because he was looking down at an angle of approximately seventy degrees he could not see through the windshield into the interior of the truck, but because the sun was low and behind him he could tell that both front seats were empty. They're back in the truck getting the money together, he said to himself. I'll give him thirty seconds.

His lips moved as he counted: "One thousand . . . two thousand . . . three thousand. . . . " He had reached twenty-three when the door of the truck swung open and Moreno stepped into the street. He was carrying four money sacks in his left hand and a revolver in his right. He turned and looked up to the top of the Johnson building, saw the men posted there and waved his gun hand. Thorsen waved back. Moreno strode swiftly to the door leading to Macy's and was lost to sight.

"Rosie . . . ?"

"Station-A."

"Look okay to you?"

"I don't know. . . . Normal, I guess."

"Think I should report it?"

"You're sure it doesn't show on your briefing-sheet?"

"Positive."

"Then you should report it."

"Regan'll give me shit," Thorsen grumbled, punching a button on his transceiver.

"Section Ten to Command."

"Go ahead Section Ten."

"Brink's armored truck on 35th, west of Broadway at entrance to Macy's. Doesn't show on my briefing-sheet."

In the Command car Regan said, "How the hell did it get past the barrier at Seventh Avenue?"

"The duty cop passed him."

"Son of a bitch," Regan snapped. "Stand by." To Lindstrom he said, "What time do we show the Brink's delivery?"

Lindstrom's fingers fluttered nimbly on a card index. "Nine, nine fifteen."

"Section Ten. The Brink's truck . . . anything out of line?"

"Looks okay. One guard's gone into Macy's."

Regan frowned. "Keep an eye on it. I'll check it out." He flipped a switch. "Command to Williamson."

"Williamson here."

"Regan. Bill, where are you?"

"35th and Sixth. East end of the Florsheim building."

"Section Ten reports a Brink's truck at the 35th Street entrance to Macy's. Looks legit but we don't show it until nine. On the other hand, the store's opening an hour early today. Can you check?"

"Will do."

"And report soonest," Regan said.

He turned to Lindstrom who was in contact with the President's lead car on an earphone. "Progress report, please."

"Half a mile east of the tunnel. Everything on schedule."

Gerry looked at the clock. It was 8:15.

Linda lay on the floor of the truck behind the driver's seat, her knees drawn up and her head pillowed on the inside of a forearm. Moreno had covered her with the blanket before leaving, pulling and tugging at it to be certain she was entirely covered and that the contours of her body were not distinguishable. When the door slammed and she heard the bolt thrust home, she had deliberately settled herself for the long wait, knowing that she would soon be perspiring beneath the blanket and that her muscles would grow stiff — but knowing, too, that she was prepared to endure it.

At first she was bothered by the amplified sounds from outside the truck. Moreno had mounted a directional microphone out of sight beneath the front bumper and had rigged a four-inch speaker under the driver's seat. It was close to her head, and loud, and conveyed the sound of the motor and the distant noises of activity from Herald Square.

In a few minutes she had accustomed herself to the tinny din, and to pass the time and still her fears had deliberately turned her thoughts to the beginnings of the sequence of events that had culminated in the unlikely circumstance of her being here in the semi-darkness beneath a rough blanket on the floor of an armored truck thousands of miles from home.

In the months during which the Central Committee of *El Mano Verde* refined the plans for the kidnapping, there were many times when it seemed the project would be abandoned. As the enormity and complexity of the problems began to be perceived, a scaling down or an abandoning of the project was argued. As was said: "Why mount a tiger when there's a horse to be had?"

The project was kept on track only by the intensity of the passion of one man, Phillipe Gomez. An old Trotskyist who relished nothing more than exploring the convolutions of a complex idea, he was exhilarated by the challenge; its difficulty made it the more intriguing. Moreover, his ego fed on the beguiling image of the solitary Phillipe Gomez confronting and besting the gargantuan power and resources of the United States. He had long resented the circumstances that had relegated him to the backwash of events — at the periphery of the revolution rather than at its heart — and he drew satisfaction from the realization that, if the plan succeeded, it would inevitably be known that the coup was the child of his brain.

Central to the execution of the plan were the personnel to carry it out. As the Committee met almost nightly, frequent reference was made to what came to be called "the task force." To the mounting exasperation of his associates, each time the term was used, Phillipe would grimace and shake his head, and when others advanced suggestions or proposals, would scornfully dissect them. At one point, the usually amiable Jaime Flores hissed at him in sudden fury, "We know what you *don't* want, Phillipe, but what in God's name *do* you want?"

Gomez, resisting the temptation to twit Jaime for invoking the Deity, answered without a moment's hesitation. "No task force: I want one and only one man, and . . . "

"And who is that superman to be?" Jaime spat. "The omniscient Phillipe Gomez?"

A smile curled the corners of Phillipe's mouth. *"No, amigo de mi corazón.* A dozen years ago, perhaps, but not today."

"Then who?"

Vallejo broke in. "Phillipe, before we get to that. . . . I have learned, as we all have, not to dismiss your suggestions lightly, but to believe that any one person could possibly . . . "

"I did not say one person, I said one man. And with that man, a woman."

The room fell silent. Gomez covered his pleasure at having so taken the others by surprise. "Think," he said, his voice rising as he continued, "think of the dramatic and irrefutable demonstration before the world of socialism's commitment to the equality of the sexes. Think, too, of the reproach to the reactionary *Yanqui* sexists when they realize they have been confounded by a woman!"

He had their attention now and knew it. He glanced at some notes on the table before him and continued:

"Why one man and one woman rather than a task force? The reasons are many, and obvious. How much less conspicuous, for instance, for a man and woman to travel and live together without creating suspicion, than for a group of men. How advantageous, too, that during the crucial hours when the President is our hostage, the enemy will suffer the handicap of a mind-set: He'll assume, because of his fundamantal bias against women, that his quarry is a male and won't think to search for a woman. Why a man and a woman? Review the plan in your mind. Think. May not a man and a woman do all that needs to be done? What need is there of muscle that can't be met by the male member of the team? What is needed in the second member of our team is not strength of arm but sinew of mind, and a different way of looking at things. We all believe that men and women must be equal in the revolutionary society, but I don't for one minute believe they *are* equal as human beings; each is superior to the other in certain ways and each complements the other. We need, not a task force but one man and one woman."

It was obvious that among the male members of the movement, Moreno was the inevitable choice. Linda was recruited by Gomez himself and was an unlikely selection. Unknown to all but her closest friends — certainly to the officials at the *Biblioteca Central* where she was assistant to the Chief Librarian — she had been a member of *El Mano Verde* for two years. Fluent in four languages — Spanish, Portuguese, English and Russian — she had been enormously helpful to Gomez when he had come to the library for specialized research, and had volunteered many evenings to translate materials he would not otherwise have been able to read. Early in their friendship she told him of her Marxist commitment. It was the result of an unhappy and turbulent love affair at eighteen with a man twice her age, a fanatical labor union organizer who had come to board at her grandparents' home. One day, without warning — although they had been lovers for a year — he was gone, but the ideas he had talked about endlessly and passionately stayed and matured. Phillipe told her about the kidnap plan, and encouraged by her excitement and interest, broached the possibility of her participation. She said she would think about it, and being well-known to the Committee was immediately approved as one of three women to be considered.

It had been decided to establish a base of operations at an isolated mountain camp where the team could be briefed and otherwise prepared. The camp was on the upper slopes of a remote mountain, a mile above an unused spur road and accessible only on foot. The life was spartan: there was only one building, a crudely constructed shack used as a kitchen, and everyone slept in tents. After two weeks at the camp, the other women candidates withdrew, and there being no one else, Linda volunteered.

She and Roberto spent the next three months at the camp. With them through the period of preparation was a rotated group of a dozen members of the movement, each assigned the responsibility of helping to prepare them in specific areas. Phillipe came for a three-day period each fortnight. Vallejo made the journey almost every weekend. Moreno was instructed daily in a variety of skills ranging from arc-acetylene welding to the handling of explosives. Both were given detailed briefings on such diverse subjects as the structure of the government of the United States, American colloquialisms, the apparatus and characteristics of the news media, even the traffic laws of New York state and Manhattan.

Moreno established for himself a demanding regimen of physical conditioning — with another for Linda — and once they had adjusted themselves to the thinner oxygen of the campsite, they pushed themselves daily to their limits until their bellies were flat, their bodies spare and hard, and their eyes and skin glowing with health.

Chapter Five

A
s Moreno waved at the Secret Service agent on the rooftop of the Johnson building and received an answering wave, he was suddenly overwhelmed by a feeling of utter certitude. As he turned to enter Macy's, his stride became almost jaunty. He would not, he *could* not, fail.

To his right as he entered the store there was a broad ascending staircase, unused for years and laden with dust. (Weeks earlier he had scouted it as a place in which to hide in an emergency — slipping unnoticed up the stairs to a landing one flight above — but had rejected it on discovering that it led to a boarded-up dead end.) Ahead and to his right there was a small, glass-enclosed office bearing the word SECURITY. It was empty. A uniformed guard was standing in the doorway leading to the store, leaning against the jam. He was a thin man, well past seventy, with his cap pushed back on yellowish-white hair. A homemade cigarette angled downward from his lips. Moreno strode toward him purposefully.

"Good morning," he said, not slowing.

The security man looked at him, blinking, confusion evident on his face, and said an automatic "Mornin'." Then, as Moreno passed, he called out, "Hey . . . ! Just a minute. Where you goin'?"

"Brink's," said Moreno.

"Brink's . . . ? Brink's comes in on 34th."

"Not today," Moreno said briskly, "34th's closed off."

The guard, Charlie Jackson, was a pensioner, called in late the previous night by John Rodemacher to help supplement the need for extra bodies. He had worked in security at Macy's for twenty-five years and in the months following his retirement had grown increasingly senile. As he often told his daughter-in-law when names wouldn't come or facts couldn't be remembered, "Sometimes it seems like my head's full of cotton wool." He remembered, or thought he remembered, that in the old days the daily money delivery was made from 34th Street, but the man before him was obviously from Brink's, and things sure weren't normal this morning. . . . It would be all right.

"Okay," he said. "Okay . . . go ahead."

"Take it easy, old-timer," Moreno said and strode off into the store.

The aisles were almost empty. A few clerks were folding dust covers, arranging merchandise and generally preparing for the day's business. They had been informed in a memorandum from the Assistant Manager, handed to all employees as they had punched out the previous Friday, that because of the political meeting in the Square the store would open an hour earlier than normally and would be busier than usual when the crowd dispersed. Overtime would be paid, the memo said, and would everyone please make a special effort to be punctual.

When Moreno was certain he was beyond the security guard's line of vision, he slipped the gun into the holster, buttoned it and veered to his left, walking close to the display counters so that the money sacks in his left hand would not be conspicuous. (He had traced the route a half dozen times in rehearsal.) Two-thirds of the way across the store he made a 180-degree turn to the left, climbed a set of five stairs, turned right and walked quickly down a broad stairway leading to the Budget Store. A few steps from the bottom there was a landing, and to the right a gray door with a metal plate inscribed MEN. He turned in.

The washroom was empty. . . . No! — a man's feet were visible beneath the door of the first pay toilet on the left, trousers billowed about his ankles. Moreno mouthed a silent curse, walked swiftly to the end cubicle on the right, entered and slid home the bolt. Swiftly, and without an unnecessary motion, he hung the money sacks on the clothes-hook on the door, placed his hat inside-up on the back of the toilet seat and began to strip off and place various parts of his uniform in it. First, the epaulets, the pocket flaps and the arm insignia — they had been basted on with light-gray thread — then the metal badge. He unclipped the holster and put it in the cap. Unbuckling the belt, he wrapped it tightly around the cap,

71

crushing it and its contents into the shape of a rough cylinder.

He was ready.

He opened the door slightly and looked across the aisle. The feet of the man in the pay toilet were still visible. He paused, tensed, barely breathing. There was a soft crackling sound from across the way . . . the son of a bitch was reading a newspaper! Moreno could delay no longer. He opened the door quietly and was suddenly struck rigid by a voice resonating in the tiled confines of the lavatory.

"Sir . . . ?" the voice boomed.

Moreno hesitated only a second; he had no choice but to answer. "You talking to me?" he said.

"Have you got the time, please?"

He looked at his watch. "Twenty past eight," he said.

Twenty past eight! — he was perilously behind schedule. There was no option; he must go ahead. He lifted the money sacks from the hook and left the cubicle. As he did, he saw the man's feet shift and a folded newpaper land on the floor. *Now!* He walked swiftly to the waste-paper container. As he reached it, the room erupted with the roar of a toilet flushing. *Quickly!* Into the container went the money sacks, but as he tried to follow them with the rolled cylinder of cap, gun and belt, it jammed; the aperture was too small. Behind him he heard a bolt slide and a door swing open and bang against the wall. With all his strength, he twisted the bundle and shoved. Resistance for a moment, then it dropped with a thud. The hinged cover swung back and forth, squeaking loudly in the silence.

Moreno turned slowly to face the person who had emerged from the cubicle. He was a boy of about sixteen in a pale-blue cotton workshirt with a leather bow tie and with the name *Macy's* stitched on the pocket of the shirt. He had a thicket of rust-red hair and a smear of freckles on face and neck and arms. His mouth was slightly open and his brows were drawn down, questioning.

Before he could react, Moreno leaped across the ten feet separating them and chopped the edge of his hand against the side of the boy's neck. His bones seemed to dissolve and he slumped in a heap on the terrazzo floor. Moreno bent over, put a knee to the back of the boy's neck, seized a fistful of hair and jerked. There was a dull crack as the vertebrae separated, and a sudden aspiration of air from the lungs. He put his hands under the boy's armpits, dragged the spasming body to the end cubicle, kicked up the toilet seat and jammed the boy's buttocks in the bowl. He backed out and pulled the door closed, but as he turned away it swung slowly open. He stepped into the cubicle, ripped a dozen sheets of toilet tissue from the dispenser, wadded them and jammed the door closed.

Striding swiftly to the paper-towel rack, he seized two handfuls of the sheets, crumpled them and stuffed them into the waste container, pushing aside the hinged cover to assure himself that they concealed the money sacks and the discarded parts of the uniform. Then, checking his appearance in the mirror, he walked from the lavatory.

On the landing, he turned right and went down the eight stairs to what an overhead sign announced was Macy's Budget Store. Walking easily, feigning a casual interest in the merchandise he passed, he attracted no particular attention. (Later, when an FBI agent interviewed members of the staff, the only person who recalled having seen him was a woman of forty, an overweight divorcée by the name of Wilhelmena Schmidt, who had noticed him because she "liked his type" and wondered in which department he worked.) At the eastern end of the store, he turned right and began to mount the broad stairs leading to the main floor, drawing a deep breath as he went. The last obstacle within the store lay ahead.

On the occasions when Moreno had studied the store and its procedures, he had observed that, although the store did not normally open until 9:45, the revolving doors leading to the street were unlocked approximately one half hour earlier, permitting customers to come in out of the weather to stand about in a roped-off area extending across the eastern end of the building. There was some passing in and out of employees, so gaps existed in the circumference of the ropes to permit access. A security guard was posted at most openings.

Now, as he climbed the stairs, whistling tunelessly, he was conscious of his heart pulsing. At the landing he stiffened imperceptibly and paused: A security guard was standing at the top of the stairs with his back to him, barring the way but as yet unaware of his presence. Moreno looked back to the lower floor, checking. Was anyone watching? No. At the foot of the stairs he saw a cleaning cart and beside it a canvas trash container and a short-handled broom. Should he retreat, pick it up and climb the stairs with it, pretending to be one of the cleaning men? No — he wasn't dressed for it, and if he was stopped and questioned he would be discovered. Should he descend to the Budget Store, cross to the stairs at the northeast corner and get to the street floor that way? He hadn't wanted to emerge from the store at 35th Street lest he be recognized by one of the Secret Service agents who had seen him enter only a few minutes before in a Brink's uniform, but he would have to take that chance.

As he turned to descend, he heard a short, high-pitched squeal. The security guard lifted the transceiver hanging from his belt and put it to his lips. Moreno could hear the faint metallic sound of a voice but could not catch the words. Could it be that the body of the dead boy had been discovered in the men's washroom and the guard was being alerted? He gathered himself for flight, and as he did the guard walked away out of sight and the way was clear.

As he reached the main floor he could see four guards in the area: three involved in an argument about a referee's call in Sunday's Giants-Dolphins game and another talking on a transceiver. He glanced at Moreno, mildly curious — he would have stopped him had he been entering the store — but when Moreno gave him a perfunctory wave and called out an easy "Good morning," he nodded and turned away.

"*Bueno*," Moreno said in a whisper as he pushed through the revolving doors and walked into the burnished morning sunlight on the thronging corner at 34th and Broadway.

The President's open limousine was parked in the blocked-off area at the western exit of the Midtown tunnel. Adam helped Joan into the car and, as she sat down in the rear seat, wrapped a heavy woolen blanket about her legs. He spoke to McGillvray who had walked back from the Secret Service lead car. "All set here," he said.

"We'll be a minute or two, sir," McGillvray said. "Have to maintain the schedule."

"Very well," Adam said.

"You might want to sit down, sir," McGillvray said. "You've got quite a bit of standing to do."

At Adam's insistence, the Secret Service had built a support into the open limousine, enabling him to stand erect while the car was in motion and leaving him free to wave to the crowds. It had been installed only the previous week and this would be the first time he would use it. It consisted of a chrome-plated tubular steel cage, padded where it contacted his body. It was attached to the rear of the front seat, waist high, and was in the shape of a horizontal oval with a narrow separation at the rear through which, by turning sideways, he could enter or leave it. Remembering how the steel back-brace John Kennedy had been wearing had kept him from slumping after the first bullet struck — holding him upright and vulnerable — the support had been so designed that it would break away if Adam's full weight were thrown against it. It had not operated perfectly in tests but this was not regarded as a serious problem since there was also a release mechanism on the instrument panel in front of the driver.

Adam was studying the apparatus. "How do you like my little Iron Maiden?" he said to Joan.

"I don't," she said. Then after a moment she added, "Adam, why can't you just sit back here with me?"

"Joan . . . let's not go through all that again."

They sat with a silence between them.

"Gerry Regan came to see me yesterday," she said.

"Gerry? To the White House?"

"He wanted me to, how can I put it, to get you not to take so many chances."

"I can see I'll have to have a word with Mr. Regan," Adam said tightly.

"But he's right, you know."

"No, Joan, he's not. I dislike discussing it because I know how it worries you, but the simple fact is that if somebody really wants to . . . to make a move, it won't make any real difference whether I'm back here or up there."

"It would make a big difference if only you would . . . "

"Joan," he said sharply. "Can we drop it?"

After a moment she said softly, "I'm not your enemy, you know. I love you."

"I know that. And I'm sorry, darling. But . . . "

McGillvray approached. "Ready to go, sir."

Out of McGillvray's line of vision, Adam patted Joan's hand, stood up and stepped into the support. The cars moved off slowly.

As Moreno walked east on 34th Street, moving with the crowd toward the platform area, he passed within fifty feet of the Command car. He went swiftly but without evident haste, turning his body sideways to slip through narrow openings, apologizing softly when he brushed against or bumped anyone. As he went, he removed a rectangular plastic-covered badge from his shirt pocket and attached it to the left lapel of his jacket. In inch-high letters it read PRESS.

He passed the area reserved for the President's limousine and edged his way through the crowd massing against the restraint of the police barricades at the southeastern end of the park. When passage was difficult, he insinuated his way through gently, murmuring the word "Press" repeatedly. Some glanced at his badge and moved aside without question, others grumbled but permitted him through. In a few minutes he had worked his way forward until he was standing in the front row.

Moreno's position had been determined only after weeks of pondering and much research. He had begun his preparation some five months earlier by searching for patterns, for predictable sets of circumstances. New York City had been selected as the site for the kidnap attempt, not only because of its potential to generate the greatest possible publicity, but because it had been observed that, in nearly every political campaign, the President made a visit to Manhattan. Moreno's research uncovered a number of traditional political practices so often repeated that they had become mandatory. He was aware of the standardized physical arrangements for public meetings, the sites used for political rallies, the Secret Service security measures, and Adam Scott's insistence on shaking hands with the public.

He had learned from a briefing-paper prepared for him by the Central Committee that outdoor political rallies in Manhattan were traditionally held in Herald Square. Three weeks after arriving in the United States, he had driven to New York City and gone to the *Daily News* building on 42nd Street, representing himself to the Chief Librarian as a writer preparing a book on the history of politics in Manhattan. Having paid the required fee, he was subsequently admitted regularly to the newspaper's morgue. There he dug deeply into the files, studying with particular care photographs of public gatherings in the Square.* He scrutinized the news stories

*Moreno did an identical study of indoor political rallies in Madison Square Garden.

of political and other outdoor rallies, making notes on any reference to the physical arrangements.

It soon became clear that virtually every public meeting of consequence held in Herald Square over the past ten years had been based on a standardized plan from which there was little significant deviation. The prefabricated platform was always the same. It was usually erected immediately to the south of the James Gordon Bennett memorial. The VIP seats were set out in two areas flanking the platform, and the provision for the featured speaker's limousine was invariably the space normally reserved as a taxi stand. There might be differences in the seating, in the speakers' stand, or in the decorations, but the essentials were constant.

The research disclosed another important pattern. If a politician wished to shake hands with the public, he had only one option: to go to the spectators ranged along the police barricades nearest to where the limousine was parked. Elsewhere, the five-foot wrought-iron fences made it difficult. In his study of Adam Scott's habits, Moreno had noted that he invariably shook hands with spectators in some part of any crowd assembled to greet him. He had carefully studied Adam's technique on television news programs; noting how the President moved quickly among or past the people — touching more than shaking hands — crossing one arm over the other as he went, and doing it with such practiced skill that he could walk at an almost normal pace and grasp or touch as many as fifty hands within fifty yards.

Moreno was aware that his plans were based on the perpetuation of a series of entrenched practices and that they could easily and unpredictably go awry, but it seemed reasonable to assume that, granted normal circumstances, his opportunity would come if he were in the right place at the right time.

Now, after months of preparation, the moment had come. All the work and all the planning had pointed toward this moment. Suddenly it broke in on him that here he was, exactly as had been prefigured scores of times in his imagination. It was as though he had lived the moment before.

He reached into the pocket Linda had sewn to the inside of his jacket and found the handcuffs. He removed them, and keeping them hidden from sight behind the waist-high crosspiece of the barricade, closed one of the bracelets on his right wrist, cupping the other in his palm. With his left hand he touched his jacket, feeling through the texture of the cloth the hard, flat shape of the bottle.

He checked his watch with the clock on the face of Macy's. According to the published schedule, the President was due to arrive in twelve minutes. As he settled down for the wait, he was totally calm.

Joan Scott's arm was tiring. Time to switch. She placed her right hand in her lap and began to wave with her left at the crowds ranging along the sidewalk in front of the Empire State building and craning from the windows above.

There was that old trouble with her cheek muscles again. She had learned that if she held a fixed smile for more than three minutes, the muscles of her jaw would cramp. She covered her mouth with a gloved hand for a moment, simulating a cough. Under the glove, she pursed her lips hard for a few seconds. When the hand went back to waving, the lips again had that lovely, slight smile for which she had become celebrated. MONA LISA OF THE WHITE HOUSE was the heading on that idiotic picture-story in *Distaff* magazine — with a half dozen close-cropped photographs of her mouth smiling alongside a blown-up reproduction of da Vinci's masterpiece. Over the years people had speculated about what was in the Mona Lisa's mind to engender that smile; what would their reaction be if they knew what the First Lady was thinking as she smiled? She was wondering if the fear was showing on her face.

The dominant fact in Oliver Hepplethwaite's life was the state of his bowels. When each day he rose from his bed and padded to the bathroom, the first focus of his awakening mind was on his lower abdomen and on the hope that the first intimations from that area would augur a successful beginning to the day.

Oliver Hepplethwaite was not happy with the bowels with which the Deity had equipped him and not infrequently said so in his prayers. Nor was his affliction to be confused with the relatively inconsequential difficulties suffered by his friends. It was not with Oliver as with those to whom he had confided his problem and who frequently irritated him by matching him symptom for symptom. No simple assistance of the systaltic rhythm with one of the multiple rows of purgatives in his medicine cabinet would serve *his* need.

So it was that Oliver Hepplethwaite began each day with, as it were, his bowels determining whether he would enter that day with joy or foreboding.

Today was filled with foreboding for he had overindulged on the weekend. So, having arrived at his place of employment — he was Assistant Manager of the Men's Haberdashery Department in Macy's Budget Store — he checked that his staff was on hand or accounted for, and as soon as was expedient, headed for the men's washroom at the landing partway up the stairs leading to the Main Floor.

As he entered, he was relieved to see that apparently no one was there: better to labor alone. He trudged to the end cubicle on the right, his favorite, eschewing the pay toilets on the left (he could see no point in the expenditure of money when he was so frequent a visitor). Oh damn . . . ! The door to his accustomed retreat was closed. Another was there. He turned in at the adjoining enclosure, and having settled down was in a position to observe his neighbor's left foot. It was twisted back and inward in an alarming fashion. Surely so contorted it must be painful. When after a few minutes the foot remained in the same position, Oliver wondered if perhaps its owner was crippled. When five minutes had passed with neither sound nor movement, he grew perturbed. Perhaps the man was sick. Perhaps he had fainted. There was no choice: he would have to investigate.

He left the cubicle and paused before the closed door.

"Hello in there. . . . "

No response.

"Hello . . . ?"

Gently he pushed on the door. A wad of toilet tissue dropped to the floor with a small thud and the door swung slowly open until it struck one of the occupant's knees. Still no response. After long hesitation, Oliver leaned forward and peered around the door. He leaped back, suddenly pale. He had seen Jimmy Turner, the red-haired messenger boy from the Exchange Desk, his buttocks jammed in the toilet bowl, his body slumped back against the wall, his head awry. . . .

"Regan here."

"Mr. Regan, this is Hans Schroeder. I'm the Chief Dispatcher at Brink's."

"Go ahead."

"Your man Williamson called me about a Brink's truck at Macy's. He told me to call you at this number."

"Yes, go ahead."

"Well, all I've got to say is that it can't be one of ours."

"Why not?"

"Well, we've only got one truck in the area at the moment — 75109 — and she's on a delivery at 23rd and Broadway."

"Are you certain?"

"I just checked. If there's a Brink's truck making a delivery at Macy's right now, there's something funny going on. It sure isn't one of ours."

Bells clanged in Regan's head. He slammed down the phone. "All stations," he shouted at Lindstrom.

Lindstrom flicked a switch. "Ready."

"Command to all stations! Green Alert! Green Alert!"

As he spoke, he could see through the windshield of the Command car the flasher-light of a police cruiser flicking its red finger across the face of the buildings not a block away, and could hear the cheers heralding the President's approach.

Chapter Six

Agreen-and-white New York City police cruiser, its roof-light flashing, moved slowly west on 34th Street. As it reached the Avenue of the Americas — known to native New Yorkers as Sixth Avenue — it turned right and proceeded north to park in a holding position at the corner of 35th. It was followed at a distance of fifty feet by the Secret Service lead car. A further fifty feet behind came the President's open limousine.

As the motorcade reached the intersection and the President came within sight, as though in response to a signal, the seated VIPs on the platform rose and began to applaud. The crowd of some fifteen thousand people burst into a full-throated roar, the sound echoing and intensified by the surrounding buildings. Patterns like wind on water swept across the Square and there was a sudden pumping, twirling and oscillating of hundreds of signs. Almost as though joining the accolade, the flags at the rear of the platform caught a thrust of wind and billowed bravely.

Adam thrust his hips forward in the chromium support-cage and raised his hands above his head, clasping them in the traditional response of boxers and politicians to their partisans. The tumult trebled. Preceded and followed by loping Secret Service agents, the limousine slowly turned right, and evoking the solemn docking of an ocean liner, cruised into the barricaded slip that had been provided and came to a stop.

At the exact second the limousine lost its inertia, one of the agents opened the rear door. Adam slipped from the support, stepped to the sidewalk and turned to offer a hand to Joan. As he did, Mayor O'Donahue and his wife — she topheavy with an over-size corsage on an oversize bust — walked from the predetermined spot where they had been positioned and the two men and their wives — for all that they had never previously met — engaged in a series of handshakes and cordialities suggestive of the reunion of old friends.

The Mayor grasped Adam's elbow with one hand and with the other indicated the pathway of red carpet leading to the platform. But Adam pulled away and both hands extended, strode briskly toward the crowd jammed against the police barricades to his right.

In an agony of tension Moreno had not drawn a breath as the handshakings were taking place. Now, as the President broke from the group and walked toward the barricades, his diaphragm ex-pelled the imprisoned air in a sudden gust. He often talked to himself in times of crisis: "Steady now," he half whispered. "Steady."

In his right hand, keeping it carefully concealed within his palm, he fingered the manacle open. With his left hand he reached into his jacket, unzipped the inner pocket and removed the bottle he had placed there before leaving the truck. Checking with his fingertips that the label was facing in the right direction, he covered the bottle with his hand, pressed it against his upper thigh and glanced down to assure himself that both hands were hidden be-hind the crosspiece of the barricade.

The President was now fifty feet to his left, reaching into a forest of outstretched hands — grasping, shaking, releasing, and approaching faster than Moreno had anticipated.

"Steady," he whispered.

In the Secret Service Briefing Manual, in order better to coordinate the actions of cooperating law enforcement agencies in the event of trouble, Regan had established two color-coded "alerts." A Green Alert dealt with an apprehended crisis and was designed to bring all security forces to a state of poised readiness. A Red Alert was to be implemented when an attempt on the President's life had been made or was anticipated. The instructions in the Briefing Manual covering each circumstance filled a dozen pages and specified the duties of each group or individual involved in the security apparatus.

Regan had observed during his years in law enforcement that it was not uncommon for major crimes to be committed when a public event of magnitude was taking place, the not unreasonable assumption of the criminals involved being that at such times the police are preoccupied and surveillance in most areas is less than usual. Consequently, when the information was relayed to him that the truck on 35th Street was not a Brink's truck — and knowing that a man disguised as a guard had entered Macy's — it immediately occurred to him that, possibly, the President's presence was being used as a diversion and that a robbery was taking place within the store. But there remained a nagging worry at the back of his mind that more than a robbery was afoot; so, having sounded the Green Alert, he called in Williamson.

"Williamson here."

"Why the hell haven't you reported on that armored truck?" he snapped. "You know it's not Brink's?"

"They told me. As far as I can tell, it's empty. No sign of anybody, although the motor's running, and running hot. I have it under surveillance."

"Can you get in?"

"Tried. Doors are locked."

"Well, keep it covered. And watch the entrance to the store. The truck could be there for a getaway. And notify Macy's security people."

"Will do."

To Lindstrom Gerry said, "Police," and on a Touch-Tone keyboard Lindstrom's fingers danced the number.

"Gerry Regan. Secret Service, Herald Square. There's a Brink's truck on 35th west of Broadway. It is not — repeat *not* — a legit Brink's vehicle. Suspect it may be getaway vehicle for possible robbery in Macy's. We're covering but passing to you. Investigate soonest. Out."

To Lindstrom he said, "All stations."

"Command to all stations. Maintain Green Alert. Maintain Green Alert."

Secret Service agent Gil Busby paced slowly along the crowd lining the police barricade. He adjusted his stride automatically to remain a distance of approximately twenty feet in advance of the President, his gaze flicking from face to face in the crowd with the swift, darting precision of the eyes of a small animal. Agent Busby was not looking for a gun or for the movement of a hand reaching for a weapon; he was studying faces. His training had taught him that in crowds at a political gathering there was a norm. All the faces would be, despite their diversity, essentially alike: eyes shining, lips smiling or open in shouting, and with usually a flush of excitement to the skin. What agent Busby was searching for in the living mosaic passing before his eyes was that one face that differed, the individual who did not fit.

His eyes came to rest on Moreno and his brows drew down in a sudden frown.

As the President turned from Mayor O'Donahue and walked toward the barricades to begin shaking hands, Jim McCurdy, who was standing at the foot of the stairs leading to the platform, muttered, "He *would*!"

In the Command car a voice broke in. "Section Five to Command."

"Command to Five. Go ahead."

"Reporting a fight at the entrance to the McAlpin Hotel."

"How many in it?"

"Two . . . it looks like."

"Could it be a diversion?"

"Pretty sure it isn't. Looks like two guys who. . . . "

"Then what the hell are you bothering me for? Call the bloody cops!" He replaced the microphone. "Dumb bastard," he mumbled.

Lindstrom said quietly, "Macy's security. Line One."

Gerry picked up the phone. "Regan here."

"Mr. Regan, this is John Rodemacher, head of Macy's security. We've got a murder here."

"Repeat."

"A murder. We've had a murder in the store. One of our employees has been found dead in the Budget Store washroom."

"What makes you think it's murder?"

"His neck's broke. His body was hid in one of the toilets." There were confused sounds on the line. Rodemacher said, "Can you hold a sec?" In a moment he was back on. "I've just had a further report from one of my guys. He was checking the john and found a gun, a badge and some other stuff in a Brink's cap, all stuffed in a waste-disposal can." Another pause; muffled excited voices. "Are you still there?"

"Go ahead."

"He says he also found some money sacks. No money in them, just wads of . . . like, stacks of paper, same size as money."

"Exactly where are you?"

"In my office. Main floor mezzanine. South side."

"Wait there." He slammed down the phone, saying as he did, "Moran. Fast!"

"Command to Special Detail."

"Special Detail. Moran."

"Moran, Gerry. A murder in Macy's. Meet their security chief in his office, main floor mezzanine. Inform police headquarters and get me a report soonest."

"McCurdy," he said to Lindstrom.

"Command to McCurdy."

"McCurdy here."

Regan's voice was low but his words were clipped. "Jim. Trouble. In spades! I've got a fake Brink's truck on 35th. Motor running but empty. I've got a murder in Macy's, apparently by a disguised Brink's guard. The whole thing's fishy as hell. Get to the President immediately. Surround him. Get him to the platform but stay on ground level until you're cleared. If you see or hear anything, *anything*, get him under the platform. Confirm."

"Confirmed."

"Then go . . . and for God's sake keep it quiet! No panic."

Agent Busby stopped and looked hard at Moreno. Within a second his inventory noted that Moreno's face was pale and shining with perspiration, and that he was wearing a gray suit with a badge reading PRESS on the lapel of his jacket. He saw, too, that both his hands were out of sight behind the barricade.

At that moment, to Busby's left, there was a sudden splintering crash and a sound of screaming. He turned and saw that, twenty feet away, one of the barricades had toppled forward from the pressure of the crowd. A dozen people had tumbled to the concrete and were struggling to regain their feet. The screams were coming from a girl of about six whose leg was trapped beneath the fallen barricade. Busby could see that the lumber beneath the fallen spectators was pressing on the child's ankle. He reacted involuntarily to the more dramatic stimulus and ran to help her. He bent over, shielding the girl from the threshing, shouting adults struggling to scramble erect, and eased her leg free.

As he straightened up, he looked back toward Moreno. As he did, he saw the President reach out his right hand, saw Moreno's hand move toward it, and glimpsed a flash of metal in the sunlight.

Jim McCurdy was at his post at the base of the platform stairs when he received the urgent call from Gerry Regan. With him were agents Quinn, Otto and Francis. He spoke one word: "Surround!" and went off on the half-run toward the President, his men following. Above the cheers of the crowd he heard a crash and a scream. He saw the barricade tip forward and fall and saw the pressure from behind send a second rank of spectators sprawling atop the first. He saw Busby sprint to help a little girl, saw the President pause in his stride and turn toward the commotion; saw him, as though in a nightmare, motionless for a moment with his right hand suspended in midair. . . . Then he saw a hand reach out from the crowd, saw it strike like a snake and saw Adam turn and look, surprised, at his wrist.

Even from thirty feet away McCurdy could clearly see the bracelet of a pair of handcuffs encircling the President's wrist and a short chain stretching to the wrist of a man he hadn't yet been able to single out in the crowd. Then a leg swung over the barricade and a tall, heavyset man in a gray suit quickly scissored his other leg and landed beside the President. There was something in the man's hand. . . . A bottle! He raised it above his head and shouted something that McCurdy couldn't hear. From the crowd: screams, panic, shoving. As McCurdy sprinted forward he saw in one glance the crowd falling back and the printing on the bottle. . . .

In large red letters was the word NITRO.

At the distant sounds of screaming from the Square, Linda Rodriguez threw aside the blanket and leaped into the driver's seat. She saw a ring of men, some in uniform, others in street clothes, surrounding the truck. Others were approaching. As they saw her — in their view, an indistinct gray figure in a guard's uniform — some drew guns and dropped to one knee, others crouched and ran toward the truck. She shoved in the clutch and jammed the gearshift into low. As the truck leaped forward she heard a thudding of bullets against metal and glass and saw sparkling pockmarks appear on the windshield as though by magic. She felt more than heard the tires rupture as lead ripped into rubber. The steering wheel bucked in her hands and it took all her strength to hold it in control. Ahead, she could see the police barricade at Broadway, and beyond it a mounted policeman, and people running in all directions.

Within the Command car Regan could hear the sounds of panic from where he knew the President must be but could not see what was happening. His first impulse was to dash from the car. His second was to call for information. He knew that to do so would bring a Babel of overlapping reports, so he contained himself, sitting in an isolation that seemed a lifetime long. Then there was a click from the speaker.

"Moran to Command!"

"Regan here."

"Brink's truck heading for the Square! Brink's truck heading for the Square!"

"All stations!" Gerry shouted into his microphone. "Red Alert! Brink's truck is enemy — repeat *enemy*! Location, 35th at Broadway! Intercept! Intercept!"

The moment McCurdy read the word NITRO on the bottle in Moreno's hand he literally skidded to a stop, spreading his arms to restrain the agents behind him. "Quinn, inform Command!" he shouted.

Only seconds had passed since Moreno had encircled Adam's wrist with the manacle, but already the two men stood in a circle of widening isolation. The crowd was falling back, shoving, cursing and screaming in panic, but the level of sound had now dropped to where McCurdy could hear Moreno's almost maniacal scream.

"Back!" he screeched. "Get back or I'll kill you all!" He shouted it again and again; his face livid, his eyes staring, the cords on his neck like ropes, the spittle spraying from his mouth.

From behind him, indistinctly, over the noise of the crowd, McCurdy could hear gunfire and the roar of a motor. There was no time to contemplate its meaning. He held up a hand of restraint to the other agents, and slowly, deliberately, began to walk toward Moreno and the President.

Moreno made as though to throw the bottle to the pavement and McCurdy halted. "Get back, you bastard!" he shrilled. "Back or I'll blow up the whole goddamn square!"

From the moment the handcuff had closed on his wrist, Adam had made no move to resist or struggle free. He looked into Moreno's face which was only inches from his own. He could see the perspiration streaming, the foam at the corners of the mouth, the fear in the eyes, and the madness. . . .

In that moment Moreno looked at him. "Tell them to get back!" he screamed. "Tell them, or I'll blow you all straight to hell!"

McCurdy began to move in once again. Adam looked into Moreno's face and raised a hand. McCurdy paused, uncertain, fighting with himself.

"Tell your men to get back," Adam said.

McCurdy stood irresolute, his face taut. His every instinct, all his training, urged him to throw himself at Moreno even if it meant death.

"That's an order, Jim!" Adam shouted.

McCurdy hesitated. He took Quinn's transceiver and put it to his lips. "McCurdy to Command."

Lindstrom came on: "He's on his way."

As he spoke, Regan burst through the fleeing crowd, paused a moment and then ran to McCurdy's side.

"Back, *you*!" Moreno screamed. "I'm warning you . . . !"

Regan looked at Moreno's face and then at the bottle. He put his lips to McCurdy's ear. "Is it nitro?"

"If it is, there's enough there to wipe out the whole Square."

"Is he bluffing?"

"Don't know."

Regan studied Moreno. After a moment he said, "I don't think he is."

From the northwest corner of the Square there was the sound of screeching tires and the roar of a motor.

"That goddamn Brink's truck!" Regan said.

As the armored truck raced toward the police barricade obstructing the entrance to Broadway, Linda could see people in the Square running in panic, fleeing the shooting in the street, the oncoming truck and the unknown horror happening at the heart of the Square. She could see a mounted policeman struggling to stay in the saddle of his mount which was rearing and turning, infected by the fear now almost palpable in the crowd.

The truck smashed into the barricade sending splintered planks flying. Linda wrestled with the wheel, fighting to avoid the policeman and his mount, but a fender struck the horse on its left flank and it went down with a scream. The officer was hurled thirty feet, landed on a shoulder and rolled to the curbstone in a boneless simulation of a cartwheel.

Sudden tears streamed down Linda's face as she tugged the wheel to the right and turned down Broadway. The crowd parted as soil before a plow. Incredibly, no one was struck, although the truck passed directly over a boy who instinctively flattened his body and was untouched.

At 34th Street, she grasped the left side of the steering wheel and pulled on it with all her weight. The truck careered to the left, the tortured rubber of the tires flapping and protesting and the rims sending off sparks as they gouged the concrete. Approaching Sixth Avenue, she saw Moreno and the President standing in the clear with a ragged circle of perhaps a dozen men surrounding them. She gave a final heave on the wheel. The truck lurched to the left, bowled over a barricade, ripped away the front fender of the President's limousine, mounted the curb and squealed to a sudden stop as she jammed on the brakes.

Moreno stepped behind Adam, pulled him against his chest and backed toward the truck. As he reached it, Linda swung open the door and he backed in, jerking cruelly at Adam's wrist, pulling until he followed. The door slammed shut.

"We've got to do *something*!" McCurdy agonized.

"Easy," Regan said. "They're not going far in *that*."

The armored truck sat before them, squat and ugly, the windshield and body pitted from the impact of bullets, the tires twisted grotesquely on the rims, the engine hissing and venting steam. There came another, a higher-pitched hiss, the sound of an amplifier, and Moreno's voice, metallic but clear, blared from the truck.

"This is a warning! This is a warning! Stay back or your President will die!" There was a strained, frantic inflection in his voice.

Regan said, "He's mad."

The truck growled into low gear and leaped forward. The crowd that had retreated to north of 35th Street fell back in a howling scramble. At 35th, Moreno hauled the wheel to the left, and as he reached Broadway, turned right, heading north.

Regan, with McCurdy at his heels, sprinted to the Command car. He seized the microphone Lindstrom handed to him. "All stations! All stations!" he shouted. "President Scott has been kidnapped and is being held hostage in a Brink's armored truck. Truck now proceeding north on Broadway from Herald Square. Do not — repeat *not* — intercept."

To his driver he said, "Follow. Flasher but no siren."

A police officer had the alertness to swing away one of the barricades. The Command car wheeled clear and within seconds was following half a block behind the armored truck as it bumped and swayed up the middle of Broadway. The side streets had been blocked off earlier in anticipation of the President's motorcade to Times Square and the street was empty of traffic. In the Command car, microphone in hand, Regan leaned forward in his seat, peering through the windshield, issuing orders and giving progress reports as they went.

The truck lurched to the right on squirming tires and was wrenched back violently to the middle of the street. Regan said softly to McCurdy, "If that *is* nitro in that bottle, I hope to Jesus he knows how to handle it!"

As the truck approached 42nd Street, Linda, who had moved to the passenger's seat, grasped the handle of the door, knuckles white against her tanned skin. Moreno was half standing, his face streaming perspiration as he fought the steering wheel. Adam, shackled to a ring welded to the wall of the van, was on his knees striving to maintain his balance.

Moreno studied the scene at the intersection. Commuters were streaming from the IRT subway exit on the southeast corner. As they saw the crippled and steaming truck — followed by the Command car, its light flashing, and beyond it a half dozen police cruisers — they stopped, transfixed. As he approached the corner, Moreno angled to the right and the truck bore down on the throng at the intersection. They broke and ran. As he came abreast of the entrance to the IRT, he braked. Linda threw the door open, leaped from the truck and darted into the stairwell. The door banged shut and the truck lumbered off.

"He's getting away!" McCurdy shouted.

"Not far," said Regan.

He punched the microphone button. "All stations. Suspect in kidnapping has entered IRT subway, southeast corner, 42nd and Broadway. Suspect wearing Brink's uniform. Stop all trains. Close all exits."

"Look!" McCurdy shouted, pointing.

A whitish cloud was pouring from the IRT stairwell. Men and women were running from the exit, coughing, gasping, rubbing their eyes.

Descending the stairway, Linda slowed her pace to avoid attracting the attention of the commuters streaming toward her. As she went she began to hyperventilate; inhaling, holding and expelling great lungfuls of air. At the bottom of the stairs there was a small foyer in the shape of an irregular rectangle thirty by twenty feet, off which there was a newspaper stand, three token-sellers' cubicles and five turnstiles leading to the subway platform. Reaching the floor level, she swung sharply left, took three strides and turned to the wall. Removing a tear-gas canister from the left-hand pocket of her jacket, she pulled the tab and dropped it to the floor. At the same moment she closed her eyes, drew a deep breath and held it.

In seconds, the crowd in the foyer was weeping and coughing, blinded and convulsed by the fumes. Linda counted to three and began a series of swift moves, actions rehearsed dozens of times, in which no motion was wasted. She ripped open the jacket — it had been closed with dome-fasteners — and shucked it off. A single jerk and the trousers broke away. With one sweep of her hand she pushed the cap from her head, and with it the wig, and her blond hair cascaded to her shoulders. She turned left, took three strides, felt for the handrail and started up the stairs. The mustache was pulled away and dropped as she neared street level.

Around her she could hear the screams, the hacking and the coughing of commuters scrambling up the stairwell. As she reached the top and turned sharply to the left, her lungs were aching. She took another three strides before she dared open her eyes, two more before she gulped in fresh air.

All about her men and women were gasping and coughing. An old woman was on her knees, retching. A child was in hysterics. Linda simulated a paroxysm of coughing, rubbed at her eyes and staggered toward the crowd that had gathered. Within seconds she had melted into it. By the time the first police cruiser whooped to the scene, she had crossed 42nd Street and was walking north on Broadway, looking like any other attractive woman in a suit with a culotte skirt, and utterly unlike the uniformed Brink's guard who, only ninety seconds earlier, had ducked into the subway stairwell.

The armored truck was now preceded by a phalanx of New York Police Department cruisers, their roof-lights flashing, their sirens emitting occasional small growls. One of the cruisers was equipped with a public address system and it blared repeatedly, "This is a police warning. Clear the Square. Clear the Square. . . . "

As the truck entered Times Square, Moreno slowed to no more than five miles an hour. Just south of 44th Street he angled to the right, and at the intersection, hauled hard on the wheel. Curving to the left in a 180-degree turn, the truck mounted the sidewalk and stopped. When Moreno turned off the motor, the truck was facing south at the exact center of Times Square.

Regan had slowed the Command car as the truck began its turn. He ordered the driver to ease to the curb adjoining the Armed Forces Recruiting Center some forty yards south of the truck's position. As he stepped out onto the sidewalk, Lindstrom powered the window down.

"What do we do now, sir?" he said.

Regan did not reply for a moment. His eyes were fixed on the armored truck squatting on its tattered tires, jetting steam and leaking coolant.

"Christ knows," he said.

Chapter Seven

The armored truck had been parked for no more than five minutes but already the perimeter of Times Square was jammed with people. They formed a ragged circle; ranging from the Allied Chemical building on the south, pressing outward against the storefronts and theaters and reaching a northernmost point at 45th Street. The circumference seemed to have been determined by an unspoken consensus; there were too few police on hand to have established it. The entire area was buzzing with hushed conversations. In the distance the muted whoop of a score of police sirens could be heard.

From his position by the Command car, Regan could glimpse occasional intimations of activity from within the dark interior of the truck. To diminish the glare from the windshield, he reached into a pocket for his polarized sunglasses and put them on. As he did, the kidnapper came from the van of the truck and slid behind the steering wheel. There was a click, the hiss of an amplifier and a voice boomed into the Square.

"Attention. Attention. Who is the person in authority?"

Regan bent down and spoke to Lindstrom through the open window of the Command car. "Public address," he said.

"Ready."

Regan put the microphone to his lips and blew on it. There was a roar from the speaker beside him.

"I'm in charge here," he said.

"Identify yourself."

"Regan. White House Detail, United States Secret Service."

He cursed inwardly at his feeling of impotence, at the need to hold this conversation in this fashion before this crowd. His entire training had been to be inconspicuous.

"I order you to surrender immediately," he said.

To his astonishment the voice from the truck responded, "I am prepared to. I will, one minute from now."

There was the amplified sound of fumbling with the microphone. Regan saw Moreno pick up a piece of paper from which he began to read in a formal manner.

"Pay careful attention. The President of the United States is my hostage. He is unharmed and will not be harmed if you follow instructions. Refuse, and he will die. This truck contains a large quantity of explosives and can be blown up at any time. . . . "

A gasp and a muttering from the crowd. The circle widened.

" . . . If anyone approaches, the President will die. You have been warned."

Regan broke in. "For the last time, I order you to surrender immediately!"

The voice from the truck interrupted. "Pay attention. I will surrender in fifteen seconds. I am unarmed. I will come out with my hands up. *Ten seconds.* For the time being, the President will remain in the truck. I will explain the conditions of his release after I surrender. *Five seconds.* A final warning . . . if anyone comes near the truck or harms me, the President will die and the responsibility will be yours." There was a pause. "I am now ready to surrender."

As Regan watched, barely able to hide his astonishment, a door of the truck opened and the kidnapper stepped out. He pushed the door closed and turned, placing his hands on top of his head.

"Where do I surrender?" he shouted. Without amplification, his voice sounded distant and subdued.

Regan passed the microphone to Lindstom. "Over here," he shouted, waving an arm.

As Moreno walked toward the Command car, Lindstrom passed a pair of handcuffs through the open window. The crowd, silent through the exchange of conversation, now seethed with excitement. As the kidnapper reached Regan he said in a formal manner, "I surrender to you as a representative of the United States government."

"To hell with that," Regan said, snapping the cuffs on the kidnapper's wrists and yanking open the rear door of the Command car. "In," he said sharply. He seized Moreno by the upper arm, propelled him into the back seat and stepped in behind him.

"P.A.," he said to Lindstrom.

"Ready."

"Your attention please!" he said into the microphone. "The President of the United States has been kidnapped. He is being held in the armored truck you see in the middle of the Square. A warning: the truck may be booby-trapped and might explode if anyone goes near it. No one — I repeat, *no one* is to approach the truck for any reason. All agents and police officers will see that this order is obeyed."

He put down the microphone and turned toward Moreno. "Now," he said brusquely, "what's your game?"

"Believe me, this is no game."

"You will release the President immediately."

"First, I will tell you our conditions. . . ."

"I'm not interested in your goddamn conditions. You are under arrest. The penalty for kidnapping is death, mister, and if you want to save your neck you'll tell me, and quick, how to get the President out of there. Now, cut all the horseshit and tell me. *Now!*"

"I'll tell you when you shut up. How can I tell you anything when you keeping shouting?"

Regan restrained an impulse to smash a fist into the face before him. He glared at Moreno. This wasn't the man he had seen handcuffed to the President fifteen minutes ago — his eyes wild, his lips drawn back and slavering, a hint of hysteria in his voice. The man before him was unnaturally calm. He's mad, he thought. And dangerous.

"Okay," he said. "Talk."

"First, about the truck. It is, in your words, booby-trapped. If anybody tries to . . ."

"We know all that."

"Second," Moreno continued, unperturbed, "I have a partner in the crowd. He has a remote-control device. With it he can blow up the truck anytime we choose. So that you know we're not bluffing, blow your horn three times."

"What the hell are you talking about?"

"You want to know how to free your President? I'm telling you. Have your driver blow the horn three times."

Regan glared at Moreno balefully. "Okay, Bob," he said.

"Blow the goddamn horn."

"Look at the truck," Moreno said quickly.

The horn sounded. A second later there was a small, muffled bang and a puff of smoke issued from beneath the hood of the truck.

"You see," Moreno said, a hint of triumph in his voice, "we don't play games. We can blow up the truck any time we want to."

Contemplating Moreno, his mind ticking off the components of the problem, Regan found himself at a loss, uncertain. He could see no options open to him. The strangely self-assured man next to him had all the cards at the moment and knew it. He, Regan, dared take no risks; the stakes were too great. He would have to mask his uncertainty and play for time.

He looked coolly at Moreno. "You're a fool," he said.

"I'm no fool."

"You're a fool if you think this ridiculous plan of yours has a snowball's chance."

"We'll see."

"You realize you're taking on the entire United States?"

"It's a simple proposition: whether or not you people are prepared to trade your President's life for mine."

"You really think it's that simple?"

"Look, Mr. Regan, I'm not here to debate with you. And you're running out of time."

"Meaning?"

"That if I'm not released in fifteen minutes, my partner blows up the truck. Now, do you or don't you want to know our terms?"

Regan feigned unconcern. "Go ahead. What the hell."

As Moreno outlined the conditions, it was obvious that he had committed the speech to memory and had rehearsed it often.

"The first condition: No one may come closer than one hundred feet to the truck. Second condition: The American people must be permitted to remain in Times Square; I have a partner and he must be able to mix with the crowd. Third condition: The United States government must prepare a ransom of fifty million dollars in gold. . . . "

"Only fifty million?"

"Fifty million dollars in gold. The gold is to be placed aboard Pan World Airways, Flight 367, departing Kennedy airport at six tonight. Fourth condition: The United States government must provide a safe-conduct on the flight for me and at least one other.

The safe-conduct must be guaranteed by and signed by the Vice-President of the United States. No passengers will be permitted, but the normal flight crew and six stewardesses must be aboard."

He paused a moment, recollecting. When he resumed, his voice was flat, deadly. "Let me warn you. If you consider diverting the plane, be aware of the following facts: There is a timing mechanism in the truck; it is connected to the explosives and is set for exactly midnight tonight. When my partner and I have arrived at our destination — a destination I shall announce to the pilot when we're airborne — a telephone call will be made to the White House giving instructions on how to release the President. If our plane is diverted, or if any other trick is tried, the telephone call will not come, the timing mechanism will blow up the truck and President Scott will be instantly killed. If he dies, the responsibility will be yours.

"There are other conditions. You'll be told what they are later. Now, you will release me." He lifted his manacled hands and looked at his wristwatch. "You have eight minutes."

Regan felt the stirrings of hope. He now knew the dimensions of the problem and his mind was already leaping ahead, pinpointing potential weaknesses.

He said, "You realize I can't accept your terms?"

"You have no choice."

"I don't have the authority. I'll report to my chief what you've said."

"I'm not interested in *how* it's done, I'm simply telling you what *must* be done. And now . . . take these off."

Regan hesitated. The thought of freeing Moreno galled him. "I don't think that would be very wise," he said.

"Why not?"

"Those people out there will kill you."

Moreno looked out at the crowd, a frown furrowing his brow. It was obviously a complication he hadn't considered. Regan pressed his advantage. "People have seen you on television. Your picture will be in every paper within the hour."

A silence hung heavy. After a moment, Moreno looked up.

"Good point," he said. "I'll accept what I believe you call protective custody. Get me a room — no, a suite of rooms in a hotel near here, and arrange a guard."

"Will the Waldorf do?" Regan said snidely.

Moreno didn't so much as blink. "It'll do fine."

Regan turned to Lindstrom. "All stations," he said.

He picked up his microphone and stepped out of the car. Off to his right he saw a police cruiser, its roof-light pulsing. He beckoned to it. Tires screamed as it started to him in sudden acceleration. It slowed as he held up a restraining hand. There were two officers in the front seat. When he explained that they were to transfer Moreno to the Waldorf, they flashed a look at each other, eyebrows raised. At the Waldorf, he told them, they would be met by a Secret Service agent with specific instructions.

He lifted his microphone. "Command to lead car. Come in."

"Lead car. McGillvray here."

"Report on your position and personnel."

"Position: Broadway at 41st. Personnel: agents Rakoff and Harvey."

"President Scott has been kidnapped. A suspect is in protective custody. I'm going to transfer him to . . . " he swallowed, "to the Waldorf Astoria Hotel on Park Avenue at 50th. You will proceed there immediately, get a suite of rooms and meet NYPD cruiser, number . . . "

"598," the driver supplied.

" . . . NYPD cruiser, number 598, at the Park Avenue entrance. Suspect is to be taken under close arrest to his quarters and a secure guard mounted on a twenty-four-hour basis. Confirm."

"Confirmed."

"All stations," Regan continued. "Suspect in kidnapping being removed in NYPD cruiser, number 598. Route is, Times Square to 42nd. East on 42nd to Park Avenue. North on Park to the Waldorf Astoria Hotel. All units en route facilitate transfer."

A voice broke in on the speaker. "To the Waldorf, Mugsy."

Regan lifted his microphone. "One more smart-ass crack like that," he snarled, "and I'll personally kick whoever's tail it is all the way to Brooklyn!"

He pulled open the door of the Command car and jerked a thumb at Moreno. "Out."

"First I signal that all's well," Moreno said. "Tell your driver to blow four blasts on his horn."

"God *damn* you. . . . !" Regan exploded. He caught himself and said to the driver. "Do it."

As the horn sounded, Moreno climbed from the car. "Take

these off," he said, raising his hands.

Regan turned the key in the lock, led Moreno to the police cruiser, shoved him in, slammed the door and turned away. As he did, his face was purple and his lips were moving.

Part Two

Chapter Eight

Air Force Two was holding over Lansing waiting for a layer of ground fog to be burned off by the morning sun. Vice-President Ethan Roberts was seated alone in the stateroom, reviewing a speech; underlining words, putting in parentheses, readying it for delivery. The Captain came quickly from the cockpit, pale, and stood by his seat. Ethan continued working.

"Mr. Vice-President . . . !" There was a slight tremor in the Captain's voice.

"Just a minute."

"I'm sorry, sir. It's urgent."

Ethan looked up, feeling a touch of apprehension. He dreaded flying.

"What is it?"

"Sorry, sir, but we've just received a message from Lansing Control that the President has been kidnapped."

The words struck him like a blow to the head. He stood up, a hand going to the back of the seat for support. The Captain handed him a piece of paper. Ethan read it in a sweep of his eyes down the handwritten scrawl.

Please inform the Vice-President that President Scott has been kidnapped and is being held hostage in New York City. It is urgently requested that he return to Washington without delay. Please forward ETA. — *James Rankin, Press Secretary to the President.*

"What do you want me to do, sir?" the Captain asked.

"Turn back, for God's sake!"

"I'm afraid we'll have to sit down at Detroit. Fuel."

"Then *do* it. But move."

The Captain turned and ran to the cockpit. Ethan was suddenly dizzy. He sat down abruptly. In a minute he buzzed for his Appointments Secretary. "Get up front and find out if I can talk to Washington," he said. "Jim Rankin at the White House."

James Walker, Secretary of Defense, was seated in his office, feet on the desk, fingertips held to fingertips. He had cleared his desk of the morning mail and with ten minutes before his first appointment was contemplating his own and the nation's navel. Now, he thought — at long last now — the political nonsense was about to end and things could get back to business-as-usual normalcy. An industrialist before he was summoned to the Cabinet, he disdained politics: it was untidy, unstructured and unpredictable, and in his view a necessary evil. As a result of Adam's junketing about the country there were too many tag ends dangling to suit his precise mind. Maybe tomorrow he could get some overdue decisions and get things tidied up.

The direct line to the President's office buzzed. Odd: Adam was in New York City. He dropped his feet from the desk and reached for the phone. The high back of his chair sprang forward and whacked him on the back of the head. "Damn," he said.

"Jim Walker here."

"Jim, it's Rankin."

"Good morning. And what the hell are you doing using the direct line?"

"Jim, listen to me carefully. The President has been kidnapped in New York City. I know it sounds mad but hear me out. . . . "

When he put down the phone a minute later he buzzed his secretary on the intercom.

"Miss Davies, put me through to General Harbison. He'll be in his office at the Pentagon. I'll stay on the line." No more than five seconds passed and Harbison was on. Walker's voice was icy calm.

"Ernie. Jim Walker. Apparently President Scott has been kidnapped and is being held hostage in New York City. Will you be kind enough, immediately, to do the following things: Bring all National Guard units to full alert. Cancel all leaves. Second, full security at all defense installations. No . . . wait a minute. Instead, put Emergency Plan-B in effect. Emergency Plan-B. That's B for Baker. Repeat it back, please. . . . Right. When you've done that, call me back. You'll be able to reach me in my car or at the White House."

He put down the phone and buzzed his secretary. "Miss Davies, would you be kind enough to cancel all my appointments for today. And have my car brought round right away, please."

Herbert Thurlow, Secretary of Agriculture, was being shown through Art R. Eagleson's Chick Hatchery, Inc., on the outskirts of Lincoln, Nebraska. As he had been driven through the gate he had read the enormous sign WORLD'S LARGEST CHICK HATCHERY, with a slogan in smaller lettering, Nobody Here But Us Chickens. Now, masking his profound boredom — the only evidence of it a glaze on his eyeballs — he stood at the threshold of an enormous barnlike room, throbbing with the melding of a dozen sustained sounds. To relieve the tedium of this particular duty call — and because he had that kind of mind — he decided, even as Eagleson began pouring out his practiced statistics, to segregate and identify each sound.

First, the canned music. Easy . . . Mantovani, who else? There was, of course, the sustained whish of the air-conditioning system. That sporadic whoosh from various parts of the room puzzled him for a moment until he identified it as feed being dumped from conveyor buckets into enormous hoppers sixty feet above, from which galvanized tin tentacles stretched to the dozens of containers below. He readily detected the clicking of the conveyor belt and the hum of the motor that powered it. There was, however, one sound he couldn't extract — a sustained, high-pitched, muted whistle. It was only when Eagleson raised the top of one of the rectangular containers to permit a look within that he realized the sound was the confined cheeping of ten thousand chicks.

" . . . In a very real sense," Eagleson was saying, with the stilted accents of a man who has parrotted a speech dozens of times, "what we have here is a factory. We manufacture a product. Just as General Motors brings many different parts together on an assembly line to produce an automobile — a machine capable of movement and sound, designed to meet a consumer's needs — so we here at Eagleson's assemble the various components, and they are many:

eggs, temperature-controlled brooders, irradiated light, fortified water, our own unique blend of feed, even environmental music . . . " He chuckled in anticipation. "Music for getting laid by, as we sometimes call it." He paused for the joke to register and then continued. "The end result is a product, a product capable of movement and sound, designed to meet a consumer's need in a very special way. . . . "

Ugh! thought Herb. I may never eat chicken again.

A girl came running toward them, her face flushed. Herb watched her, admiring the movement of her breasts beneath her sweater and the bounce of her long blond hair as it streamed behind.

"Excuse me, Mr. Eagleson," she said breathlessly, "but there's a long-distance call for Mr. Thurlow. It's from Washington, sir. The White House, sir. They said it was very urgent."

Herb turned and went off, loping toward the door through which the girl had entered. Eagleson said, "Excuse me," and barged past to take the lead. Herb thought, he even *runs* like a chicken, the way his rump swings back and forth.

He took the phone that was handed him and said, "Thurlow here." A voice said, "Oh, good! Will you hold please?" Jim Rankin came on.

"Herb?"

"I'm on. Go ahead."

"Herb, the President's been kidnapped. . . . "

"He's been *what*?"

"Now look, Herb, let me go ahead and I'll fill you in as fast as I can. He was kidnapped this morning in New York City. As far as we know he's okay. We don't have many facts. We don't know who the kidnapper is and it isn't clear yet what they're going to do. But believe me, Herb, it's no hoax. . . . "

"Jim, look. . . . "

"Please don't ask questions. I'm trying to track down all the Cabinet and I can't take the time. The important thing is this: Get here as fast as you can. The airlines have been told to make every plane available, even if they have to bump passengers. So get out to an airport and get in here. Send word on your arrival time."

"Jim, listen. . . . "

"Sorry."

There was a click and then a sustained buzz. He put the phone down.

"Great jumpin' Jesus!" he said.

Barney McCrory, Secretary of Labor, was just too damn content even to consider getting out of bed. He tugged at the rumpled sheet, pulled it up over the thickly matted hair on his enormous chest, dropped a second pillow behind his head and lay in lassitude watching the girl through the kitchen door where she was making coffee.

Three times, he thought. Twice last night and just now again. What a broad! He'd have to call Keith when he got back to Washington and tell him he sure steered him right. He looked about the apartment. Very nice. But why not? — at what she charged she could afford it.

The only troubling thought that intruded into his enormous sense of well-being was the nagging knowledge that he had to make a luncheon speech to the CIO brass at the Sheraton-Cadillac, hold a press conference at the Labor Temple at 3:30 and, tonight, argue the Administration's case in an open forum on local television at Cobo Hall. So he *was* Secretary of Labor; couldn't the Secretary of Labor talk to somebody else but workers on something else but labor problems . . . ?

Janet came to the door of the bedroom — naked as a jaybird, dammit! — and smiled.

"Mr. McMillan. . . . "

"Barry."

"Barry, would you mind if I put on the radio?"

"Hell no. Anything you want, baby."

Barry McMillan — right? He'd have to remember. Matched the initials on his briefcase. Everything was copasetic. He'd sure have to find a reason to get back to Detroit as soon as . . . The radio broke in on his thoughts:

"*. . . A crowd of about five thousand now rings Times Square. In the center is the armored truck in which the President is being held hostage. As far as is known at this time, he is unharmed. Mr. Scott was seized by his abductors at 8:42 this morning just as he arrived for an election rally in Herald Square. The White House has announced that members*

*of the Cabinet are being summoned to Washington where a meeting has
been scheduled for eleven this morning. . . . "*

Barney McCrory, alias Barry McMillan, was already zipping up
his trousers and stepping into his shoes.

Charles Garvin, Secretary of Housing and Urban Development,
was, to put it simply, stealing a day, and had constructed an elaborate rationale to justify it. This is how it went:

By luck, and with the assistance of a sympathetic secretary, his
calendar for the day was clear. And because he was undoubtedly
the worst public speaker in the Cabinet — with an infinite and
ingrained skill for putting both political feet in his mouth — he had
no assignment from the Speakers Bureau. And because he happened to be in California, partly to meet tomorrow with the California Mayors Association and partly to vote, and because he had
heard that The Big Ones were being taken in record numbers off
Baja California, and because, if he chartered a Lear jet, he could
leave Los Angeles at two in the morning, get in at least six hours
on the water and be back by early afternoon, and because there
really was no compelling reason why he *shouldn't* go, he went.

He had been careful to ensure that nobody knew where he was
— "It's really none of their damn business; heaven knows the
country's getting its pound of flesh ninety-nine percent of the time"
— he had informed only his secretary. And that was why when he
had just nicely tied into an approximately one hundred and twenty-
five pound sailfish and was beginning to pump it in, and heard the
ship-to-shore rig buzz, and had to unbelt and get out of the chair
and pass over the rod, he was red in the face with anger.

When he emerged from the cabin no more than two minutes
later, the blood had ebbed, and if anything he was pale beneath his
tan.

Diego, rhythmically pumping and taking up slack, got ready to
turn back the rod.

"She's a beauty, Mr. G."

The United States Secretary of Housing and Urban Development squinted against the sun and watched as the great fish thrust
its length clear of the water, hung for a long moment, lashing and

106

glistening in the morning sunlight, and fell back to the foaming surface of the ocean.

"Cut her loose, Diego," he said sadly. "We're heading back."

Henrietta Cown had just had her hair shampooed. The girl was applying the silver rinse when Mr. Maurice himself pushed aside the brocaded drape that covered the doorway and, Princess phone in hand, entered the cubicle.

"I'm dreadfully sorry, Madame," he fussed, "I really am. But they *insist* they must talk to you."

He placed the phone delicately on the plastic cover on her lap and plugged in the jack.

And that is why the Postmaster General wore a kerchief on her head that entire eventful day.

So, from the bumpy air over Michigan, and from Eagleson's Chick Hatchery, Inc., and from an expensive whore's bed, and from the fantail of *Diego's Luck,* and from Mr. Maurice's, and from a half-dozen other places and circumstances, the United States Cabinet was assembled.

Chapter Nine

The President of the United States was on his knees. He had discovered that if he moved as far forward in the truck as the handcuffs would permit, and dropped to his knees, he could see the Trans-Lux reader-lights on the north face of the Allied Chemical building.

The handcuff Moreno had snapped about his right wrist was still there. At the end of six inches of chain the other manacle was attached to a metal ring welded waist-high to the wall of the truck almost at the center point. He was unable to stand erect — the roof being less than five feet above the floor — and his freedom of movement was limited to a half-circle with a radius of approximately three feet, but, crouched, he could scuttle about and was able to sit without serious discomfort on a cheap gray blanket on the floor. Against the wall, within easy reach, was a two-quart glass jar filled with water, a loaf of sliced white bread in a commercial Pliofilm wrapper and an enameled metal chamberpot, within which reposed a half roll of toilet tissue.

Leaning forward, peering through the windshield, he strained to read the traversing news bulletins. It was made difficult by the fact that the narrow north end of the building displayed only six letters at a time and because the pocks dug in the windshield by the bullets each had filaments of light radiating from it. He squinted at the moving letters:

PRESIDENT SCOTT BEING HELD HOSTAGE IN ARMORED TRUCK IN TIMES SQUARE . . . . . 50 MILLION DOLLAR RANSOM DEMANDED . . . . . CABINET TO MEET IN SPECIAL SESSION AT

The steel bracelet was biting into his wrist. He scuttled back and
sat on the blanket with his back to the wall.

Adam Scott, who was much given to introspection, was interested to observe that he was neither frightened nor unduly worried.
He had heard Moreno voice the threat that he would blow up the
truck if his demands were not met but, whatever his demands —
and apparently he was asking fifty million dollars and a safe-conduct
— it seemed to Adam they would pose no serious problem if the
Cabinet decided to accede. The question was, of course, whether
or not they would. And knowing his colleagues as he did, he could
imagine the intensity of the debate that would ensue when they
confronted the issue. He put the question to himself: What would
his attitude be if he were in their position? Normally, his almost
automatic response would be to oppose yielding to extortion no
matter what the circumstances; but, he wondered, would his reaction be so immediate and so unequivocal with his own neck in the
noose or if one of the members of his Cabinet was in similar
jeopardy? Suppose, he thought, they found a way to put the question to him. Troublesome possibility . . . he'd have to think his way
through that later.

He looked at his watch. Just past ten. The news bulletin had said
the Cabinet would meet at eleven. He smiled grimly. By God,
there must have been some scurrying at the White House when the
news of the kidnapping first broke. He wondered how many members of the Cabinet they'd be able to round up; they were scattered
all over the country. His smile broadened: Wouldn't it be something if they couldn't muster a quorum. He could see them assembled in the Cabinet room with Ethan Roberts in the chair: "Gentlemen, I regret to inform you that since we do not seem to have a
quorum we cannot deal with the question of getting our esteemed
leader out of hock. Meeting adjourned."

Not funny!

The news of his abduction must be having a traumatic effect on
the country. He recalled the profound shock that followed the news
that John Kennedy had been shot. Millions of people had been
emotionally immobilized by the enormity of the event. He remem-

bered his own reaction: utter disbelief followed by a vague feeling that something in the substructure of life had come apart. Surely the first reaction to his kidnapping would be a similar incredulity — "It *can't* be! Surely it's a macabre joke!" — followed by a profound and terrible fear.

His thoughts turned to the election. If he were still in the truck tomorrow, how would it affect the voting? That it would, he had no doubt. It would be impossible for the people to make objective decisions; indeed, many would be so unnerved they wouldn't be able even to contemplate going to the polls. The men who had drafted the Constitution — even those who in 1967 had written the 25th Amendment, providing as it did for the possibility of the President being incapacitated — had never, he was certain, so much as considered a circumstance in which on election day the President would be held hostage in a booby-trapped armored truck by some refugee from the loony bin! He shook his head; the whole thing was insane.

Joan . . . ? She'd be all right. She was a resourceful woman and a courageous one, and she didn't panic easily. He'd seen that many times in their years together. But she'd be frightened, and she'd worry about him. He'd have to find some way to get word to her that he was all right.

But was he? He analyzed his personal peril. There was probably no immediate danger. If the truck was booby-trapped — and certainly that box in the corner and the care with which the kidnapper had handled the bottle of nitro argued that it was — his life depended on the skill of the man who had done the wiring. He could only conclude that the reason neither Regan's men nor the police had approached the truck was because the possibility existed that the explosives could be detonated from a distance. In this there was jeopardy, of course, but it seemed reasonable to believe that the people who had devised the elaborate plan by which he had been abducted wouldn't have done so had they not believed they could get the ransom and get away. And they would realize that they would have no chance of success unless his safety was assured. He felt some reassurance in the knowledge that they, too, had a stake in preserving him unharmed.

There was one unsettling possibility: that some eager beaver out there would appoint himself a hero and try to outwit the kidnappers and thus bring about a confrontation and force everybody's hand. That, he decided, was a possibility he did not care to dwell on at the moment.

Gerry Regan stood, hands on hips, contemplating his and the President's predicament as it lay below him. From his vantage point he could see the entire Times Square area. He had commandeered the National Theater on the east side of Broadway midway between 43rd and 44th streets, exactly opposite the armored truck, and was standing on the Loge-mezzanine level in an opulent lobby stretching the width of the building. Behind him, four sloping tunnels led to the theater itself. Before him was an entire wall of tinted glass 160 feet long and 30 feet high, permitting him to look out but leaving him almost invisible from the street.

Behind him to his left, a cacophony of sound flowed up the stairway and escalator ramps from the Orchestra level — it being, roughly, a duplicate of the area in which Gerry was standing. It was swiftly being transformed into a Command Center and was a confusion of concentrated activity. Cables snaked off and down the stairs to the street. Technicians from the New York Telephone Company were industriously installing individual telephones and tying them in to a portable switchboard. Three Xerox telecopiers were already in operation and a serviceman was running tests. A supervisor from Western Electric was peering over his half-spectacles as a small army of technicians set up a bank of Teletype machines, a Watts-line unit and a wirephoto receiver against the south wall. At the other end of the area, a group of uniformed Army Signal Corpsmen were unpacking battered crates and assembling an intimidating miscellany of transmitting and receiving equipment. Off the stairway at the south end, the manager of the theater stood with a bewildered look on his face; he had just been ejected from his private office which was rapidly being transformed into a headquarters for Regan.

Times Square, from Regan's point of view, presented an extraordinary sight. There was so little movement that the illusion was created of an enormous photograph. At the center of the area, solitary and somehow menacing, sat the armored truck. There was an intimidating quality to the truck as it squatted there on shredded tires, scarred from the impact of bullets. It stemmed from its apparent impregnability and the stunning knowledge that the President of the United States was a helpless captive within. That realization had induced a strange solemnity in the crowd that was growing with every minute and was now clotted in the side streets leading to the Square and north and south on Broadway for two hundred yards. Regan could see them, thousands of them, drawn to the scene by curiosity, or morbidity, or by the desire to be present as history was being made, or by a compulsion to lend the support of their presence to the unseen prisoner.

An unbroken line of police barricades had been placed around the Square as a restraint, and policemen, afoot and mounted, patrolled the perimeter. But there was no thrusting against the barrier. A brooding hush hovered over the crowd. Conversations were few and whispered. The people in the front rows stood silent and unmoving, staring numbly with unblinking eyes at the truck.

At the southern end of the Square, crowded on both sides of the City of New York Information Center, three giant television mobile units were parked. At the far northern end, the New York City Fire Department had positioned an enormous pumper unit and a ladder truck.

Above the street, in the office buildings facing on the Square, no activity could be seen; the occupants had been evacuated almost immediately after Moreno parked the truck. But the millions of colored bulbs and the miles of neon tubing were still flashing their flamboyant invitations and the Winston billboard still puffed its smoke rings, sometimes almost settling one about the truck.

Ranged along each rooftop, members of the armed forces — helmeted and in battle dress, with guns slung over their shoulders — stood like statues. At each end of the Square, three thousand feet above the street, Army Sikorsky helicopters hovered like ungainly eagles, their rotating wings thudding against the air.

As Regan studied the scene, for all the enormity of the problem lying heavily on him he could not restrain a reluctant smile: Moving through the crowd across the way he could see a man in a white linen coat selling hot dogs from a steaming metal container, and below to his left, a fuzzy-haired and straggle-bearded youth was stroking his guitar and singing.

Regan turned, walked swiftly down the stairs to the Orchestra level, put his head in what would soon be his office and crooked a finger at his secretary and Special Agent Ziggy Mayer, who were supervising the setting up of the facility. Continuing on, he passed

Jim McCurdy, deep in conversation with a group of workmen, called out, "Jim," and turned into one of the tunnels leading to the semi-darkness of the theater. Indicating a front row of seats, he waited, pivoting restlessly on the balls of his feet until the group was seated.

"Looks like this is the only place we can talk privately," he said, "and there's lots to do." He looked at his secretary. "Meg, got your notebook?" She held it up. "Okay," he said. "Let's start."

He paced back and forth, gathering his thoughts. "I won't take the time to specify who's to do what," he began, "I'm simply going to talk out some of the things we've got to get moving and you people can sort them out. First, fill me in: Jim, have you worked out the coordination with the FBI and the police?"

McCurdy nodded. "There are some arguments about jurisdiction and a few noses out of joint, but everybody's cooperating."

"Good. Get in touch with a guy by the name of . . . I think it's Hamilton. He's in charge of the CIA's Latin American desk. Get him in here. If he can't come, get him on the phone. He called earlier this morning about a tip the CIA had on a plot to kidnap the President. I'm hoping he can come up with a file on our man. In the meantime, get a photographer over to the Waldorf, take a grab-shot of him and rush the prints here.

"While we're talking about pictures: get pictures taken every hour of every section of that crowd out there. Use telephoto lenses so nobody will know what you're up to. Then make blowups and circle the faces of people who show up in the same general location in each picture. Could help us narrow it down."

Walking back and forth before the little group he snapped out an unbroken string of orders. "I want an exact duplicate of that armored truck out there. Talk to Brink's. I want the man who designed it, or somebody who knows everything there is to know about it. I want a meeting at the earliest possible minute with the best available experts on explosives, on arc-acetylene welding, on heat and vibration sensors, on remote-control electronics, on ultrasonics and lasers . . . the whole thing. I want another meeting with either medical men or scientists, or both, who know all there is to know about human physiology and neurology. Talk to the Pentagon and get their top guy on nerve gas and systemic poisons and any new bacteriological agents they may have — I mean the incapacitating or killing kind." He broke off his pacing. "What I want to do is to put together a think tank of the the best brains in the country. I want them to come up with a way to incapacitate or, if we have to, to kill that guy out there ready to blow up the truck."

He was pacing again. "Find out what's *under* the truck," he said. "There's a series of metal gratings running down the middle of the Square — probably vents for the subway system, but I want to know. Find out whether it's possible to come up through them under the truck. Find out what else is down there. . . . Sewers . . . ? Cables . . . ? Find out."

He looked at McCurdy. "Jim, talk to the police and the FBI. I want every plainclothes man and woman we can round up out there in the crowd, moving around, watching, listening. Set up a system for getting and evaluating reports on anything that seems significant. But, for God's sake, warn them to make no move without specific approval from me. I don't want any whiz-kid trying to make a name by taking it on himself to solve the whole problem and in the meantime getting us all blown to hell."

When the final plan for the abduction of the President had been agreed upon, Linda was given definite instructions by the Committee to guide her during the crucial hours when she would be on her own in Times Square. She had reviewed them many times — by herself and with Moreno — and they were fixed in her mind. She was to be as inconspicuous as possible. She was to speak to no one. She was to avoid the front rows of the crowd that would gather. She was to keep both hands in the pockets of her suit; her left hand on the remote-control mechanism at every moment. She was to determine as early as possible the location of any headquarters set up by the enemy and to so position herself that she could simultaneously observe it and the armored truck. She was to post herself close to one of the four shops on the Square selling television sets so that she could monitor news reports and hear the coded messages Moreno would feed to the television networks.

She was standing now with her back to the marble facing, to the right of the entrance to the Paramount building. A few feet to her right, in the window of the Times Square Tee-Vee-O-Rama, a bank of television sets displayed identical pictures of Robertson Kirk speaking into camera, his voice blaring into the street from a speaker mounted over the door.

"Just in, an announcement from the Secret Service Command Headquarters in the National Theater. As had been rumored earlier, the leader of the group of kidnappers is being held under what is described as protective custody at the Waldorf Astoria Hotel. The announcement says he's being kept there for his own safety . . . pretty opulent safety. There is also a request from a spokesman at Command Headquarters that all the news media communicate the following message. I'm quoting: Schedule Three is operative. The message is signed with what is obviously a code-name: Cormorant.

I'll repeat that: The message is, Schedule Three is operative, signed Cormorant.

We have no way of knowing, of course, but I would presume the message is to inform the kidnapper's accomplice on some matter known, at this point, only to them. It's all very cloak-and-dagger.

I've just been told that an attempt is being made to communicate with President Scott, so we'll go to Times Square and Tom Healey. . . . "

Gerry Regan was standing in a clutter of electronic equipment on a small balcony used to support the marquee, above the entrance to the theater. He was wearing earphones. In his right hand was a bullhorn. Crouched at his feet was a member of the Army Signal Corps directing a three-foot-wide, dish-shaped antenna toward the armored truck in the Square below — the type of directional-microphone sports fans have become accustomed to seeing on the sidelines at football games. Regan's eyes were on a Corpsman who was kneeling before a portable field-amplifier adjusting dials. He nodded and Regan raised the bullhorn to his lips.

"President Scott . . . ?"

The volume of the sound of his voice startled him as it re-sounded and ricocheted off the surrounding buildings. He began again. "President Scott. . . . This is Gerald Regan. If you can hear me, would you please respond by counting slowly from one to ten?"

On the phones he heard Adam's voice, faintly at first, then as the operator made adjustments, hollow and muffled but clear.

"Thank you, sir," he boomed.

Adam, who had been startled by the sudden sound of his name, regained his composure and said, "Am I to understand that you can hear me? Clearly?"

"Loud and clear, sir."

"Am I audible to everyone?"

"No, sir, only to me and the operator here. We're picking you up on earphones with a directional-mike."

"Well then, Mr. Regan, the first thing I'd like to know is, when do I get out of this damned steel box?"

Regan gave him a swift, succinct rundown.

"As I understand it," Adam said, "you're saying that I'm going to be here until late this evening."

"I'm afraid so, sir."

"All right. Now that that's established, what can I do to help?"

"I'm sorry to bother you, sir, but . . . "

"Skip that stuff, Gerry. What do you need from me?"

"Yes, sir. First, tell me everything you think is significant about the interior of the truck."

"Significant . . . ? I'm not at all sure I know — this *is* my first time inside one of these things. Anyway, here goes. The most significant thing as far as I'm concerned is a wooden box in the far corner . . . that's the northeast corner. It's rectangular, about eighteen inches high, two feet wide, and maybe three feet long. It's where, I presume, the explosives are. I don't know that for certain, but it *is* the box into which our kidnapper friend put that bottle he had."

Gerry interrupted. "A question."

"Go ahead."

"How did he handle the bottle?"

"Very carefully. And when he put it in the box he seemed to fit it into some kind of receptacle."

"Back to the box itself — any wires running from it?"

"None visible."

"Anywhere else explosives may be hidden?"

"Nowhere I can see."

"Go ahead."

"I suppose I should report on my own situation. I'm shackled to a metal ring welded onto what would be the western wall."

"Sorry."

"Nothing to be sorry about; it's how it happens to be. I can stand up if I crouch. I can move about a bit. There's a blanket to sit on."

"Anything else?"

"Well . . . let's see. One thing: the entire interior is covered with plywood. I don't know whether that's normal or not."

"All the walls?"

"The walls, the ceiling, the floor."

"Anything else?"

"There are two devices of some sort mounted on the ceiling. I don't know what I can tell you about them except that one is rounded, like a hemisphere, the other is rectangular, about one by three inches."

"Any wires running from them?"

"Can't see any. But then they're mounted on the plywood and the wiring could run behind it."

"Anything else?"

"No, that's about it."

"Anything you can tell me about the kidnappers? Did they say anything that might be useful?"

"No, not a word. You've talked to one of them; the other had his back to me."

"One other thing, sir. We were wondering whether you can see the news-bulletin lights on the Allied Chemical building?"

"I can, but it's difficult."

"It occurred to one of our people that we could keep you in touch by communicating to you with the lights."

There was a pause while Adam considered the suggestion. "No," he said. "But I'll tell you what you can do. I'm wearing a wristwatch — you might use the two minutes or so at the hour and the half-hour to keep me informed. Then I won't be hanging on the end of this damn chain all the time, or worrying that I should be."

"Will do, sir."

"And, Gerry. . . . "

"Yes, sir."

"Will you get in touch with Mrs. Scott immediately and let her know that I'm all right? She'll be worried, so I'd like you to reassure her."

"Yes, sir. Right away."

"And please do it personally . . . first-hand word, you know."

"Right."

"One other thing: How do *I* get in touch with you?"

"We'll have a man monitoring the truck at all times. Any time you want to get out a message just tell him."

"You mean I'll be listened to all the time?"

"Yes, sir."

"I shall have to be careful then not to make any rude noises, shan't I?"

"Ah . . . I suppose so, Mr. President."

"At any rate, that's it for now. Thank you . . . or Roger, or whatever I'm supposed to say."

"Thank you, Mr. President."

Chapter Ten

The 25th Amendment to the Constitution of the United States was ratified February 10, 1967. Its purpose was to provide for such circumstances as might afflict a President who, despite every precaution taken to preserve his body from disease, his mind from undue fatigue and his person from the assassin, is mortal and more subject than most men to pressure, anxiety and danger.

In Article One, provision is made for his death, his resignation or his impeachment. In such circumstances the Vice-President becomes President.

In Article Three, provision is made for the possibility that the President might become too ill to fulfill his duties, or through some other cause become incapacitated while yet remaining in command of his mental faculties. It reads:

> *Whenever the President transmits to the President pro tempore of the Senate and the Speaker of the House of Representatives his written declaration that he is unable to discharge the duties of his office, and until he transmits to them a written declaration to the contrary, such powers and duties shall be discharged by the Vice-President as Acting President.*

But, as the men who framed the Amendment recognized, there remained the possibility that the President might not be able to transmit a written statement declaring his incapacity — having perhaps suffered a stroke, or being in a coma. For such contingencies, Article Four was provided. It reads:

Whenever the Vice-President and a majority of either the principal officers of the Executive departments, or of such other body as Congress may by law provide, transmits to the President pro tempore of the Senate and the Speaker of the House of Representatives their written declaration that the President is unable to discharge the powers and duties of his office, the Vice-President shall immediately assume the powers and duties of the office as Acting President.

Ethan Roberts was familiar with every reference to the Vice-Presidency in the Constitution. He could quote each passage verbatim, not because he had troubled to commit them to memory but simply because he had a retentive mind and the matter was of particular interest to him. From the moment of his inauguration he had been keenly aware of the cliché, "The Vice-President is but a heartbeat away from the Presidency."

Ethan wanted very much to be President. Not, of course, at the cost of Adam's life but because he was, as most politicians are, an ambitious man, a man with a sizable ego who knew that the Presidency enshrined a man in history. More, Ethan knew that many of the men who had been thrust into the office by the death of the incumbent had risen to the challenge and acquitted themselves well. He had always felt a particular sense of identification with Harry Truman and was certain that were he propelled into office as Truman was on the death of Franklin Roosevelt — scorned by the press, the pundits and his own party — he, too, would demonstrate his capacity to govern.

Eight times in the history of the United States the elected leader has died in office — four times from natural causes, four times from assassination — and the Vice-President at the time became the nation's chief executive. The first four — Tyler, Fillmore, Andrew Johnson and Arthur — were relatively undistinguished men who, being eminently forgettable, have been forgotten by all but historians, political scientists and schoolchildren. The others — Theodore Roosevelt, Coolidge, Truman and Lyndon Johnson — filled the role so suddenly thrust on them with such distinction that when they sought the approval of their respective parties for the nomination in their own right, and of the nation for a further mandate, they were successful.

John Tyler was the first Vice-President to be elevated on the death of the incumbent. In 1841, when William Henry Harrison died only a month after his inauguration, Tyler was sworn in. He was a failure as President. His policies led to the resignation of most of his Cabinet and to a public repudiation by most of his party. At the end of his term, not only did he not seek renomination, he retired from public life.

Millard Fillmore became President when Zachary Taylor died suddenly after sixteen months in office. He, too, was a failure. He was not a strong leader and could not cope with the dissension in his party or the nation over the issue of slavery. He was defeated at the nominating convention in his bid for a second term.

A bizarre and malevolent coincidence then entered American political history. Since Fillmore, every American President who has been elected or re-elected in a year ending in a zero has died in office. It began in 1865 when Abraham Lincoln, in his second term, was struck down by bullets from John Wilkes Booth's revolver. His death elevated Andrew Johnson to the Presidency. But Johnson was an incompetent who soon alienated his fellow Cabinet members and the Republican majority in the House. Finally, he was impeached. Despite his acquittal, he did not seek renomination.

The jinx then cut down James Garfield in September, 1881, in his first year in office, and Chester Arthur was sworn in. The achievements of Arthur's Administration were considerable: the introduction of standard time, the organization of the American Red Cross Society, the completion of three transcontinental railways and the establishment of Alaska as a territory. Yet, when he sought his party's renomination it was refused him, the defeat being not so much a rejection of the man as a grass-roots protest against Republican party politics at the time.

Twenty years later, William McKinley fell to the assassin's bullet while campaigning in Buffalo. The man thrust into the breach was Theodore Roosevelt. He served out the remaining years, sought and was given the party's nomination and was re-elected.

The malevolent pattern repeated after Warren Harding was elected President in 1920. He died while returning from a trip to Alaska in 1923 and was succeeded by Calvin Coolidge. Coolidge completed the unexpired term and was re-elected in his own right.

Franklin Delano Roosevelt was in his fourth term in 1945 when he was suddenly stricken by a massive stroke and the unprepossessing Harry Truman became President. Almost against his party's will he was nominated in 1948 and scored an astounding upset victory over the Republican nominee, Thomas E. Dewey. He did not seek a second term.

When John Kennedy, having come to the highest office in 1960, was killed by fire from Lee Harvey Oswald's rifle, Lyndon Johnson was sworn. Some eight months later when Johnson sought a mandate in his own right, he swept the country and achieved an enormous majority. Four years later, bedeviled by the war in Southeast Asia, he decided not to seek renomination and retired to his native Texas.

In the plane returning to Washington, Ethan Roberts reviewed all these events. He reviewed also the options available to his Cabinet colleagues under the Constitution. They might not consider the President to be incapacitated — despite the fact that he was obviously unable to discharge his duties — and simply ride along with events. However, with the nation in potential jeopardy, it was entirely possible they would move to name him Acting President even though his tenure might be only hours long. Ethan knew also that there was the terrifying possibility that Adam would be killed. He felt the skin on his scalp draw taut in the realization that before the day was out he might be President of the United States. How ironic, he thought, when only hours ago he had feared that his political career was over.

Looking down from the window, he watched the fertile geometric patchwork of Pennsylvania unreel from beneath the trailing edge of the wing, and he prayed. He prayed for the decisiveness, the resolution and the unflappable temperament of Harry Truman. He prayed for Adam Scott. He prayed for the United States. And when he placed his briefcase on his lap and began to make a series of notes on a scrap of paper, his mind was calm and his handwriting firm.

Despite the fact that Joan Scott was commonly described in Washington society and by journalists as First among the First Ladies, her upbringing had left her unsuited to be the wife of a politician. By all but her immediate family and her closest friends she was believed to be as perfectly mated to her responsibility as to her husband, and since Adam's accession to the Presidency, she had been the object of the same kind of adulation that had been heaped on Jacqueline Kennedy in her White House days.

It might be said of Americans that they abhor the monarchy but adore royalty, and as surrogates have elevated motion picture stars and superlative athletes to those pinnacles of national veneration occupied elsewhere by a beloved king or queen. During her husband's tenure, Jacqueline Kennedy was frequently termed by newspaper editorialists Queen Jackie the First; if she was, Joan Scott was in a direct line of descent.

The fact was, however, she detested every minute of her public life. It was not that she felt herself superior to either the task or the trappings — she had an acute sense of history and realized the importance of what Adam was doing and of her part in it — it was simply that her entire upbringing had shaped her into an intensely private woman who, despite herself, felt resentment when the unavoidable responsibilities of her position required that she put herself on display, or when the insatiable curiosity of the public led journalists to peek and pry and penetrate into her personal and private life.

Joan had made few close friends in Washington. Rather, she had kept alive and refreshed her relationships with the associates of her Bryn Mawr and Philadelphia days. It was not aloofness or an unfriendly disposition, it was simply that, with few exceptions, she did not find in the wives of the politicians or the women of Washington society the cerebral, cultural and sensual kinship she needed in a friend.

Politicians' wives, she had discovered, were of three essential types: those who hated politics and hated their husbands for being politicans; those who had their own needs and drives and exulted in the automatic homage and public attention that came to them through their husbands; and those who, engrossed with other concerns — children, family, hobbies, sometimes liquor — played only a peripheral role in their husbands' careers.

Politicians themselves, she had learned, ranged the spectrum from saint to rogue. Most, she discovered — somewhat to her surprise for she had believed the common canard that most politicians are corrupt — were honorable men who spent themselves in longer labors than men of other professions and made zealous efforts to serve their constituents well.

After she had been in Washington a year, Joan worked out categories for the politicians she met, and gave them names. When they were alone, she would sometimes delight Adam by assigning new acquaintances to the appropriate pigeonhole. The largest group she named the Dudley Dogoods: earnest, unnoticed men who went about their tasks with little attention being paid their small achievements and whose principal concern was to keep the political fences mended in their home constituencies. The second group she named Troglodytes: incredibly uninformed and misinformed purveyors of half-baked opinions on any and every subject who, as she put it, "make up in thunder what they lack in lightning." Then came the Mini-messiahs: men who tended to believe the times were out of joint and that they had been appointed by some deity — never clearly distinguishable from their egos — to set things right. The politicians Joan disliked most she described with the term Hum-buggars. They were the pompous, the self-important, the declaimers, the constant seekers of center-stage. Those she liked most, for reasons she couldn't specify, she called Pussycats. There was something about them — though some were twice her age — that stimulated maternal feelings in her.

Everything Joan Scott disliked about politics was distilled in the predicament in which she now found herself. She was standing in the open atop the marquee of the National Theater with an electronic megaphone in her hand, headphone hemispheres on her ears, two Army Signal Corpsmen kneeling before heaps of mysterious equipment a few feet away, television and film cameras peering at her and a sheet-lightning storm of flashbulbs flickering in the crowd of some twenty thousand massed in and about the Square below. In such circumstances she was expected to talk to her husband, her voice braying and metallic, her sentiments leaping around the world. She had asked Regan to inquire if the television networks would grant her privacy from their peering. The response was simple incredulity: "The President's wife's going to talk to the President while he's a hostage and you ask us not to carry it? You must be out of your skull!" It would have been unthinkable to go ahead were it not for Adam's frightening isolation and his need for her.

She raised the bullhorn to her lips and pressed the trigger as she had been instructed.

"Adam . . . ?" *Adam . . . Adam . . . Adam* went the echoes.

His voice was loud, although hollow and muffled. "Hello . . . is that Joan?"

"Surprise."

"What a lovely surprise."

"How are you, Adam?"

"As well as can be expected. How about you?"

"Oh, I'm fine." She knew she was sounding stiff and cold and wanted to communicate her affection, but couldn't bring herself to it.

"Are you very uncomfortable?" she said.

"No, I'm fine. Don't worry. I see where the fellow on the other end of this bizarre affair is staying at the Waldorf."

"Yes, but I'd better not say anything about that. Everyone in the world can hear what I'm saying, you know."

"Can they hear me?"

"Only the men on the equipment here, I think."

"Hold a minute, Joan. I'm now addressing myself to whoever's monitoring this conversation. If it isn't absolutely mandatory that you do so, please get off. And will you tell Mrs. Scott if you can?"

The serviceman, his face crimson, removed his earphones and nodded to Joan. "It's okay," he said.

"Adam . . . ? Do you still hear me?"

"Perfectly."

"Apparently it's all right. You aren't being monitored now."

"So I can say what I please?"

"I believe so."

"Then let me tell you what I've been thinking sitting here. I've been thinking about that weekend we spent at Camp David last New Year's. Remember?"

"Very well."

"Do you remember what you said to me about the Constitution not defining all of the President's powers?"

"Adam . . . !"

"Well, pretty lady, you might be interested to know that when I get out of this prison . . . "

"Adam. I'm not sure you should . . . "

"To hell with that. As I was saying . . . "

Joan felt a hand on her shoulder and turned. It was Gerry Regan, his face pale. "Tell him to hold it," he shouted, his face close to hers.

"Just a minute, Adam," she said quickly. "Gerry Regan is here."

"I don't want to talk to Gerry Regan."

"Adam, will you please wait a minute?" She pushed aside an

earphone so she could hear Regan's voice. "What's the matter?" she said.

"The television people," he said. "They've set up their own directional-mikes and they're carrying both sides of the conversation. I thought you should know," he finished lamely.

Joan flushed. She replaced the earphones.

"Adam. . . ."

"What's the problem?"

"Mr. Regan was explaining to me that the television people have arranged for their own directional-microphones, I believe they're called. They're broadcasting our conversation."

"*Both* sides?"

"Both sides."

"Ah . . . yes. American know-how, I believe it's called."

"Yes."

"You might thank Mr. Regan on my behalf for keeping me abreast."

"Yes. I shall."

There was an extended uneasy silence. Joan had a mental picture of millions of people smirking. "Is there anything you'd like me to do?" She said.

"Can't think of anything."

"Well then . . . I suppose I'd better go. . . . "

"Not for long. They expect to have me out of here by midnight."

"Adam . . . ?" Her eyes were wet.

"Yes."

She forced herself to say the words. "I love you."

"And I you," he said.

There was another silence. "To think," Joan said, feigning a lightheartedness she did not feel, "it was only yesterday you were complaining about not getting any time to yourself." She heard him laugh. "I'll be going now," she said.

"See you tonight."

"Yes. Good-by."

Chapter Eleven

When the Cabinet assembled at the White House at 11:05, Ethan Roberts walked toward the conference room with a resolute step. There was no indication on his face that his mind was in tumult and his stomach constricted. He had planned to take the President's chair at the center edge of the great oval table as he did when Adam was out of the country or on vacation but as he entered through the open double doors his resolve faltered. And when Chester Harrison, Secretary of the Treasury, saw him and beckoned and patted the chair beside him and called out, "Robbie, come here a minute and fill me in," he did so.

Harrison was embarrassed and enraged and admitted it. The Secret Service is administratively a part of the Department of the Treasury, and when he had telephoned the Director to be brought up-to-date, he had been given the runaround by Morris's secretary. It was only after he had used some very earthy language that he had been able to extract the information that the Director was out of town bird watching, that a helicopter had been sent to pick him up and that he would be back in the city by ten.

Henrietta Cown, self-consciously adjusting the kerchief on her head, entered the room hurriedly and took her seat. The other members of the Cabinet — who had been standing about in small clusters talking — moved to their chairs. There was an awkward pause. Ethan seized on it.

"Gentlemen and Miss Cown," he said. "May I suggest that we begin by getting a report on those of our colleagues who are not present. Jim Rankin is standing by. Perhaps we might bring him in."

He didn't wait for assent but stepped from his chair, opened one of the great oak doors and beckoned to Rankin. As they walked to the table he said, "Just give us a rundown on where the fellows are."

"Good morning," the Press Secretary began. "First, the Secretary of State is en route from London where he has been meeting with Prime Minister Bradshaw on the coordination of our new trade agreements with the Common Market countries. He's due in at 3:00. The Secretary of the Interior is on his way back from Alaska. He's expected around 2:30. The Secretary of Commerce may not be able to attend; his father was taken to hospital at 2:30 this morning suffering from a massive stroke and remains in a coma . . . " There was a brief mutter of comment around the table. Rankin waited for it to subside. "Mr. Garvin is on his way back from the West Coast. I don't have his expected time of arrival yet. The Attorney General, Mr. Rosewald, is in the city and on his way. He should be here within the next few minutes."

"Thanks, Jim," Ethan said.

Rankin hesitated. "I wonder if you could give me some instructions for the press?"

"What have you done to this point?" Jim Walker asked.

"The absolute minimum. I've released the essential facts about the kidnapping, no more, and have announced this meeting."

Ethan picked it up. "I think," he said, looking slowly about the table, "it would be well to leave it at that for the time being. We may have a statement for you later. Are we all agreed?" There were no objections so he said, "Thanks again, Jim. Stay within reach."

Rankin turned and left the room, pulling the door closed behind him. Again there was a moment of general hesitation. Chet Harrison broke it.

"Well, fellows," he said briskly, "let's get to it. We haven't come here to hold a wake and time's a-wasting. We need a chairman. I move the Vice-President assume the chair."

"Second," said Henrietta Cown.

There was a ragged chorus of "Agree." Ethan rose, picked up his papers and moved to the President's chair. He sat down and arranged his papers, the ruled pad and the half dozen sharpened pencils on the table before him, and deliberately gathered himself. When he began, his voice was quiet but authoritative. "The meeting will come to order," he said.

"We should," he continued, "have an agenda. Let me propose that we deal with the following matters in this order: First, though it's a bit irregular, I suggest we invite the Director of the Secret Service to join us to give us a report on what the precise situation is. That is, if that's agreeable to you, Chet?"

The Secretary of the Treasury nodded.

"Second," Ethan said, "we'll need to discuss the actions of the kidnappers and try to determine the full extent of the threat they pose to the security and order of the nation. For all we know at this point, the abduction of the President may be only the first of a number of crimes. Third . . . "

Jim Walker broke in. "Mr. Chairman, if you'll permit me . . . ?"

"Go ahead, Jim."

"I'll be brief. Let me simply inform this meeting that at 8:57 this morning, having been notified by Jim Rankin that President Scott had been kidnapped, I presumed to be in touch with General Harbison, Chief of Staff at the Pentagon, and because it seemed prudent, ordered Emergency Plan-B put into effect. For your information, Emergency Plan-B brings all the armed forces and the various law enforcement agencies of the country to a full alert. I'm fully aware that my action was taken without proper authorization, but it seemed to me the appropriate thing to do. I have here," he said, removing a number of bound folders from the attaché case before him, "copies of the specifics of Emergency Plan-B, and if you have no objection, Mr. Chairman, I would like to distribute them."

Ethan nodded and the folders were passed from hand to hand around the table.

"That's all I have to report," Jim Walker concluded, "other than to ask that this meeting ratify the action taken. Perhaps I should add that I have personally spoken to the Director of the Federal Bureau of Investigation and to the Supervisor of the Washington Field Office of the Secret Service — I was unable to contact Mr. Morris — and have notified them of the action taken."

Ethan made a note on the pad before him. "Thank you, Jim. I'll add it to the agenda and we can vote later as to whether there is concurrence.

"Now, to continue. The next item for the agenda, I would suggest, is the need to decide on our response to the kidnappers, and to weigh carefully any jeopardy President Scott may be placed in as a result. Finally, we will have to consider the ramifications of the incarceration of the President as they may affect the fact that tomorrow is election day."

There were murmurs of assent around the table.

"I take it then," said Ethan, "that the first item of business should be a briefing on the situation in New York City, and I take it to be the sense of the meeting that we invite the Director of the Secret Service to join us. I believe he's standing by."

He picked up the receiver of one of the two telephones before him and pressed a button. "Ask Mr. Morris to come in, please."

There was a knock on the door and Herbert Morris entered. He was dressed in hiking boots, an old pair of brown slacks and a yellow waterproof shell, the zipper open at the neck to reveal a red hunting shirt. His face was flushed and he was clearly self-conscious about the inappropriateness of his attire. Ethan indicated a chair at the end of the table. Morris shook his head. "If you don't mind, sir, I'll stand," he said.

"Mr. Morris," Ethan said, "I'm going to ask you to dispense with non-essentials in your report. We all know the basic facts. What we'd like from you is your appraisal of the situation and anything else you think we need to know. Please proceed."

Morris placed a thin briefcase on the table in front of him. He was about to begin when he realized to his surprise that the saliva in his mouth was thick and dry. He took a sip of water.

"Gentlemen," he began, "as requested, no preamble. The President is being held hostage in an armored truck which is, to use the vernacular, booby-trapped. It would seem that the doors have been so wired that any attempt to open them will activate a circuit and detonate a quantity of explosives within the truck. At least one of the kidnappers is among the crowd of approximately twenty thousand now gathered in and around Times Square. Apparently he has a remote-control device — some kind of transmitter — which, if activated, can detonate the explosives."

"How many kidnappers are there?" asked Henrietta Cown.

"We're not certain. At least two, possibly more. There is one, as I say, in the crowd that has gathered. The man who did the actual kidnapping is at this moment in protective custody in a suite at the Waldorf Astoria Hotel." He flushed slightly.

Jim Walker broke in. "A question: Why don't we send in troops or the police and clear the crowd out of the Square? In so doing you'll be rid of the accomplice and reduce your problems by one."

Morris looked at him ruefully. "Unfortunately, one of the kidnapper's demands is that we *don't* do that. The crowd provides a cover for his accomplice and we've been told that if we attempt to empty the Square, he'll trigger the explosives before he goes."

"Is he bluffing?"

"We don't know. It's my view that he's not."

Morris looked at Ethan. "I don't suppose, Mr. Vice-President, you wish me to detail the various actions being taken to resolve the situation?" Ethan shook his head. "Let me merely say then that every facility at our command and the full complement of our staff has been assigned to find a solution. I might also mention that we are being given complete cooperation by the FBI and the local and state police. I feel sure we'll soon be able to effect President Scott's release."

"You'll excuse me," said Dr. Jonathan White, Secretary of Health, Education and Welfare, "you say you feel sure. On what ground? Is your confidence based on more than hope? It's quite clear that we're up against a clever and resourceful group of men here, men who, it would seem, have to this point remained one jump ahead of your people and the police."

Morris turned and looked into Dr. White's face. He was not a bigoted man but he tended to resent any black man who was his superior in authority. When he replied, his voice was flat and cold.

"My confidence, Dr. White, is based on the performance of the Secret Service over many years."

"Those years would include the times when President Kennedy and Senator Kennedy were assassinated, would they not?" Dr. White said acidly.

Morris glared at him and was about to reply but changed his mind.

"Mr. Morris, I have a question," Henrietta Cown said. "Is there any possibility that the kidnapping could be . . . well, could it be just a first step, so to speak? Have there been any other incidents?"

"To this moment, Miss Cown, none. However, we're not discounting that possibility. I might say that I have assigned agents to provide security for each of you and I would ask your cooperation in this."

"Have you been able to communicate with the President?" Ethan asked.

"Yes."

"How?"

"In two ways. We have commandeered the Trans Lux light display on the Allied Chemical building at 42nd Street, and plan to send messages to him by that means. Also, the Army has brought in a sound system consisting of a loud-hailer and a directional-microphone. This permits us to speak to President Scott, and because the directional-microphone equipment is very sensitive, to hear anything he says from within the truck."

"You'll have to speak in generalities though, won't you? Everyone will be able to read the lights or hear what's said on the loud-hailer."

"That's correct, sir."

"Who'll be responsible for what is communicated?"

"I was planning to take care of that, sir . . . after clearing it with the Secretary, of course," he said, looking at Chet Harrison. Harrison made no response, and Morris flushed again.

Ethan glanced around the table. "Any further questions?" No one spoke. "Then let me thank you, Mr. Morris, for your report. Before you go, I'd be interested to hear your view on paying the ransom."

The Director placed his hands, fingers spread, on the table. When he spoke, he kept his eyes down. "I don't want to be guilty of presumption, sir," he said quietly, "but since you've asked me, I would urge one thing on you . . . *do not* pay the ransom."

"Even if it means endangering the President's life?" asked Herb Thurlow quietly.

"Please understand, I'm not indifferent to that possibility; indeed, it's my principal concern. It's simply that if there is one thing I have learned in more than thirty years in law enforcement, it's that you don't make deals with criminals."

There was a brief silence. Henrietta Cown broke it.

"Just a minute," she said. "*I* don't agree with that at all. And I hope it's not what we intend to do. It doesn't matter *what* we have to pay, we can't take any chances with Adam's . . . with the President's life. These men are criminals. They're desperate. Who knows what they may do!"

"I agree," said Chet Harrison.

Ethan broke in. "Perhaps we can discuss the question later."

"Fine," said Dr. White. "But in the meantime I would like some assurance that nothing will be done that will endanger Adam's life."

Morris looked at him coldly. "You have my assurance," he said.

Ethan turned to the Director. "Again, Mr. Morris, our thanks. May I ask that you keep us informed."

"Thank you," Morris said. He turned and left. As the door closed behind him, Herb Thurlow turned to the Secretary of the Treasury. "Why the casual duds on your boy, Chet?" he asked.

Chet Harrison literally spat out the words. "He was out bird watching."

Barney McCrory exploded. "Did you say bird watching?"

"I said bird watching."

"Holy jumpin' Jesus!" Barney said and shook with laughter. After a moment everyone in the room, even the Secretary of the Treasury, had joined in.

Chapter Twelve

Mr. Regan?"

"Yes, Mr. Morris."

"I've been trying to reach you."

"We've been installing equipment."

"Any significant progress since we last talked?"

"I'm afraid there's not much new. It's one devil of a . . . "

"It *is* a difficult problem."

"Yes, sir."

"I was planning to join you in New York City but it now seems wiser to stay here."

"Very good, sir."

"I understand you've arranged for a direct line from your head-quarters. Let me see now, you're at . . . "

"1500 Broadway. The National Theater."

"I've made a note of that."

"There'll be a telex, too. With a scrambler. In about half an hour, I would think."

"Yes. Ah . . . Mr. Regan . . . "

"Yes, sir."

"I've just come from a meeting with the Cabinet. There seems to be, I must say, a disposition to pay the ransom."

"Yes, sir."

"I might say I expressed another opinion."

"I would hope so, sir."

"I might say further that the thought of a group of men — men indifferent to the law, criminals — abducting the President of the

United States and getting off scot-free is something I view rather dimly. You understand?"

"Yes, sir, I understand."

"If anything, it seems to me it will only serve to encourage further criminal activity of the same kind. Wouldn't you agree?"

"Yes, sir. I would."

"We've seen evidence of that in recent years."

"Yes, sir."

"I would like you to keep this in mind as you pursue the matter."

"Yes, sir."

"We must not, of course, do anything that would endanger the safety of the President."

"I understand that, sir."

"You understand that?"

"Yes, sir."

"On the other hand, it would be equally reprehensible if everything possible to apprehend the criminals responsible was not done."

"I agree, sir."

There was a pause.

"I'm sure you're aware, Mr. Regan, that the Service is under something of a cloud as a result of what has happened. Critical reference was made in the Cabinet meeting. It is imperative, of course, that we avoid any course that would add fuel to that fire."

"I understand."

"We don't want an aftermath like the one that followed Dallas."

"No, sir."

"The Warren Commission, the Treasury investigation of the Service. . . . "

"Yes, sir. I remember."

"I have every confidence in you, Mr. Regan. I would, however, ask that you inform me in advance of any . . . shall we say, any extraordinary measures you may propose to take."

"I will, sir."

"Thank you. Good-by."

The possibility that the kidnappers might escape troubled Gerry Regan profoundly. Not only would it underscore a major failure by his department — which would undoubtedly lead to his being fired or demoted — but, far more important, it struck at the very essence of his life.

Regan had been born in Regina, Saskatchewan, at the height of the depression. His father had immigrated to the United States in 1901 from Ballymena, a town some twenty miles from Belfast. In a typical example of his native obduracy he had scorned going to Canada as many of his friends had done (to settle in Toronto and work for Timothy Eaton in his department store, where the word was: "If you're a Ballymena man and can spell your name, you'll be taken on."). Instead, he had taken ship for New York City.

A big, restless, gregarious man, Gerry's father had worked at a variety of jobs in half a dozen cities, had managed to marry a pretty Belfast girl he met on the Chicago "El," and happened to be in Fargo, North Dakota, delivering a new car from the Studebaker plant in South Bend, Indiana, the day the stock market collapsed. With the economy foundering, it made no sense to return to Chicago, so he cashed in his return train ticket, sent the money to his wife, Maureen, and wrote that he was going to scout the possibilities in the middle west.

Maureen sold what furniture they owned and arrived in Fargo as a passenger in a moving-van driven by a friend. Three years and half a dozen temporary jobs later — stony-broke and with Maureen pregnant with Gerry and "looking like a horse and buggy" — the two of them hitchhiked to Regina at the invitation of an old Ballymena friend. There he was hired on the spot as night watchman at the Robert Simpson Company Ltd.

Regina was a small, pleasant prairie city in 1933 and an ideal place in which to grow up. The times were hard but they made no impression on Gerry's young mind. As soon as he was old enough, his father took him shooting and Gerry learned how uncomfortable the hunter's pleasure can be: lying in the pre-dawn darkness on the stiff, wet, wheat stubble, waiting for the move of prairie chicken or partridge, or by a pond for ducks to come in. His father even took him along on a hunt for the elusive coyote whose howling in the moonlight made the boy shiver; and on wild chases by touring car of the fleet jack rabbits that, to Gerry, seemed as big as dogs.

Then the idyl ended.

His father was making the rounds one early morning and came on two men who had managed to jimmy open a metal door at one of the loading bays. They fled, blundered into a cul-de-sac, and as he followed, fired a single shot. It smashed through his cheekbone into his brain and killed him instantly.

Gerry had never seen a dead human before. He looked at the distorted, waxen face of the man in the coffin — the repairs to the shattered cheek botched by a drunk mortician — and felt not sadness but revulsion, and a shuddering sense of horror.

Gerry's mother, using the ten thousand dollars paid by the Metropolitan Life Insurance Company, paid off her husband's creditors and the burial costs, and the day after the funeral, bought two tickets for Chicago.

As the boy matured — raised more by his grandparents than by his mother — he became solitary and a constant reader, with a particular interest in books on crime, criminals and law enforcement. He collected souvenirs of the Royal Canadian Mounted Police until they covered the bureau top in his bedroom. After finishing high school, he studied for a bachelor's degree in criminology at the University of Chicago. Within a week of graduation he married and was enrolled in the Federal Bureau of Investigation's training course, completed it with distinction and spent the next six years working out of the Bureau's Chicago office. A friend from his university days importuned him on a number of occasions to come to Washington and join the Secret Service. He considered it, but decided to remain with the FBI where he was building an enviable record for the thoroughness of his investigations and the relentlessness of his pursuit.

At 12:42 on the afternoon of November 22, 1963, he was at work in his office when the bulletin bell on the Teletype outside his door began to ring with an abnormal insistence. He joined a dozen others clustered about the machine to learn that John Fitzgerald Kennedy had been shot by an assassin in Dallas, Texas.

One week later he filed an application with the Secret Service and three months later moved with his young family to Washington. He played a major role in planning the controversial security arrangements at President Nixon's residences in San Clemente and Key Biscayne, and at the height of the controversy was commended by the Director for his thoroughness. His capacity for detail and his imaginative preparation for exigencies were the principal reasons why Herbert Morris appointed him to head the special White House Detail assigned to guard the President.

He inherited a well-organized security system and improved it even further. His years spent in the Bureau helped him in developing a new apparatus for coordination between the Secret Service and the FBI, both of whom had jealously husbanded particular prerogatives in areas where their responsibilities tended to overlap.

Gerry Regan took an enormous pride in the organization that screened the President from harm, and observed its smooth operation with great personal satisfaction. Consequently, he regarded the kidnapping of Adam Scott as being of the nature of an attack on himself; a direct and personal affront. And as it became clear that there was the possibility the Cabinet would accede to the kidnappers' demands and give them a safe-conduct, putting them beyond reach — in effect, rewarding them for their crime — a rage began to kindle deep in his gut where it grew and contorted and burned.

Regan ripped a sheet of paper from the Teletype and turned away in near apoplexy. "Oh no, no, *no!*" he groaned.

Jim McCurdy half ran toward him. "What is it?" he said anxiously.

"Read this," he said, thrusting the paper at McCurdy. "As if we didn't have enough."

It was an Associated Press news bulletin:

LITTLE ROCK, ARKANSAS, NOV. 6 (AP) - A RADICAL BLACK-POWER ORGANIZATION, THE ATTICANS, HAVE KIDNAPPED A BLACK EMPLOYEE OF THE LITTLE ROCK CENTRAL POST OFFICE, 18 YEAR OLD ROBERTA JEAN KING, AND ARE DEMANDING 50 MILLION DOLLARS FOR HER RELEASE. THE ATTICANS, NAMED AFTER CRISPUS ATTUCKS, A BLACK, THE FIRST CASUALTY IN THE BOSTON MASSACRE OF 1770, HAVE ALSO DEMANDED A SAFE-CONDUCT TO AFRICA FOR FOUR MEMBERS OF THEIR GROUP.
THE RANSOM NOTE SAYS, "IF THE UNITED STATES REALLY IS A DEMOCRACY IN WHICH ALL ARE CREATED EQUAL AND NOT AN ELITIST SOCIETY WHERE ONLY WHITE MALES ARE EQUAL, THEN THE GOVERNMENT MUST PAY THE SAME RANSOM FOR ROBERTA JEAN KING AS FOR THE PRESIDENT. THEY ARE BOTH AMERICAN CITIZENS AND EMPLOYEES OF THE GOVERNMENT OF THE UNITED STATES."
LITTLE ROCK POLICE CHIEF, WILLIE JERMYN, SAID THIS MORNING THE FBI HAD ENTERED THE CASE BECAUSE KID-

NAPPING IS A FEDERAL CRIME. "I'M AFRAID THIS IS A VERY SERIOUS MATTER," CHIEF JERMYN TOLD REPORTERS. "THE ATTICANS HAVE BEEN INVOLVED IN AT LEAST THREE MURDERS IN THIS AREA IN THE PAST YEAR."

From end to end, interrupted only by doorways, the walls of the National Theater's Loge-mezzanine were covered with blown-up photographs, overlapped to avoid duplication and stapled to the walls in a continuous horizontal strip; the impression was of endless lines of people standing behind a barricade. Pacing slowly, scrutinizing the photographs, Jim McCurdy was reminded of the photographs commonly taken at large gatherings by a panoramic camera, sweeping from one end of an assemblage to another and producing an extended horizontal print. He smiled, recollecting how as a boy he had posed at one end of a crowd, and when the lens had moved past, had ducked behind to outrace the sweep of the camera to position himself at the other end, and so appear in the photograph twice.

The strips on the walls — so positioned that the areas represented matched each other — were mounted one below the other, each strip representing photographs taken an hour later than the one above. Girls, some standing on portable aluminum ladders, were circling, with grease pencils, faces in the crowd duplicated in each earlier photograph. There were now four horizontal strips — representing photographs taken hourly from ten that morning — and the number of encircled faces in the bottom strip was considerably fewer than in the ones above.

It was Regan's theory that the kidnapper's accomplice would post himself at a predetermined position and not move from it. He based this conclusion on two assumptions: that the site would have been carefully studied in advance and an advantageous position selected, and that the chief kidnapper would want to know the exact location of his accomplice in the crowd.

As McCurdy scanned the bottom strip of pictures, such hopes as he had held that the plan would provide a means of identifying the accomplice were almost extinguished. Despite a surprising mobility among the spectators, after four hours the circled faces still comprised about twenty percent of the crowd.

He saw Ziggy Mayer approaching, his face animated.

"It's a girl!" he said, excitement in his voice.

McCurdy arched his eyebrows. "You just had a *baby?*"

"I mean the accomplice is a woman. I just got a call from the FBI's forensic lab. They found some long blond hairs in that wig left at the IRT."

"Long blond hair doesn't necessarily mean it's a girl, old buddy."

"No, no. There's a difference in the structure of the hair, or something. They can tell."

McCurdy felt a sudden surge of hope. He clapped his hands loudly. "Attention, everybody!" he shouted. "Attention!"

The clatter of talk and other activity subsided immediately except for an area at the far end of the room.

"*Quiet!*" Ziggy roared.

McCurdy stepped up on one of the ladders. "Let me have your attention," he said. "We've just learned that the second kidnapper is a woman. . . . "

There was an excited buzz of comment.

"Hold it, please. As I explained to you earlier, we believe there are only two people involved, so will you all please eliminate from the bottom strip of pictures all males. Understand me now: You are to eliminate the circles on the faces of all males and confine your search to females only. Is that clear?"

There was a nodding of heads and a general murmur of assent.

"Okay, everybody. Back to work. Let's find her!"

"Mr. Regan?"

"Yes."

"Did they tell you who's calling?"

"They told me."

"I'm calling from the Waldorf."

"I know that. What do you want?"

"I just want you to know I'm not satisfied with the way things are progressing."

"You're not."

"No, I'm not. Do you have a pencil?"

"A pencil?"

"I've made a list of my complaints. I want you to write them down so you can pass them on to your superiors."

"I won't need a pencil for that. And you don't deal with my superiors, you deal with me."

"You don't seem to realize . . . "

"Skip it. What is it you want?"

"First, I've decided this isn't a good place to be. I want you to have me moved to a hotel room or an office; some place that overlooks Times Square."

"You're not happy with the service at the Waldorf?"

"Mr. Regan, your humor isn't funny. You will move me to Times Square. I don't trust you."

"I'm pained."

"Mr. Regan, if you . . . "

"You said you had a list. What else don't you approve of?"

"The most important thing is that you and your superiors aren't keeping our agreement. You're stalling. I've been watching the television here and they just said the gold hasn't been shipped from Fort Knox yet."

"The reason for that is simple; we haven't decided to pay you yet. And we don't have what you call 'an agreement.' "

"But the Cabinet said the gold was going to be shipped to Kennedy airport. And now your Mr. Kirk says it hasn't even left Fort Knox. I think it's a trick."

"Let me ask you something, buddy: Do you have any idea how much fifty million dollars in gold weighs? Do you realize . . . "

"At the current price on the world's gold markets, somewhere around twenty-five thousand pounds."

"All right. But do you think I can pick up twelve and a half tons of gold like I'd send out for coffee? The shipment has to be authorized. It has to be protected. A plane with enough lift to carry it has to be laid on. It has to be transported from the vaults to the airport. It has . . . "

"I know all that. But it is now going on two o'clock. The flying time from Fort Knox to Kennedy airport is around an hour and forty-five minutes. If I haven't heard that the gold is on its way here within an hour . . . "

"You'll do what?"

"Let me remind you, Mr. Regan; any time I choose I can blow that truck into a thousand pieces."

"And let me tell *you* something, Mister, you'll do nothing of the kind and you know it. We're *both* in this now, and you're going to have to sweat it out with the rest of us. We have your conditions and we'll decide to meet them or we won't. In the meantime, I don't want any more lousy ultimatums from you. Understand?"

"Regan. . . . I'm warning you . . . !"

"Okay. Go ahead. Blow up the goddamn truck! But remember, Mister . . . the minute you do, *you're* dead, too!"

Regan slammed down the phone, reached into a pocket, pulled out a handkerchief and wiped away the perspiration that was beading on his forehead.

The Cabinet had debated for a full hour the question of whether or not to pay the ransom, and was deadlocked. The discussion had begun solemnly but with a general amiability, views being presented reasonably and equivocally, but as the arguments mounted, tempers shortened and the initial positions taken by the seven men and one woman present hardened. In favor of paying the ransom and granting an unconditional safe-conduct were: Chester Harrison, Secretary of the Treasury; Henrietta Cown, Postmaster General; Barney McCrory, Secretary of Labor; and Dr. Jonathan White, Secretary of Health, Education and Welfare. Opposed were: James Walker, Secretary of Defense; Herb Thurlow, Secretary of Agriculture; Charles Garvin, Secretary of Housing and Urban Development; and Saul Rosewald, Attorney General.

Ethan had refrained from participating in the debate. His stated reason was that, as Chairman, he must be impartial. His unstated reasons were more important, intensely personal and as yet unresolved in his mind.

He was facing a terrifying dilemma. The essential question — whether or not the ransom should be paid — presented no difficulty. It was of a kind he had faced many times in his political career: whether to yield to pressure for reasons of expediency. He had answered such questions negatively without equivocation dozens of times.

Listening to the discussion around the table, he recalled an appearance he had made on a national television show in 1972 when aircraft hijackings had been epidemic. He had argued with vigor and some heat that no concessions of any kind be made to the criminals or madmen who seized aircraft for political, financial or other reasons. The three other members of the panel had attacked him at what he knew was the weak point in his argument: that if one were inflexible, innocent passengers might well lose their lives. He had been booed by the studio audience and had received an avalanche of mail the following week, mostly critical, after he had shouted, "Better to take that risk than to reward criminals and encourage further crime. You do not," he had thundered, pounding the desk until the microphone bounced and the program host winced, "you do not bend the knee to the tyrant, be he petty or be he strong!"

The thought of paying fifty million dollars to a gang of criminals and then guaranteeing their escape stirred a swift anger in him, an anger intensified by the temerity of the kidnappers in demanding that he personally sign the safe-conduct.

Ethan's dilemma was infinitely more complex than his colleagues'. If, in obedience to his conscience, he was forced to break the tie and vote against paying the ransom, he knew that his action could bring about Adam Scott's death, and Adam's death would have far greater consequences for him than for the others. If Adam died, Ethan would be President of the United States. If Adam died, the Springlass problem, with its potential to force his resignation, would disappear. Conversely, voting to pay the ransom would not only require him to go contrary to convictions he had held and advocated throughout his public life, it would probably bring an immediate end to his political career, for he knew now as he had known early that morning, pacing the streets of Washington, that when he and Adam next met he would have no alternative but to tender his resignation.

An angry interjection from Herb Thurlow broke in on his thoughts.

"I've had it up to here, with these bleeding-heart arguments. Let me get on the record here and now: If we vote to give that bunch of thugs fifty million tax dollars and a plane ride home, I'll resign and fight the issue publicly."

"The voice of the democrat is heard in the land," said Barney McCrory. "He'll abide by the majority decision *if* it goes his way."

"I don't need any lessons in democracy from anyone in this room, and certainly not from the Secretary of Labor," Thurlow snapped.

"Can't we stop these personal remarks and get back to the point?" Henrietta Cown said, her voice plaintive. "The only thing that matters here is Adam's safety. Not because he's the President but because he's a human being. There is no principle, no amount of money, no *anything* important enough to justify putting him in danger."

"He's in no small danger now, Henrietta," Jim Walker said acidly.

"That's not what I mean and you know it," she retorted. "What I'm saying is this: Nothing is as important as a human life, in this case Adam's life, and it's our responsibility to see that he comes to no harm. It's as simple as that."

"You'll excuse me, Henrietta," Walker said wearily, "but it *isn't* as simple as that. I wish to God it were. Let's hypothesize that we do as you suggest: namely, pay the ransom and give the kidnappers a plane ticket home. What happens then? Right away, somebody says to himself, 'Hey! — isn't *that* a beautiful bonanza for the taking.' And first thing you know, nobody in public life is safe."

"You'll have opened a Pandora's box," murmured Saul Rosewald.

Dr. White held up a hand. "Let me pose this question," he said. "What would Adam say if the problem were put to him?"

"*I* don't have any doubt on that score," Charles Garvin said. "He and I talked about the possibility of an attempt on his life not six months ago. It came up on our way back from that Dallas trip. Adam said he'd settled the question long ago. He figures the risk is part of the job. 'It comes with the territory' was the way he put it."

"But that's not the same thing," said Dr. White. "Assassination is something you can't control. You take every possible precaution but there's always the chance. What we're facing today is another thing entirely. In this instance it *is* within our control to protect him. So I put it to you again: What would Adam say?"

"Exactly," Henrietta Cown said. "Surely *he* should have a say. It's *his* life at stake. Why don't we ask him? We can get word to him somehow."

"We could, you know," Chet Harrison mused. "As Herbert Morris said, the boys have set up some kind of loud-hailer to talk to him and a directional-mike so he can answer."

Jim Walker exploded. "You're not seriously proposing that we take a bullhorn and bellow the question into the wind? You're not suggesting that, in the hearing of every spectator in Times Square, of everyone watching on television and listening on radio around the world, we shout, 'Adam, old boy, give us your objective and unbiased judgment as to whether we should buy your freedom.'? Good God!"

"It's a ridiculous suggestion," said Saul Rosewald, "and I for one am opposed to it. It's buck-passing of the most craven sort. As Harry Truman used to say, 'The buck stops here' . . . with the man in charge. Which means that, this time, it stops here in this room."

"I'm reluctant to agree with you, Saul," Dr. White smiled, "but in this case, you're right."

There was a break in the flow of the argument and Saul Rosewald seized it. "Mr. Chairman," the Attorney General said slowly, "I wonder if I might be permitted a minute or two to try to put the entire matter in perspective?"

Ethan nodded.

"Let us examine for a moment the nature of the crime we're dealing with, then perhaps our response to it may be more clearly discerned. The crime is what the law describes as extortion: the obtaining of money by force or threat or fraud. Kidnapping, blackmail and what I believe is called 'the protection racket' are all generically alike; they're all forms of extortion. In each case the criminal has the power to hurt you and requires that you pay him money so he won't. The protection racket is a threat, usually, to your business. Blackmail is a threat, usually, to your reputation. Kidnapping is a threat, usually, to a loved one — or at least to human life. But they're all extortion. In each, a person with criminal intent is saying, 'Do as I say or I shall do something decidedly unpleasant.' On an international scale, it's precisely what Adolf Hitler was saying to the civilized world in the 1930's. And that, friends, is my point: so long as people and nations acceded to his demands he continued to make more and larger demands. Appeasing him didn't satisfy him — as Neville Chamberlain learned to his sorrow. The civilized world found itself faced with the unpleasant necessity of saying, 'Thus far and no further,' even though to do so meant war and the suffering of the innocent. Mr. Chairman, in my view, what's happening in New York City today is completely analogous. We must stop such actions *now*. To fail to do so will intensify rather than diminish the problem."

"Saul," Chet Harrison said, "I'm reluctant to take you on in matters related to law or justice. That's your field and an area in which you've served with distinction over the years. . . . "

"Thank you, Chet. I take it then that you're prepared to alter your position?" Saul said, smiling.

"On the contrary. It seems to me that what you've done is to state admirably the case as it relates to law, but that's not the relevant point. You said you wanted to get down to the essence; all right, let me have a go at doing just that."

He paused to suck on his pipe and vent a stream of smoke. "Why do men form a democratic society, a free society? To be specific: Why was our Republic formed? Wasn't it so that men, consenting together, would thus be enabled to do everything within their collective power to protect the life, the liberty and the opportunity to pursue happiness of each individual member of the group? So, if the society exists to protect and benefit the individual, surely any member of that society has the right to require of the society that it do what it was established to do — namely, to protect, so far as it is able, his life and liberty. Now, here we have the First Citizen of this Republic. He has already been deprived of his liberty and stands in danger of being deprived of his life. It seems to me he has a claim on the society. He has the right to ask the society to do everything in its power to succor him. And I'm not, mark you, talking about tendering aid to some *hypothetical* individual who *may* some day in the future be in jeopardy under some *general* set of circumstances. I'm talking about our responsibility to render aid to a particular citizen of this Republic under a specific set of circumstances here and now. What you've been arguing, Saul, with respect, is legalism, pragmatism. What we're face to face with is the right of a human being, a man in jeopardy through no fault of his own, to his life and the liberty to pursue his personal happiness. And it seems to me that our responsibility in this specific instance is the greater because the citizen in this case is one who is endangered *because* he was serving the society."

Henrietta Cown applauded. "Bravo, Chester! That's it exactly. Where would all this talk about principle go if the person kidnapped was one of our own family?"

"Right," echoed McCrory. "The United States was set up to protect the rights of the individual. That's basic."

"No, no," Saul Rosewald replied. "It was set up to protect the rights of the *greatest possible number* of individuals. That's why we restrict the rights of any single individual. He's not free to do anything that encroaches on the collective rights of others. That's why we have laws prohibiting speeding, prohibiting theft, prohibiting dozens of things. The individual's rights are *not* supreme; the rights of the greatest possible number of individuals come first."

"Abstract theory," grumbled Henrietta Cown. "For the life of me, I don't know why you can't get it through your head that we're not talking about some hypothetical somebody, we're talking about Adam."

"We've been over that ground a dozen times," Charles Garvin said. "It's time we took a vote. The question please, Mr. Chairman."

"That's not fair," Henrietta Cown protested. "You know we're evenly divided and you know where Ethan stands. You want to get your way by closing off debate."

"Henrietta dear, if a tie-breaking vote is required, it's the Chairman's duty to cast it."

"Well, he doesn't have to yet."

"Question. Question."

"Oh shut up!" Henrietta snapped.

Ethan picked up the gavel and tapped it lightly. "Order please," he said smiling. "The Chairman does have a couple of things he'd like to say at this point. First, however, while I do appreciate your vote of confidence, Charles. . . . " He looked at the Secretary of Housing and Urban Development, "you really ought not to presume you know the Chairman's mind. . . . "

"I didn't *say* what you'd do, Ethan."

"But you know," Henrietta broke in.

"Excuse me, Henrietta," Ethan said, "he doesn't. I'm not one of Pavlov's pups; I may not salivate automatically because someone sounds a familiar tone. But let's leave that for the moment." He put down the gavel, leaned his elbows on the table and sat rubbing his palms together. "The fact is, gentlemen and Miss Cown, I don't want to cast a tie-breaking vote unless I have no option. I won't duck my responsibility but I'm certainly not going to seek it when so much hangs in the balance. Consequently, I have two suggestions to place before you: First, that we postpone the vote until Jim Hilliard and Arnie Gustafson get here. They're due, I believe Jim said, around three this afternoon. . . . "

There was a flurry of objections.

"Hold on a moment," Ethan said. "Hear me out. My second

suggestion is that, in the meantime, we take the necessary steps to get the gold shipped to Kennedy airport so that, in the event our decision is to pay the ransom, there'll be no delay."

"But that's as much as saying we're going to pay," Herb Thurlow protested.

"What does it matter? If we finally decide not to pay, it doesn't matter what we seemed to say. And if we decide to pay, the money will be on hand."

There was a moment of quiet around the table as each weighed the suggestions. Saul Rosewald broke the silence. "If you'll accept my putting it this way, Ethan, it's a solution worthy of a Solomon."

"I agree," said Dr. White.

"Then, if there's no objection," Ethan continued, "I suggest we table the question until our absent colleagues join us. With your permission I'll have Jim Rankin draft a press release to the effect that we're bringing in the gold from Fort Knox pending a decision by the Cabinet. I think we can trust Jim to put it in such a way that it won't be misunderstood."

There was a general murmuring of "Agree."

Ethan turned to Chet Harrison. "I wonder, Chet, if you'd be kind enough to make the arrangements at Fort Knox and to communicate our decision to Mr. Morris and through him to Gerry Regan. I think they should be made aware of our thinking."

"Will do," Harrison said.

"Mr. Chairman," Jim Walker said, "I have a question. Why in hell does this decision lie with us? Why should a matter of such importance be settled by, at most, nine people? And by what authority do we do it? Shouldn't we talk this over with the Speaker of the House and the President pro tempore of the Senate? Surely they have an equal or greater responsibility than we. They're the elected representatives. The only person here who's been elected to office is you yourself, Mr. Chairman. Shouldn't we give some thought to that side of things?"

"I have thought about it," Ethan said. "I talked to Chauncey Howe by telephone this morning — he's back home in Richmond — and a conference call with him and Travis Johnstone is being set up for later this afternoon. I raised the question with Chauncey that you've raised here. It was his view that there is no practical option; it's almost a physical impossibility to poll each member of the Congress. At any rate, Chauncey wanted some time to think about it and said he'd give me his decision when he and Travis and I get on the phone."

There was another silence.

"I must say, Mr. Chairman . . . Ethan," said Dr. White, "it's a very difficult situation. Especially for you."

"I agree. But I'm afraid that's the way it is."

Henrietta Cown said, "There is one other matter we should discuss. . . ."

"Yes?" Ethan said.

"The kidnapping of that girl in Little Rock. We're going to have to make some kind of response."

"Look," Herb Thurlow said impatiently, "it's a ploy, a device. It's being done just to embarrass the government. I say we don't even respond."

"Send the FBI in and clean 'em out," Barney McCrory yawned.

"I'm afraid that's not possible," Ethan said. "We must say something. The press boys will want an answer."

"The thing to do is stall," Thurlow said. "Have Rankin say that we're giving it serious consideration but won't be able to make a decision until tomorrow . . . something like that."

Barney McCrory rose to his feet. "Look friends," he said, "I'm starved. I move we adjourn at the call of the Chair."

"Second," said Herb Thurlow.

Ethan informed them that a buffet had been laid on in the dining room. "If it's agreed," he said, "we'll reconvene at two o'clock."

Times Square. The neon lights, the flashing lights, the sequenced lights have all been turned off; and in the daylight, with their distraction gone, the tawdriness of the Great White Way is suddenly emphasized. *Dark* — the neon is whorls and convolutions of tubing caked with dirt. *Dark* — the patterns of the light bulbs are like faded patches of pebbled color on a dusty palette. Darkened and shuttered with metal grillwork, the souvenir shops, the amusement arcades, the skin-flick movie houses, the bargain stores and the music bars are shoddy. It is as though everything that is sleazy in America has been transplanted to these few acres at the heart of the world's greatest city. Even the sky is dirty: slate-gray and tinted with a soiled saffron.

A wind has risen and is tumbling and chasing papers, candy-wrappers, oddments of cardboard and cellophane and dust in erratic eddies. It has flattened a page from the *Times* against the side of the armoured truck. The eight-column headline on the normally restrained page is visible from the crowd:

PRESIDENT HELD HOSTAGE
IN BOOBY-TRAPPED TRUCK

The hush that had hovered over the Square earlier in the day has gone. The pervasive murmur of thousands of conversations mingles with the hum of the generators in the television mobile units, the shouts of hawkers and the fretful crying of children. Portable radios multiply the staccato urgency of news bulletins. Faces frown into a thousand newspapers. A youth in a hand-tooled leather hat strokes his greasy guitar and improvises nasally about loneliness. In a tight circle, a dozen drably dressed men and women are praying, their interjections increasing as their zeal is cranked by their leader's importunities.

In the front row of the crowd, his massive upper thighs pressed against the police barricade, a burly black man stands, his elaborately ornamented sport shirt open at the neck. He has been staring unwaveringly at the truck for many minutes, his eyes filling with tears until from time to time they overflow to course unnoticed down his cheeks. Oblivious to the people around him, he swallows hard and begins to sing. The voice is cloudy and unsure at first. It quickly clears and swells and grows in volume and power. It is a resonant, untrained voice, melodious but with an edge of roughness, and the sound pours from his open mouth.

"My coun-tree 'tis of thee,
Sweet land of li-ber-tee,
Of thee I sing. . . . "

The people around him have picked up the song and it rises above the hubbub.

"Land where our fa-thers died,
Land of the pil-grims' pride. . . . "

Now a thousand voices join, and other thousands, and the song mounts and swells until it echoes and reverberates in the Square.

"From e-e-vry-ee moun-tain side
Le-et free-dom ring."

In the truck, Adam Scott is singing too.

Chapter Thirteen

Adam Scott was troubled. Five minutes earlier, at exactly two o'clock, he had strained against his leash to read the news reports on the running lights on the Allied Chemical building. The final bulletin read: WASHINGTON SOURCE SAYS CABINET SPLIT ON PAYING RANSOM . . . . . DECIDING VOTE MAY REST WITH VICE-PRESIDENT . . . . .

He crawled back to the blanket and sat down, kneading his wrist where the manacle had bitten into the flesh. Wasn't *that* a hell of a note, he thought: a split in the Cabinet and the tie-breaking vote up to Ethan! It was a circumstance he hadn't contemplated. In fact, he had brushed aside the likelihood of serious debate over the payment of the ransom. He should have known better; it was a legitimate issue.

Adam now realized that he was in considerably greater jeopardy than he had assumed. If the ransom weren't paid, his safety came down to a question of the firmness of the kidnappers' resolution. The man now in protective custody — and probably the other kidnapper, too — would be arrested, charged and confronted with the fact that kidnapping carried the death penalty. Undoubtedly, pressure would be applied. A promise would be made that the death sentence would be commuted to life if he, Adam, were released unharmed. But even as he was reviewing the possibilities, Moreno's face, as he had seen it that morning — flecked with sweat and spittle and touched with madness — materialized in his memory and chilled him. This was not the sort of man to yield to importunities or threats; he was a fanatic. It suddenly came home to Adam that if the ransom were not paid he might die.

The ironic complication was the fact that the decision whether or not to pay might rest with Ethan Roberts. What a tumult there must be in his mind. No one but the two of them knew of their conversation yesterday afternoon, or of the Joe Springlass affair, or of the ultimatum that he, Adam, had laid down. Surely, in the debate going on in Cabinet, Ethan would feel required to declare that he had a conflict of interest and disqualify himself from voting. What Adam could not know was that the Vice-President had no such intention.

Ethan had met Joe Springlass in the spring of 1974 at a fishing lodge in Canada. Bob Williamson, a partner in Ethan's former law firm, Roberts, Holcomb, Smythe and Williamson, had importuned him each year to join a fishing party of four that flew every May to a camp on the Upper Humber River in Newfoundland for Atlantic salmon fishing. The invitation had little appeal for Ethan: He did not know the other members of the group, was not a practiced fisherman and had long made it a rule not to put himself in situations where he might appear inadequate. Consequently, he turned down the invitation and had planned over the Memorial Day weekend to fly out to Indianapolis for the Indy-500, and while there to do "a bit of political fence-mending."

But for a combination of reasons the plan had fallen apart, and Ethan realized with a flush of irritation that he was faced with spending the first spring weekend alone in an empty Washington: Emily was going to Virginia to see her mother, and the children had their own plans. It was a prospect that did not please. So, when on the Wednesday evening Bob Williamson telephoned to tell him that one of the fishing foursome had canceled because of the death of a relative and urged him to join the group, he agreed.

To his surprise he enjoyed himself enormously. The two other members of the group, Joe Springlass and Clayton Edgerton, were relaxed men of approximately Ethan's age and he was soon at ease. Edgerton was a pipe-smoking expert on corporation law who ten years earlier had stopped practicing law to write textbooks and lecture to learned societies and university audiences. Ethan had once referred to two of Edgerton's books while preparing a brief and remembered them as abstruse, pedantic and dust-dry. He had expected Edgerton to be the embodiment of his writing style, and

153

on being introduced to him just prior to boarding their chartered Lear jet at National airport, concluded that indeed he was. It was not until the party had arrived at the camp, settled in, and was doing some serious drinking before an enormous fieldstone fireplace, that it became evident Edgerton was the possessor of a seemingly endless collection of barrack-room jokes which he told with consummate mastery; spinning them out in hilarious detail and couching them in earthy language — the stories being borne forward on great gusts and spasms of laughter until the punchline was reached. Ethan had a fondness for subtle ribaldry and normally was reluctant to encourage what he termed "dirty stories," but Edgerton's skill as a raconteur swept away his inhibitions and left him at the end of the first evening half sick with laughter.

The other member of the foursome, Joe Springlass, was an importer and evidently a man of great wealth. When Ethan asked Williamson what the cost would be for the weekend he had been told, "Forget it. Joe says if you're coming, he's picking up the tab."

"The bill for the charter? The accommodation . . . ?"

"The whole shmear."

"For everybody?"

"Everybody."

Questioned, Williamson was vague on how Springlass had made his money — "He's an old friend and a fishing buddy, and we don't talk business." All he knew was that Springlass employed a large team of buyers who scoured various parts of the world purchasing a variety of exotic products — everything from rattan furniture to semi-precious stones to Peruvian ponchos. These were retailed through a chain of unornamented warehouse-type stores under the name Shipboard USA. "What matters is, he's got more money than he needs," Williamson said, "and the way he spends it, more than he wants."

Ethan warmed to Springlass immediately. The importer was an ebullient man of forty-five, craggily handsome, tanned and quite clearly fit, with an easy gregariousness that Ethan had always envied. But what he found particularly attractive was Joe's interest in politics. There was nothing of the sycophant about him, but it was evident that he had long admired Ethan, had followed his career closely, and was able to talk about it in a manner which, while flattering, was not obsequious.

By the time the party returned to Washington with a freezer full

154

of salmon, sunburned forearms and faces and a variety of hang-overs, Ethan and Springlass had become friends, and the politician had accepted an invitation for the following weekend to join the businessman aboard his 52-foot cruiser for a jaunt on Chesapeake Bay. The developing friendship was enhanced when Emily Roberts and Estelle Springlass found an easy camaraderie.

In subsequent months the two couples became each other's closest friends and spent at least an evening a week in the other's home, or weekends aboard the cruiser. Springlass owned a sumptu-ous oceanside vacation home at Lyford Cay in the Bahamas, and shortly after the Robertses had spent a weekend there as guests, completed an unfinished wing and made it available to Ethan for work or relaxation.

Ethan, who received much more from the relationship than he gave, or was able to give, had for the first six months anticipated a request for a favor. But when a year passed and Springlass had not so much as asked him if he could use his name as a reference, nor hinted that Ethan speak to someone in government on his behalf, Ethan began to feel self-conscious about the material kind-nesses being given. He raised the subject as they sat at poolside on a hot Sunday afternoon.

"Joe," he began, "it occurred to me the other day that there might be something I could do for you on the Hill. If there is, I hope you won't hesitate to ask."

Springlass was slow in responding. "Thanks," he said. "That's very kind, but no thanks."

"I didn't mean anything out of line," Ethan said quickly. "It's just that if I can ease a logjam or light a fire under a bureaucrat, all you have to do is let me know."

Joe cleared his throat and when he spoke there was a trace of huskiness in his voice. "Ethan," he said, "the only thing I'll ever ask from you is the honor of calling you a friend. If you'll put up with my being maudlin for a minute . . . the best thing that ever happened to me was meeting you on that trip to Newfie. I can't tell you what your friendship has meant to me."

"If we're going to be candid," Ethan said, "perhaps this is the time to say that I'm a bit embarrassed by the kindnesses you and Estelle show us. There's no way I can begin to return them."

"You mustn't think of it like that. See it from my side. I'm a businessman and I've been lucky, very lucky. I work less than one day a week and I'm rewarded handsomely. But look at you: You're a public servant. You work long hours every day, and what do you get out of it? — in financial terms, I mean. Very little. If anybody should feel guilty, it's me."

The subject was awkward for both sides and was quickly dropped.

The growing friendship would prove important to Ethan for he had decided to seek the Vice-Presidential nomination at the convention scheduled for July in Miami. He broached his intention to political associates in his home state. The response was, as Ethan put it, "underwhelming." The sum of their counsel was: hold steady till you see how the fight for the Presidential nomination shapes up.

But Ethan was not prepared to play the waiting game. He knew that aspirants to the Vice-Presidential nomination seldom campaigned actively until the eve of the convention. He knew, too, that it was irregular to seek the post and that it could militate against him, but he had observed in his years in politics that diffidence was seldom rewarded. Political lightning tended to strike where there was a mutual attraction; you had to be available to be found available, even though tradition required that you disavow your intention.

He talked the matter over with Joe Springlass on a blustery April Saturday when, having been driven from the tenth tee at the Burning Tree Country Club by a pelting rain, they were sipping a cognac and coffee in a secluded corner of the clubhouse. Joe shook his head in disbelief as Ethan recounted the lack of encouragement he had met with.

When he was finished, Joe said, "Well, what are we waiting for? We'll start without the bastards. We'll set up our own organization. We'll hire a PR guy. We'll light a fire. . . . "

"Hold a moment, friend," Ethan said, smiling at Joe's enthusiasm. "You can't go at it that hard, or that openly. It's got to be subtle as hell."

Springlass sat silent for a moment, circling with a forefinger the rim of his glass. "Why don't we do this . . . ? I've got a public relations firm I use, and they're damn good. What say we get the president of the company down here — guy by the name of Jake Gruneau — and have an exploratory talk?"

So it was that Jake Gruneau, the forty-year-old president of Gruneau Associates, joined them for dinner at the Springlass home the following Tuesday.

Gruneau was unlike any PR man Ethan had ever met. He looked like a college man not long out of a California university. He was well over six feet, affected a crew-cut, was gangling and awkward and had a laugh like the bellow of a bull.

During cocktails, while Ethan was trying to figure him out and Jake was engaged in his apparently unending search from pocket to pocket for a pack of cigarettes, he shot an arched-eyebrows look at Springlass and got a cryptic smile in return. They were not halfway through the meal before Ethan realized that Gruneau was a wizard of his kind and that he *must* have him on his team. He so informed Joe after their guest had gone and was told with a grin, "It's all arranged."

"All arranged?"

"All arranged. I knew if you met him you'd buy him."

As a consequence of the application of Jake's skills, Ethan's name was soon constantly to be read in the public prints, and radio and television reporters commonly pushed microphones in his face and sought his views. Equally important, he began to gather around him a band of volunteers who, for all the variety of reasons that stimulate people to work in politics, offered their services.

Shortly after Gruneau had gone to work on his behalf, Ethan raised the question of his remuneration. Springlass dismissed it by saying that Jake was more than adequately taken care of through the retainer Shipboard USA was paying him, that his work for Ethan was part-time and that it had not required the expenditure of a single additional dollar.

By early summer, it became increasingly evident that Adam Scott was the front-runner for the Presidential nomination. By mid-June there were no fewer than nine declared or unofficial candidates in the race; four of them serious, the others being "favorite sons," wanting or needing the publicity.

Adam had built up a strong lead in the primaries and would have had a clear path to the nomination had it not been that the three other leading candidates were of a kind, and seemed ready to form a "coalition of conservatives" with one purpose: to effect their will on the party's Platform committee. There was general agreement among the political pros and the press that, if they could deny Adam a first-ballot victory, and if on subsequent roll calls the others could swing their support to one of their number — probably Caleb Thornton of California — they could deadlock the convention.

Ethan's political savvy told him that Adam would win the nomination. He had decided some months back that, at what seemed an appropriate time, he would make an approach and try to work out an arrangement based on mutual interest. He had some bargaining power: he was in a position to deliver somewhere near 150 votes, an impressive amount of clout.

Three weeks before the convention he arranged a meeting with Adam. To avoid speculation they planned to lunch in a private dining room at the Mayflower hotel. It was agreed that each would bring one aide. Ethan invited Bart Manning, a congressman from his own district whom he had named Chairman of his Strategy committee. When they arrived at the rendezvous, Adam introduced them to his chief aide, Jaz Osterwald.

The meeting was unsatisfactory. There was, it seemed to Ethan, too much ambiguity, too much general conversation. A half dozen times he sought to focus the conversation and each time Osterwald took it in another direction. The meal over, the four men sipping their coffee and dipping into bowls of fresh strawberries on ice cream, Ethan decided on a frontal attack.

"Adam," he began, a touch of formality entering his tone, "the purpose of our getting together today is to explore ways in which we may be useful to each other at the convention. I'm prepared to throw a considerable body of support behind you, and it has been my hope that you would be willing to give some indication — only within the party, of course — that I have your confidence as your running mate. There are, as you know, four of us. . . . "

"Yes," Bart Manning interrupted. "Kevin Whiting, Mike Harlow, Ralph Morton, and of course, Ethan here."

"It was my hope," Ethan continued, "that we could work out some kind of accommodation."

Adam was, it seemed, preoccupied with the lighting of a cigar. Jaz made as though to speak but an almost invisible lifting of Adam's hand stopped him. There was a silence until Adam got the cigar properly lit.

"Well now," he said slowly, venting great puffs of fragrant smoke toward the ceiling, "perhaps we should begin at the beginning. We can forget about Harlow . . . reactionary bastard." He took another pull on the cigar, contemplating the ash. "I'm afraid," he said, turning to Ethan, "you put me in a difficult position. Kev Whiting is an old friend. Beyond that — and I'm sure you'll understand me in this — it isn't good politics to commit yourself early. One needs room to maneuver. There's the geographical balance of the ticket to consider. And further," he said, looking levelly at Ethan, "let me ask you a question: Wouldn't it be a bit indelicate for me to specify who I want as my running mate before I'm nominated?"

"It's been done," Bart said.

"Hardly ever," Jaz countered.

"I'll tell you what I *can* do," Adam said. "When and if I'm asked, I can say that you and Whiting are both men I'd be happy to have with me on the ticket. In the meantime we can keep in touch, and if and when the time comes, we can examine the situation as it is at that time."

"It seems to me . . . " Ethan began.

Adam cut him off. "I'm afraid that's as far as I can go at the moment. Perhaps we should leave it there for now."

Chairs were pushed back. The meeting was clearly over.

When Ethan and Bart compared notes, they agreed that Scott favored Whiting, that he wasn't declaring his whole mind and that, if it came to a showdown, the nod would go to Whiting. It was Bart who offered to sound out Caleb Thornton. Ethan agreed, with the proviso that Bart make it clear he was speaking without authorization. A week later, Bart was on the telephone.

"I talked to our friend," he said ambiguously. (Since the Watergate bugging incidents, much Washington telephone talk was cryptic and non-specific.)

"And?"

"Problems. H. has the inside track."

"Is your man persona non grata?"

"No, but definitely second-string."

"Not good."

"Not bad, actually. In a deadlock I'd rather be everybody's second choice than front-runner."

"That's presuming there'll be a deadlock."

"Maybe that's what we work for."

"I follow you," Ethan said, concerned that too much had been said. "We'll talk later."

At the convention, a behind-the-scenes battle had been joined between the conservative and liberal factions in the party. The contention was over a number of progressive planks in the first draft of the report of the Platform committee. Committee sessions were barred to the press but delegates leaked the proceedings to the media and they trumpeted the schism in the newspapers and on television. Adam's supporters held a slim majority in the committee and fought bitterly to achieve a document that would create the enlightened image Adam wanted to present when he went to the country. But the conservative forces gained their immediate objective through a variety of parliamentary devices and a series of stalling tactics: namely, to push back the presentation of the report to the convention until after the nomination of the Presidential candidate. The chairman — under pressure from the television networks and anxious to have the balloting take place during prime time — finally ruled that nominations would proceed and the convention would receive the report of the Platform committee later.

On the first roll call, no one name dominated. After four ballots, Adam's total was close to a majority but static, with no sign of a breakthrough. At 3:40 in the morning, Adam, with Jaz Osterwald, climbed the four flights of back stairs to Caleb Thornton's suite in hope of finding a way out of the impasse. Thornton made two demands: the removal or the softening of five planks in the platform, and the selection of Mike Harlow as the Vice-Presidential candidate. Adam exploded. He was prepared to discuss the platform but would not, under any circumstances, accept Harlow as his running mate. Thornton was equally adamant in rejecting Kevin Whiting — "That goddamn left-wing turncoat." The argument was loud and often heated. It ended when they settled on Ethan Roberts as a compromise.

The confrontation over the Platform committee report took longer. Pencils came out. Phrases were tortured, synonyms were employed, ambiguities were agreed upon. With Jaz Osterwald proposing, altering, arguing, cursing, pleading and sometimes conceding, and Adam silent and watchful except for two identical interjections — "No, I will not buy that!" — the matter was settled.

Word was telephoned to the floor of the convention where the Chairman, fully aware of what was happening, had been marking time despite taunts and cadenced shouts of "Vote!" from the galleries. He gaveled the sagging convention to order and called for ballot number five. As the roll call began, Alabama yielded to California and a rumpled and sweaty Caleb Thornton went to a microphone to withdraw in favor of Adam. As the call of the delegations droned on, each state chairman leaped for the bandwagon and Adam Northfield Scott was nominated. The following afternoon the hastily revised Platform committee report was rammed through despite scattered shouts of "Betrayal." That same evening Ethan Roberts was acclaimed as the Vice-Presidential nominee.

The victory was sweet on Ethan's tongue. It was soured only by the knowledge that under the almost unendurable pressures of the convention he had authorized expenditures far beyond his budget. When all the bills had been tendered he found himself almost thirty thousand dollars in debt and was reminded that a candidate is legally responsible for expenditures made in his name.

An approach to the party's National committee yielded the response that, while they would finance his election campaign, they could not assume any responsibility for deficits incurred in getting the nomination. In response to personal appeals by members of his Executive committee, a few thousand dollars trickled in, but the amount owing at the bank leveled near the twenty-five-thousand-dollar mark. Over the next few weeks, under increasing pressure from the bank to secure the note, he met with the manager, who was honored and sympathetic but also adamant. Ethan saw no option but to take out a second mortgage on his home. A troubled Emily confided her concerns to Estelle Springlass and the following day Ethan received a phone call from Joe: Could he drop by that evening on an urgent matter?

He went to the Springlass home curious as to the reason for the summons. Joe, clearly in an expansive mood, made affable conversation and poured a series of drinks. When an hour passed with no reference to the reason for the meeting, Ethan raised the question.

"What the hell goes on, Joe?" he said. "I get this urgent request to come over — 'Drop everything' I'm told — and now, for an hour, you've been encouraging my already ingrained tendency to alcoholism while saying precisely nothing."

Joe looked at him and smiled — they were both feeling the liquor. "Is a friend permitted to meddle in the affairs of a friend?" he asked.

"Go ahead and meddle."

"Okay. Estelle tells me you're going to put a second mortgage on your house. True?"

"Oh, that woman of mine!" Ethan groaned.

"That woman, nothing. She's worried. And I can understand why." He tilted back his head and downed his drink. "The point I want to make is this: If that's what you *have* to do, for God's sake don't go to the bank. They'll charge you an arm and a leg. I'll put up the money and you can pay me back any way you want."

"But I couldn't let you do that."

"Why'n hell not? How come you can owe the bank but not me? Tha's a hell of a note." He chuckled loudly.

Ethan, his mind slightly fuzzed, pondered the question. The bank rate for a second mortgage was outrageous. The worry was obviously lying heavily on Emily; he could see it in her face and demeanor. Springlass resolved his indecision.

"Look," he said, "if it bothers you to borrow from a friend, we'll draw up a document. Okay? And if you feel you *must* add an interest charge, okay again. But in the meantime get the thing off your back. And Emily's."

The following evening when Ethan arrived home, Emily met him at the door, excitement in her eyes.

"A man brought a package for you an hour ago. Said he was a messenger for Shipboard USA. Some messenger service! — he was driving a Cadillac."

He unwrapped the sealed package. Inside was a cardboard box. He lifted the lid and Emily gasped. There, in neat, segregated piles, were stacks of currency in denominations of twenty, fifty and one hundred dollars. He made a swift tally — twenty-five thousand dollars.

The document on the repayment of the loan was never drawn. Joe and Estelle Springlass were killed three days later with 178 others when a Pan World Airways 747-B flew into a wooded hill in a thunderstorm some twenty miles south of Gary, Indiana. There were no survivors.

Ethan discussed with Emily getting in touch with the legal firm handling the Springlass estate but concluded that — the twenty-five thousand having been sent to him in cash, and there being no receipt or document of any kind — it might be awkward to explain. He decided to wait until he was contacted and in the interim set up a bookkeeping allocation of five hundred dollars a month in his personal records.

Eight months later, while at breakfast, he read in the *New York Times* that the will of Joseph Marvin Springlass, importer, had been probated. He had left his entire estate of almost three and a half million dollars to his wife with the provision that, in the event of her death, the residue be dispersed among a half dozen universities for the endowment of scholarships in political science.

Almost fifteen months later Ethan arrived at his office early on the Sunday before the off-year elections, planning to clear his desk so that nothing would be pending during his western trip or on election day. He had only begun to go through a stack of mail when the intercom buzzed.

"Yes?" he said, irritation in his voice. He had impressed on the lone girl at the switchboard that he did not want to be interrupted.

"The White House on the line."

It was Jaz Osterwald. "I wonder if you could drop by this afternoon about 4:30," he said. "The President has something he'd like to go over with you."

"Of course," Ethan said.

"You might come to my office in the EOB before you go in."

"Right. See you at 4:30."

Ethan replaced the phone and paused before returning to the stack of mail before him. Contrary to what is commonly believed outside Washington, the Vice-President is not the constant confidant of the President. Apart from Cabinet meetings, Ethan seldom had private conversation with Adam Scott. Pondering the reason for the summons, he concluded that it probably bore on policy matters Adam would like emphasized on his western trip. As was his custom, he dismissed the matter by an act of will and returned to his work.

At precisely 4:20 he climbed the stairs to Jaz Osterwald's office in the Executive Office Building.

"What's on his mind?" he asked.

"Haven't the slightest idea. The reason I asked you to drop by before going in is because the Soviet Ambassador is with him and we figured there might be the need to push back the appointment schedule a few minutes. But apparently all is well; I've just had the alert he's leaving. You can go right over."

Ethan strode across the street from the Executive Office Building to the White House proper, passed a security check and walked to the hallway outside the President's oval office. Adam was standing in the open doorway bidding his guest good-by. There were a number of handshakes and much smiling and nodding. Ethan hung back until the Russian had gone, and as Adam turned back to his office, crossed the hall.

"Good afternoon, Mr. President," he said.

"Ethan," Adam said, "good to see you. Come in."

They entered the office. Adam, without further word, gestured Ethan to a chair, went to his desk, sat down, opened a drawer and took out a manilla file folder.

"You'll forgive me if I go right to the point," he said, opening the file. "I've got a press conference in fifteen minutes." There was silence as he leafed through the file.

"Now," he said, looking up, "to the matter at hand. Am I correct in my understanding, Ethan, that you knew Joseph Springlass quite well?"

"I did indeed," Ethan said, surprised at the reference to his dead friend. "I think you could say he was my closest personal friend."

Adam cleared his throat. "All of which makes my task more difficult. Ethan, I'm going to ask you a few questions. Some of them you may find objectionable. I hope you'll understand that I'm only doing what I have to do."

"Of course," Ethan said, sensing a slight tension in his stomach.

"First of all, what did you know about Springlass's business?"

"Very little, actually. He was an importer. He was president of a company called Shipboard USA."

"Did you know any of his business associates?"

"No. As a matter of fact we almost never discussed his business. He gave very little time to it; didn't seem interested in it. Apparently he had an excellent second-in-command."

Adam was flipping pages in the file, obviously seeking a particular document. Ethan felt a mixture of apprehension and anger growing in him. "You'll forgive me, Adam," he said, "but what's this all about?"

Adam removed a paper from the file and placed it before him. "I'll try to explain," he said. "Perhaps the best thing to do is start at the beginning. You may not know that the Federal Aviation Administration did a careful examination of the plane crash in which Springlass and his wife were killed. There were rumors of sabotage, but apparently they were without foundation, and the case has been closed for some months now. However, about a week ago, a boy playing in the woods not far from where the crash happened, found a locked attaché case, with the initials JMS, lodged in the branches of a bush. Apparently, it had been flung there by the impact. Because the FBI had been interested in the crash, the briefcase was forwarded to them. It turns out that it belonged to the late Joseph Marvin Springlass and it contained a letter to him from you on White House stationery . . . this letter I hold in my hand."

Ethan felt his entire system react. The blood drained from his head. His heart leaped into an erratic acceleration and he was suddenly cold. Adam, reading the letter, did not see his reaction. Ethan's mind went back almost two years. He saw himself at his desk at the end of the day, his secretary gone, pecking out on an official letterhead a thank-you letter to Joe. Good Christ! — what had he written?

Adam's voice brought him back. "I should tell you that no one has seen the letter other than the Director and me. I've spoken about it to no one and I told the Director this morning that he could forget the matter, that I'd clear it up."

He held up a single sheet of waterstained letterhead embossed with the legend The White House. To the right were the smaller words, Office of the Vice-President. "The letter is yours, isn't it?"

"Yes."

"If I may, I'd like to read an excerpt or two and ask you about them." He found the place. "I'm quoting: 'I couldn't let the day go by without letting you know how much I appreciate this latest expression of your thoughtfulness. Emily gave me the package you sent around to the house yesterday. I tried to reach you a number of times today, but no luck. I really don't know how to thank you.' "

Adam looked up. "Would you mind telling me what was in the package?"

Ethan's mind was now crystal clear. His every sense was alert. The letter was ambiguous; there could have been anything in the package. He would feel his way forward.

"Adam," he said, "I find this whole thing quite incredible. You have there a letter of mine, a personal letter to a friend, and you're reading from it and asking me questions about it which, with all respect, are my business and nobody else's."

"Ethan," the President said, his voice patient, his manner gentle, "I quite understand what you feel. But the fact is — and I regret having to tell you this — your friend Springlass has long been known to the FBI, the Customs department and the CIA. Not only did he have a number of unsavory associations in his business, some being Mafia connections, but there is also reason to believe he was tied in with the smuggling of narcotics into the United States. It's never been proven, I grant you, but our people say that, while his company, Shipboard USA, may not have done any actual smuggling, it was involved in financing such operations."

Ethan's face had gone gray. His eyes were wide and unblinking. "I simply cannot believe it," he said slowly.

"I'm afraid there isn't any doubt about it," Adam said. "You'll understand now why I must go over this letter with you. I thought it better that I do it than someone at the Bureau. So, let me ask you again, Ethan, what was in the package?"

Ethan concentrated on regaining his composure. There was no point now in umbrage. "It was a loan," he said softly.

"A loan?"

"Yes."

"In a package? I don't understand . . . unless it was an amount in cash."

"It was."

"But why cash?"

"I don't know. That's the way he sent it. I had no idea it would be in cash until it arrived."

"Didn't it seem strange to you?"

"Yes, it did."

"What was the amount?"

"Twenty-five thousand dollars."

"That's a large loan. What was it for?"

"I ended up after the convention owing the bank twenty-five thousand dollars, and Joe, Mr. Springlass, offered to loan it to me instead of my going to the bank for a mortgage."

"Has it been repaid?"

"No."

"You have some kind of a note covering it?"

Ethan could feel perspiration running down the sides of his

chest. "I'm afraid it's a complicated thing," he said. "He loaned me the money three days before he was killed. There was no chance to draw up a note."

"But surely you have an agreement, since drawn up, with the executor of his estate."

"I'm afraid not."

Adam ran his fingers through his hair, slowly shaking his head. "It would seem to me then, that the only way to view the money would be as a gift, a contribution." He paused. "Have you declared it as such?"

Ethan squirmed. "I'm afraid not."

"Not to the Internal Revenue people? Not as a contribution to your campaign?"

Ethan shook his head. Adam's face was suddenly flushed with anger. "But why in heaven's name would you do that?" he said. "You know the law; all contributions to any campaign must be reported."

Ethan made no reply. Adam picked up the letter again, his hand trembling. "I wonder if you'd explain what this means," he said stiffly. " 'Your gift will help out immeasurably. . . . ' You do say 'gift.' "

"I meant loan."

" 'Your gift will help out immeasurably, as has the other assistance you have so freely given whenever you could.' " He put the letter down. "What assistance are you referring to?"

"Oh . . . dozens of things. Serving on committees, personal counsel. . . . "

"Was any of that assistance gifts of money that were not reported?"

Ethan locked eyes with the President, staring at him fixedly but saying nothing. Adam was betraying signs of mounting anger. "Will you please answer me, Ethan," he said strongly. "Did Joseph Springlass give you any other sums of money that were not reported?"

"No."

"Did he give any monies to your campaigns? Did he pay off any debts on your behalf? Did he provide professional services at no cost? Anything?"

Ethan sat motionless. Adam looked into his eyes for a moment, then he looked down and rubbed his palms together for a time. An extended silence fell on the room. The faint distant sound of a jet could be heard through the window.

"Ethan," the President said finally, "I have to go now. I'm overdue at the press conference. But let me say this before I go: We can both recall very clearly the Watergate prosecutions. One would have hoped that no one holding high office would ever again accept contributions without filing the appropriate declaration. Now, your reasons for not doing so may be entirely proper — and I'm not your judge — but what I must do is require of you that, by Tuesday noon at the latest, you furnish me with a statement specifying those reasons. I regret to say this, Ethan, but if those reasons aren't sufficient, I shall have no option but to request your resignation."

He rose, but remained standing behind the desk. "I'm sorry, Ethan," he said quietly but in a firm voice, "but I simply can't have a Watergate in my Administration."

He turned and walked from the room. Ethan sat for a moment, his eyes on the place where the President had been. Then he got out of the chair and walked slowly from the room, pulling the door closed behind him.

Chapter Fourteen

The man from the Central Intelligence Agency sat, knees pressed together, an attaché case on his lap, a manilla file folder open on top of it. Holding out his CIA card, he had identified himself to Regan as Melvin Hamilton and had explained that CIA activities in Central and South America came under the supervision of his office. He reminded Gerry of his telephone call earlier in the day, and during his first five minutes in Regan's office, said at least a half dozen times that the Agency was pleased to cooperate with the Secret Service and would welcome the opportunity of providing any assistance within its capacity.

"As for the man you describe as the chief kidnapper," he continued, "his name is Moreno. Roberto Saldivar Moreno. Born Antigua, Guatemala, July 7, 1936. Father a radio repairman. Poor. Died when Moreno was seventeen. Mother unknown. From the age of seventeen he's lived in a variety of places, mostly in Central America. I'll leave his file with you. It has the details. That is, unless you'd like them now . . . ?"

Gerry shook his head. "All I want at the moment is anything that'll help me know who I'm dealing with and what his motives are."

"Right. Now, as to the man you're dealing with. . . . I suppose you could best describe him as a professional revolutionary, a communist. But let me hasten to add, not a traditional communist. He's one of the underground guerrilla types, modeled on Ché Guevara more or less. What motivates him . . . ? It isn't patriotism; he's been active in countries for which he has no emotional attachment." He shrugged and spread his hands. "What can I say? — he's a revolutionary. I don't know why. There are thousands like him in Latin America. Dedicated. Hate capitalism. Hate the United States . . . " He smiled tightly. "Hate the CIA."

"Would you describe him as mentally ill?"

Hamilton looked at the sheet before him and pondered the question. "No," he said slowly, "I wouldn't say mentally ill. I'd describe him as a fanatic."

"Okay. Is there more?"

"He has some expertise in electronics; studied for two years at the *Escuela Electrónica de Guatemala.* Familiar with explosives; has done a fair amount of demolition work. Speaks perfect English. He's bright and he's tough, but not bright enough to have dreamed this thing up by himself. It's quite obviously a scheme hatched and financed by *El Mano Verde.*"

"*El Mano Verde?*"

"The Green Hand. It's a left-wing revolutionary group, one of those agrarian-reform parties — that's where the name Green Hand comes from. It's run by a ragtag group of has-been leftist intellectuals who are trying to exploit the exploited peasants; organize them in order to get enough votes to take power legitimately. Their biggest problem is, they're broke, and that's undoubtedly the reason for the kidnapping."

"Anything on Moreno's accomplice? You know it's a woman?"

"So your Mr. McCurdy tells me. The fact that she's a blond and a member of *El Mano Verde* helps. That suggests to us that she's one of two women: a Linda Rodriguez, born Oaxaca, Mexico, 1947, or a Carmelita Hernandez, born 1943 in Cuba. The Hernandez woman has dropped out of sight for a year or two and I doubt that it's her. My guess would be Linda Rodriguez, especially if she speaks fluent English. But that's pure hunch; unfortunately, we don't have much on her. The only photo we've got is a pretty fuzzy snapshot. I'll leave you the file on each of them."

"That's very helpful," Regan said. "And I appreciate it. I wonder if you'd do one more thing. Would you be kind enough to go with Mr. Mayer here to the Loge-mezzanine and take a look at some photos we've been taking of women in the crowd? See if you can spot the Rodriguez woman, or the other one."

He stood up. Hamilton placed two file folders on the desk, snapped his attaché case closed and rose from his chair. They shook hands across the desk.

"We think finding the woman is priority number one," Gerry said. "If we can single her out, maybe we can lick this thing."

The CIA man walked to the door, stopped and turned.

"Perhaps I should add one more thing to what I've told you," he said. "You and your people should know that this man Moreno is perfectly capable of killing the President. He's not a major revolutionary figure, not by any means, but one thing is clear: he can be ruthless. He has killed before. By hand, as a matter of fact."

"Yes," Gerry said, "we know."

"Here is a bulletin from the White House. The United States Cabinet, meeting in emergency session this morning following the kidnapping of President Scott, has just reconvened after a brief lunch break. Reliable sources at the White House say that the seven men and one woman present for this morning's session remain hopelessly divided on whether or not to pay the ransom. It's understood that a final decision has been postponed until this afternoon when two of the three absent members will have arrived back in the capital.

"White House Press Secretary, James Rankin, told reporters a few minutes ago that the fifty million dollars in gold demanded by the kidnappers is being transported to Kennedy airport in New York City under heavy guard. Rankin emphasized that the shipment of the gold in no way indicates that the Cabinet is prepared to agree to the kidnappers' demands. It is being sent to New York so that it will be available if — and he emphasized the 'if' — the Cabinet decides to pay the money. The plane is scheduled to leave Fort Knox within the next half hour and is due . . . "

Gerry Regan turned down the sound on the television set, went to the door of his office, stuck his head out and called, "Jim, Ziggy."

As the two special agents entered and were seated, Gerry walked to the window overlooking the Square and said, almost to himself, "Time. I've got to buy some time."

He turned from the window. The ordeal was showing on his face: his eyes were encircled with shadow, there was the beginning of a stubble of beard on his chin, his hair was rumpled and there was an oily sheen on his brow.

"Okay, fellas," he said, "let me tell you what's on my mind. I'm convinced we can lick this thing if we have enough time. We've got to find a way to stall. So, what I want the three of us to do in the next few minutes is to put our heads together and see what we can come up with. Talk out whatever comes into your mind. It doesn't matter how wild the idea is, out with it — and maybe we can come on something."

He turned to McCurdy. "Jim?"

McCurdy shifted in his chair, his brow furrowed. After a long silence he said, "Suppose we say we can't get that much gold together that fast."

"Won't work. They've got almost twelve billion dollars' worth of gold at Fort Knox, all of it in gold bars. Fifty million is peanuts."

"We say they can't get it ready in time."

"If the Cabinet says move it out, it moves out. They know that as well as we do."

"So the vaults down there are on a time-lock system and they can't get at the gold. It could be, you know."

"A time lock that closes the vault in the middle of the day?"

"Oh, yeah." McCurdy sank back in his chair.

Regan turned to Ziggy Mayer who was sitting, head in his hands, elbows on his knees.

"Ziggy?"

"It's a rough one, Gerry. . . . "

"I know that."

"Let's see. . . . Suppose we say the President has been taken ill — heart attack, or something — and we've got to get him to hospital."

Gerry pondered the suggestion.

"If the President dies they don't get their money," Ziggy added. "And they've lost their edge. Right?"

Gerry shook his head. "Won't wash. Among other things, how would we get word to Mr. Scott to fake it? And he wouldn't go for it anyway."

McCurdy leaned forward in his chair. "Look, Ger," he said, "I think we're all being had; I've thought so from the beginning. I don't believe there's nitro in that bottle. I don't think they can blow up the truck. I think the whole thing's a big fat bluff. We're being conned. They figure they'll get away with it because they're sure we won't take chances with the President's life. And that's exactly what's happening."

"So, it's a possibility. We all know that."

"Then why don't we test the possibility?"

"Like how?"

"Well, to start, suppose we send in troops and clear out the Square. Move everybody out, including the woman."

"But suppose we're *not* being conned. Then what? And remember what happened when we gave those three beeps on the horn." He punched a fist into his palm. "Bang!"

"That's a part of the con. Ger, look, why have they gone to all this trouble? — and God knows they've gone to a helluva lot. What for? For the gold, right? Does it make sense that they'll kill the President, destroy their only chance to get the money and save their own necks, unless their backs are right up against the wall?"

Regan pursed his lips. "Could be. Could be."

"Gerry, we're in a spot, but so are they. They don't want to kill the President. He's their one ace in the hole. If they kill him they're through. I say we call their bluff."

"Okay, so we clear the Square. Then what?"

"We cross that bridge when we come to it."

"Oh come on, fella! With everything that's at stake here you don't take step one until you know what step two will be."

"Okay," McCurdy said, with less assurance, "so we go over to the Waldorf and work our kidnapper friend over a little . . . see if we can convince him he should cooperate. . . . "

"No way," Gerry said flatly. "Have you considered what might happen if his next hourly message doesn't get carried on the television and radio?"

"Then we have a go at trying to get into the truck."

Gerry shook his head, turned and began to pace. There was an extended silence, each man locked within his own thoughts. Suddenly Gerry stopped and wheeled, excited. "I've got it!" he shouted. "The plane from Fort Knox. . . . Pile it up! Crash it!"

The two agents looked at him aghast. "You mean, *literally?*"

"Literally."

"With the gold?"

"Of course not with the gold. Get it offloaded on the quiet. Have the pilot and the crew parachute, and ram the damn thing into some mountain."

"But Gerry. . . . "

"Do it, dammit! The plane's expendable." He reached for the phone. "And be sure it gets reported to the television people as soon as it happens."

On the phone he said, "Get me Mr. Morris on the scrambler line."

"It may surprise you, Mr. Regan, but the steel on the walls of these armored trucks is only approximately one-eighth of an inch thick."

Gerry Regan and Anthony Zucker were standing beside the open door of a Brink's truck similar to the one in which the President was being held. Earlier, when Ziggy Mayer had called Brink's and asked them to send over a truck identical to the one in the Square, he had received an immediate acquiescence and then, ten minutes later, a worried telephone call.

"Mr. Mayer, we're anxious to do anything we can to help, but we've just taken a look on the television, and that truck's a real old-timer. More than that, it's not one of ours; they've just tried to make it look like it is."

"Can you send over one like it?"

"I don't know. It's at least fifteen years old. . . . "

"So, try."

They had finally managed to find one in Newark, New Jersey, where it was sitting, rusted, without license plates and out of service in the company yard. There had been apologies about the delay and the truck's condition along with a definite promise that it would be delivered by two that afternoon, and with it, "Tony Zucker, who knows everything there is to know about the security business."

Now the borrowed truck stood just within the police barricades at 43rd and Broadway, and Gerry Regan was examining it.

"What do you mean the steel is only an eighth of an inch thick?" he said. "I can see it here at the door frame; it's at least an inch and a quarter."

"No, Mr. Regan. What you're looking at is the thickness of the wall, not of the armor-plate. The wall is, in effect, a sandwich. First, there's a sheet of cold-rolled steel. . . . "

"Cold-rolled?"

"Steel that's been specially handled at the mill to harden it — it's rolled without the application of heat."

"Go ahead."

"Right. First there's a sheet of steel, then approximately one inch of batting, and finally another sheet of steel."

"Batting? You mean cotton batting, the stuff used in bandages?"

"Not exactly, but that's close enough. It's the batting, not the steel, that stops a bullet. A bullet from a high-velocity rifle could easily penetrate the steel; that is, if it struck pretty well dead-on. If it struck at an angle, it would simply make a dent and ricochet off . . . just as you can see over there." He pointed at the other truck.

"So if a bullet strikes at approximately ninety degrees it will penetrate the steel?"

"It depends on the type of bullet and its velocity at impact, of course, but the answer is, yes. But by the time it penetrates the batting, its inertia is reduced to the point where it can't get through the inside sheet."

Gerry tapped the windshield with his knuckles. "The glass . . . is it thin, too?"

"No. Actually it's better than an inch thick. It's commonly called bulletproof, but it really isn't. Once again, a bullet striking it dead-on might go through, although it'd be pretty well spent. Its purpose is to deflect anything that strikes it."

"Wouldn't it shatter — like the safety glass in a car?"

"No, it gets pitted. Although it can crack . . . as you can see on the President's truck."

"If I wanted to get in from the outside, would it be difficult to remove a window?"

"Pretty well impossible, unless you took a sledgehammer to it. The glass is mounted in a steel frame and the frame is riveted to the body on the inside of the truck."

"Let's get in," Gerry said.

Gerry climbed in and sat in the driver's seat. Zucker walked around the engine and got in on the other side. The passenger seat was separated from the driver's by about three feet and was set back far enough to permit passage in and out of the door. Zucker pulled the door closed, shot home a bolt and reached across to flip three switches on the dashboard. There was a series of thunks as bolts leaped into place.

"I've just locked the two front and the rear doors," he said. "On this model there are three ways to lock or unlock each door; from the outside with a key, with the bolt you saw me throw and with the bolts activated by these switches. The guard making a delivery has a key and he can open the door from the outside, but not if the electric lock has been activated. If it's out of order, the man on the inside can always throw the bolt manually."

"If you were going to booby-trap the doors, those electric switches would be damn convenient," Gerry said sourly.

"Made to order."

There was a sign on the door immediately above the interior door handle. In black letters on a rectangular yellow background, it read:

DANGER!

IS HE YOUR MAN?

"What's that mean?"

"Well, let's say the guard making a delivery has been ambushed inside the building. And let's say the criminal involved puts on his uniform or his cap and approaches the door. The sign is to remind the driver, before he unlocks the bolt, to make doubly sure it's his partner and not just some guy in a Brink's uniform."

Gerry climbed out of the seat and moved into the van. He had to crouch; the ceiling was no more than four and a half feet high. Immediately behind the driver's seat was a box made of sheet-steel, two and a half feet high, two feet deep and three feet long. The top was hinged and there was a hasp by which it could be closed. Zucker saw him examining it.

"We call it a safe. Actually it's a strongbox. The idea is to delay anybody who manages to get inside. We don't want to make it easy for him. Incidentally, there's usually a wall between the cab and the van where the money is. This is one of the last of the two-man trucks."

Gerry examined one of the gunports. There was one on each of the three doors and on each wall. He pressed against a spring and the circle of steel that covered the opening pushed outward. He twisted it and it moved down and clear.

"Can they be opened from outside?"

"It wouldn't be easy. First, you'd have to drill a hole — and that's tough steel — then you'd have to insert some kind of tool that would allow you to pull and turn at the same time."

"I was just wondering whether, if I got it open and then reached in with a long stiff wire — the same way you get into your car with a coathanger when you lock in the keys — could I throw those switches and unlock the doors?"

"Interesting," Zucker said, blinking. "It hadn't occurred to me."

Gerry stamped his foot. "Is the floor armor-plated too?"

"Yes. And the ceiling."

"Ventilation?"

Zucker reached over and threw a switch on the dashboard. There was an instant hum and a soft rush of air.

"Is the outside air drawn in?"

"No, the air in here's expelled. Fresh air comes in through those vents over the windshield and below the roof at the back."

They climbed out of the truck. Gerry walked to the front, reached in, released the catch and raised the hood. The engine was surprisingly compact. "Looks like the motor on any small truck," he said.

"That's because it is. The trucks are built to our specifications on a standard truck body. As you can see, this one's a Ford."

Gerry slammed down the hood and stood off, looking at the truck. "Do you people have any idea how our kidnapper could get one of these things? Did he steal it?"

"No. There's no record of one being stolen, at least not that we've heard of."

"Then where would he get it? What do you people do when you're finished with a truck?"

"Well, when Brink's is finished with a truck we don't just scrap it — we cut it up with acetylene torches. First, we strip it of anything worth salvaging, then it's taken to a scrap yard and cut up. The man who does the cutting is required to take a Polaroid picture before he starts, another when he's half done, and another when he's finished. The pictures, with a record of the truck, are sent to our Chicago office and filed."

"Then how the hell would somebody get one?"

"He wouldn't get it from Brink's. That's for sure."

"Could he get it from some other company?"

"It's possible. Some banks have their own. Years back, some of the big department stores had their own. I know a few of those were sold to the public."

Zucker paused. "There's one other possibility," he said. "There's a story around about a welder who was supposed to cut up one of these things some years back, but didn't do it. What he did was take extra pictures of a truck he was destroying, save some of them, and turn them in on the next job, letting on they were the pictures of the truck he was supposed to turn into scrap. The way the story goes, he then sold the truck and put the money in his pocket."

They turned to leave.

"I don't know whether it's true," Zucker said, "or just one of those stories that gets around. But what in the world would anybody want with a worn-out armored truck?"

Gerry gave him a withering look.

Chapter Fifteen

Assembled on the stage of the National Theater were a group of seven men and one woman, the best-qualified experts in a variety of the sciences living within an hour's flying time of New York City. For all their eminence, they were not, as a group, prepossessing, in part because of the lighting. Most looked ghastly, some almost cadaverous, for the theater lights, having been found inadequate, had been supplemented in the wings with four naked 500-watt bulbs on spindly stands, the type normally used to illuminate a theater for cleaning women. They were seated on folding chairs, arranged in an erratic half-circle, and were buzzing with animated conversation; each trying to learn from the others the reason for the urgent summons that had brought them together. All they had been told was that the meeting was extremely important and that they would be given a full explanation later. They had been warned not to discuss the summons with anyone, even their families.

Present were: Dr. Michael Palermo, neurologist, Presbyterian Hospital, New York City; Dr. David Chan, physiologist, Harvard School of Medicine; Dr. Oleska Royko, physicist, Massachusetts Institute of Technology; Major General Raymond Taylor, the Pentagon, Washington, D.C.; Dr. Herbert Brodkin, Westinghouse Research Center, Pittsburgh; Elmer Stickley, consultant in electric energy, New York City; Andrew R. H. Ruddle, Monsanto Chemical Corporation, St. Louis, Missouri, who chanced to be lecturing at Princeton University; and Dr. Greta Olsen, psychologist, Columbia University, New York City.

At 3:05, five minutes late, Gerry Regan strode down the aisle of the theater, followed by Jim McCurdy and Ziggy Mayer.

"Gentlemen and Dr. Olsen," he said briskly. "I'm not going to waste my time or yours with preliminaries other than to say that my name is Regan and I'm with the Secret Service. You've probably guessed why I've invited you here, but in case you haven't, I'll explain. As you know, President Scott is being held hostage in that armored truck you saw as you came in. The truck is booby-trapped. We believe the following devices are being used: an electric circuit attached to each of the three doors, a heat detector mounted on the ceiling, and a vibration sensor, also on the ceiling. We don't know for certain, but we believe that each of these devices is wired to a box in the van of the truck containing some form of dynamite and a quantity of nitro-glycerine . . . approximately twenty fluid ounces. There are no wires visible, but the walls, ceiling, and floor are covered with plywood and, presumably, the wires run behind it. The kidnapper has a woman accomplice in the crowd with some kind of portable transmitter capable of detonating the explosives by remote control."

He paused, fished a pack of cigarettes from his pocket, shook one loose and lit it, his eyes ranging over the group. "I've asked you people here because I need to find a way to get around the system I've just described. The President's life is in jeopardy and, in a word, I desperately need your help."

He glanced at a notebook in his hand. "Let's begin with one of the simpler problems," he said. "Which of you has some knowledge of the properties of nitro-glycerine?"

There was no response.

"Friends, listen to me," Gerry said solemnly. "This is not the moment for modesty. We haven't time for that luxury."

A hand was raised. "Identify yourself, please," Gerry said.

"Andy Ruddle, Monsanto."

"Good. Now Dr. Ruddle. . . . "

"Mr. Ruddle."

"Okay, Mr. Ruddle. How great an explosion would be caused by, say, twenty fluid ounces of nitro-glycerine?"

Ruddle spread his hands, palms up, and shrugged. "Poof! — no truck. Undoubtedly the steel plate would contain the explosion somewhat, but the probability is the blast would not only destroy the truck, it would kill everyone within a hundred yards. Combined

180

with the dynamite, it could very well damage the surrounding buildings. Perhaps as many as a thousand of those people out there might be killed or injured."

"It's my understanding that nitro is very unstable. True?"

"Indeed it is. Nitro-glycerine is a very uncomplicated but enormously powerful explosive. It's the principal ingredient in dynamite and it's made simply by treating glycerine with nitric acid. There it poses no problem, but in the liquid state it's so unstable that, under certain conditions, it may explode from the slightest shock. The great problem in using it is its unpredictability."

"Then it's possible that our kidnapper was bluffing. He carried a bottle of it on his person and was waving it around pretty vigorously this morning. Surely he wouldn't take that risk if a slight jar could set it off?"

"Not necessarily, Mr. Regan. You see, if the bottle was entirely filled, with no air space whatever, the liquid wouldn't be affected by his movements, even sudden movement. All he'd have to avoid would be banging the bottle into something, or dropping it. Not only that; if the nitro was at a low temperature it would be less volatile — farther away from what you might call its critical threshold. It's certainly true that he *could* have been bluffing. Nitro is crystal clear and the liquid in the bottle could be tap water, even gin." He smiled. "There's no way of ascertaining that by simply looking."

Regan shot a sideways glance at Jim McCurdy, who was standing to one side. "It may be a foolish question," he said, "but is there any way to render it impotent?"

Ruddle shook his head. "Not unless you can get it out of the truck. Otherwise . . . " he shrugged.

Gerry made reference to his notebook. "Let's go on to electronics," he said, looking about. "Who?"

Two men raised their hands — Dr. Brodkin and Elmer Stickley. Brodkin said quickly, "I yield to my friend Stickley."

"Mr. Stickley," Gerry said, "the kidnapper's partner is a woman. She has some kind of remote-control device small enough to hold in her hand. Is there any reason to doubt she could use it to trigger the explosives?"

"I wouldn't think so. It's a simple enough thing to do."

"How can I stop her?"

Stickley ran his fingers through his rumpled and thinning hair.

"That's a difficult question," he said. "There are so many imponderables. It depends on what kind of device she's using. It could be a low-frequency electromagnetic transmitter, but I would presume that to be unlikely. Too big. It could be an ultrasonic device, but I would think that too is most unlikely . . . mostly because it can be so easily blocked. You need a line of sight to operate it, you see, and all you'd have to do to negate it would be to interpose something substantial between it and the truck. A human body might do it. The probability is that what she's using is a simple high-frequency transmitter of the type people use to turn their television sets on and off. It's activated by closing a circuit — in other words, by simply pressing a button."

"Okay," Gerry said. "Now, what I need you to tell me is what I can do to foul it up. And please keep it simple."

"I'll try to. First, there has to be a receiver, a mechanism which when activated will detonate the explosives. The probability is that it's inside the truck. . . . " He paused. "Do you know the location of the explosives?"

"A wooden box on the floor in a rear corner of the van."

"Fine. Now, the steel walls of the truck pose a problem — not to you, but to the person with the remote-control device. The likelihood is that they would interfere with the signal, so there's probably an antenna somewhere. . . . "

"There is," Jim McCurdy broke in. "There's what looks like a steel wire projecting from one of the vents in the rear."

"I would expect something like that," Stickley said. "Now, if you could manage to short that antenna, her transmitter probably wouldn't have enough power to penetrate the steel walls of the truck."

"The problem is, getting close enough," Gerry said.

"Could it be shot off with a gun?" McCurdy asked.

Stickley shook his head dubiously. "Cutting a steel wire with a bullet . . . ? That would be quite a feat of marksmanship," he mused. "More important, didn't you say there was a vibration sensor mounted on the ceiling?" Gerry nodded. "Then, I wouldn't recommend shooting at the wire. The shock when it's struck could be transferred directly to the vibration sensor. Steel, as you know, is an excellent conductor."

"What other options do I have?"

"Before we go on," Stickley said, "I have a question — is the

President wearing shoes?"

"Shoes?"

"I simply mean that, if he is, he should be told to take them off. And he should be warned not to do anything that will set up shock waves, even insignificant ones. Vibration sensors can be set to activate with very little stimulus."

Regan turned to McCurdy. "Jim. . . . " he said. McCurdy loped from the stage and left the theater.

Gerry nodded and Stickley continued. "One way you could interfere with the operation would be to incapacitate the woman's transmitter. You could short it out, or perhaps fuse the mechanism with a high electrical charge . . . but if it's in her pocket, how you'd accomplish that escapes me." He puzzled a minute. "The only other thing that occurs to me is pretty far-fetched: If you could place a metal barrier between her and the truck you could probably stop the signal. . . . "

"How?"

"Frankly, I don't know. . . . Lower it from a helicopter, perhaps?"

"Too slow. She could trigger the thing before we even got near."

Dr. Brodkin broke in. "Incidentally, for what use it is, you can find out whether she's transmitting constantly simply by passing near her with a portable oscilloscope. I'm sure your Army Signal Corpsmen have one."

Gerry turned to Mayer. "Ziggy, go find out."

"Anything else?" he said.

"Can't think of anything at the moment. Nothing she couldn't counter by simply pressing the button."

"Let's investigate that," Gerry said. "One of you is a neurologist?"

"I am," said an enormously fat man seated spread-legged on a groaning chair. "Dr. Palermo. Presbyterian Hospital."

"You understand human reflexes?"

"I know a bit about them. So does my colleague here, Dr. Chan. He's a physiologist."

"How fast is a human reflex action?"

"It varies with the circumstances and the individual."

"Average."

"Average . . . ? I presume you're thinking of the young woman

183

with the device. Well, impulses travel over the nervous system to and from the brain at approximately the speed of light. Any measurable delay would come in the period between the time the brain perceives and the hand reacts. It depends on the individual. It can be very swift; possibly less than a tenth of a second."

Gerry looked at the floor, his demeanor betraying the fact that he was ill at ease. "I'm going to apologize once and only once about some questions I have to ask you people," he said. "I'll be raising some pretty unpleasant possibilities and I can only ask that you don't jump to conclusions; I'm merely scouting every option open to me. Do we understand each other?"

There was a general nodding of heads.

"Okay then." He turned back to Dr. Palermo. "Dr. Palermo, if a person was to be, say, shot through the head — killed instantly, as we say — would there be sufficient time from the impact of the bullet to the cessation of consciousness to press a button?"

Dr. Palermo did not change expression. "Probably not." He looked at Dr. Chan, who nodded. "There is, however, another problem. There are two fundamental kinds of reflexes: the voluntary, which we've been discussing, and the involuntary. In the event of a bullet entering the brain it's entirely possible, indeed it's likely, that there would be an involuntary reflex action and it might trigger the device."

"Is that certain?"

"Well, it's not as sure as death or taxes, but it's highly likely."

"Dr. Chan?"

"I'm afraid so, Mr. Regan." He paused. "I'm reluctant to mention it, but there *is* a way by which it might be possible to stop the involuntary reflex Dr. Palermo referred to. It's a rather grisly option. . . ."

"Please go ahead."

"Well, if the spinal cord were cut at, say, the back of the neck — between the brain and the hand — the reflex action might not take place."

"I would agree," said Dr. Palermo. "The probability is that the muscles would go flaccid."

"It should be added, however," Dr. Chan said, "that there can be no assurance the muscles of the hand won't go into spasm . . . in which case you have a problem."

Dr. Brodkin broke in. "May I make a suggestion?"

"Of course."

"It's a bit out of my field, but I've been listening to your discussion and it occurs to me that if what you're after is to keep the woman from pressing the button, wouldn't the best way to achieve that be to induce an unexpected and terrible pain so that her reflex action would be *away* from the device?"

"Specifically?"

"Specifically, if you were to, let's say, create a sudden intense pain in the eye — the kind of pain that would make her immediately and involuntarily bring her hands to it — you might achieve your purpose without doing serious damage."

"Tell me more."

"We do a fair bit of work on lasers, and as you probably know, they're quite portable now and can be aimed more accurately than a rifle. Suppose you were to use a Q-spoiled laser and fire a pulse — fire a burst, if you like — so that it struck the subject's eye, but at an angle so as not to penetrate the brain. I would think the pain would be such that a person would forget all about the triggering device and immediately put her hands to the eye."

Gerry turned to Dr. Palermo, his eyebrows raised in an unspoken question.

"I'd be disposed to agree with that. We tend to be very protective of the eye, and certainly that area is one of the most sensitive parts of the body. You would in all probability achieve what Dr. Brodkin says."

"One problem," Dr. Chan interjected. Gerry looked at him, questioning. "Simulate it," the physiologist said, "and I think you'll find your normal reaction would be to put, not two, but one hand to your eye. Unfortunately, that would leave the other hand free to trigger the device."

Gerry frowned, took a pen from his pocket and made a note. He looked up. "Any other suggestions?" His eyes ranged across the group. No one spoke.

"Major General Taylor, isn't it?" Gerry asked.

"Yes, sir."

"You people are familiar with the new tools of physiological warfare . . . the nerve gases, the bacteriological agents. Has anything occurred to you?"

The officer cleared his throat. "You'll understand if I don't go into specifics, Mr. Regan," he said apologetically. "Much in the area you refer to is classified, and . . . "

"In generalities then."

"There *are* a number of gases that kill or incapacitate almost instantaneously. Unfortunately — I mean, unfortunately as it relates to your question — none of them so swiftly there wouldn't be time to react."

"How quickly do they act?"

"As I say, in seconds. But there's nothing new there . . . cyanide gas has been around for a long time and it kills within four seconds."

"But only if you breathe it."

"On the contrary, it can enter through any of the body orifices, although the action would be slower."

"You have nothing instantaneous?"

"Only a very old-fashioned thing."

"Yes?"

"A bullet."

Gerry referred to his book. "Dr. Royko?" he queried.

"I'm Royko," said a nondescript man in the rear. You'd certainly never guess to look at him that he's a Nobel prize winner, Gerry thought. "Any suggestions?" he said.

Royko stood to his feet. His speech was slow, halting, accented and confused. It was almost as though he were mentally retarded.

"I must say, I'm sorry . . . I mean, I regret being here," he began, flushing at being the focus of attention. "Nothing that I could contribute . . . I mean, I don't have any suggestion that would help. But what I would like to say . . . what I'd like to do is . . . is to go on record that I don't approve. . . . I mean, that I don't agree with what's being done here." He picked up a battered old-fashioned briefcase from beside his chair, crossed the stage and left the theater. Gerry, betraying no reaction, waited until he was gone and then turned to the one woman present.

"Dr. Olsen?"

She smiled at him. "First of all, let me say I have no compunction about being here," she began. "But I'm a psychologist; I'm not sure what I have to contribute."

"Well, I've got to get to this woman somehow," Gerry said. "I was wondering if I could use her motivations in some way?"

Dr. Olsen smiled at him again, a radiant smile. Gerry thought: Man, those brains sure are beautifully packaged. "Perhaps I might mention certain elementary drives," she said. "The most powerful emotions in a normal woman are the will to live, love, the sexual urge, the maternal instinct, acquisitiveness. . . . "

"Stop there just a second," Gerry said. "Let's take them one by one and see if we can find a possible chink in her armor. Let's see, the first was self-preservation. . . . ?"

"I can't see much hope there," she said. "She's obviously willing to risk her life or she wouldn't be doing what she's doing."

"How about love?"

"I would presume that's already motivating her. Certainly there's a devotion to the cause she's a part of." She smiled: "You could always send in Paul Newman to woo her away."

Gerry didn't smile. "The sexual drive?"

"Neither the time nor the place is conducive."

"You mentioned acquisitiveness?"

"Yes, but I hardly think she's vulnerable there, with a ransom of fifty million dollars within reach."

"Now, what else was there?"

"The maternal urge. I don't know what the possibilities are there. If you had her child, presuming she has a child, and you were holding it as a counter-hostage, you'd undoubtedly have some leverage. But that's purely hypothetical."

Perhaps she *does* have a child, Gerry thought, and perhaps he could find out through the CIA. He made a note. "Could we get at her through somebody else's child?" he asked.

"How?"

"I don't know. Off the top of my head: Say there was a baby near the truck, or in it, or something like that, would that be likely to deter her?"

"It's possible, but only possible. The problem is we have no data on which to make a judgment. We don't know enough about her."

"Yes," said Gerry gloomily, "and how the hell would we get a kid near the truck anyway?

"Any other suggestions," he said, looking about. There was no response. "I've got to go," he said. "You all know the shape of the problem. I'd like you to stay here and put your minds to it. Quite bluntly, friends, if we don't find a way to resolve it, there's a very real possibility that President Scott will be killed. Give it your best shot, will you?" he said, and strode from the stage.

Chapter Sixteen

It's her, all right."

Melvin Hamilton and Gil Purdom of the CIA were standing with Ziggy Mayer before the extended strip-photographs, now seven deep, of the crowd in the Square. Hamilton had been examining them carefully, supplementing his vision from time to time with a hand-held magnifying glass.

"How do you know?" Ziggy asked.

Hamilton turned from the photographs. "I don't want to do a Sherlock Holmes," he said with a slight smile, "but it's a simple matter of elimination. First, we restricted our search to areas from which she would have a coincidental view of both the truck and your headquarters. Second, we concentrated only on blond women in their early thirties. Third, the people at the forensic lab informed me that they'd discovered some brown wool fibres on the inside of the uniform discarded at the IRT. Consequently, we've limited ourselves to . . . " he ticked off the list on his fingers, "youngish, blond women in brown clothing. There are only three women here who meet all these conditions." He turned back to the photographs and put a forefinger on one of the encircled heads. "According to the reports I've had from our people, this one is Linda Rodriguez."

Ziggy Mayer turned and was off on a full run, headed for Gerry Regan's office.

Robertson Kirk on the television screen:

"*. . . The plane, an army version of the Boeing 727, en route from Godman army field in Fort Knox to New York City's Kennedy airport, went down in a heavily wooded area approximately forty miles from Allentown, Pennsylvania.*

"No announcement yet as to whether there were any casualties. There is a report that the plane was carrying the fifty million dollars in gold demanded by the kidnappers for the release of President Scott. Government sources refuse either to confirm or deny the report. . . . "

Chauncey Howe had been President of the Senate for more than a decade and despite his eighty-two years had lost little of his intellectual vigor and none of the charm that had made him respected not only in Washington and in his native Virginia but everywhere in the United States. In appearance he was very much the stereotype senator — looking not unlike the representation of Colonel Sanders on the familiar Kentucky Fried Chicken packages — his cherubic face, snowy hair and courtly manner offering no hint of the Jovian anger that could move him to thunderous imprecations against opponents in the Senate chamber. But, for all his passion, in his forty-three years in Washington he had never been known to argue a position solely for partisan reasons, and for this — and for his enormous contribution to the well-being of the nation — he had come to be revered beyond almost anyone in American public life.

On receiving the news of the kidnapping, he had begun to puzzle over the potential ramifications of the crime. He was exercised not only because of the jeopardy in which an old friend, Adam Scott, had been placed, but also because of the possible adverse influence of the situation on the electoral process. A lifelong student of the Constitution and a zealous guardian of the democratic process, he was concerned lest the Congressional elections be affected in a way that would militate against the free expression of the will of the electorate. Some five minutes into the conference telephone call with Ethan Roberts and Travis Johnstone, Speaker of the House, he raised the question.

"I take it, then, we're agreed that the decision as to the payment of the ransom is to be left with the Cabinet. Am I correct in that?"

Ethan and Travis voiced their assent.

"Good," he said. "May I move then to a matter which, while nowhere nearly so dramatic, is of equal importance: namely, the effect of today's events on tomorrow's elections. There is no certain way of knowing what may happen today — what action the Cabinet may take, or what the kidnappers will do in response — but one thing *is* certain: whatever happens, the nation will be profoundly affected. As I understand it, if the President is freed, it will not be until shortly before midnight, and with the concern that will mount in the hearts of the people until his safe release has been effected, there can be little doubt that there will be an enormous surge of sympathy in his direction — and quite understandably so. If on the other hand — and may God in his wisdom forbid it — some injury or even death is inflicted on our friend Adam, the shock, the trauma, will make it impossible properly to conduct an election. Not only impossible, but undesirable. Do you not agree, Travis?"

"I do. I remember what it was like when Jack Kennedy was killed. The country was in shock."

"In addition to that, the nation would officially be in mourning," Ethan added.

"Indeed. Indeed," the Senator said. "Now, that being so, it is my view that we must seriously examine the possibility of postponing tomorrow's election."

There was a silence on the line. Neither of the others had considered the possibility and were taken aback. Ethan responded first.

"I'm not sure that's possible," he said slowly. "Offhand, I can't recall any provision to that end in the Constitution."

"You're quite right," Senator Howe said. "The reason being that the voting date for federal elections is not laid down in the Constitution. It was determined by an act of Congress in 1845."

"Of course."

"Consequently, and fortunately, it would not be too difficult to change. If an Amendment to the Constitution were required it would take months . . . years."

"I take it you've given thought to the necessary procedures," Ethan said.

"I have. Do you wish me to outline them?"

"Please."

"Very well. If my understanding is correct, under Article One, Section Four, of the Constitution . . . and I'm quoting: 'The times, places and manner of holding elections for Senators and Representatives shall be prescribed in each State by the legislature thereof; but' — and I emphasize the but — 'the Congress may at any time make or alter such regulations.' End quote. Now, this has already been done — back in 1845, as I mentioned a moment ago — when

190

Congress named the first Tuesday after the first Monday in November as the date. It was done, actually, to end the confusion that then obtained because each state set its own election date. Consequently, gentlemen, not only is there authorization in the Constitution to change the date, there is precedent."

"But there's a practical problem," Travis said. "We aren't in session and it would be virtually impossible to get in touch with and assemble the more than — what? — five hundred members of the combined Houses."

"It would be difficult in the extreme. I grant you that," said Senator Howe. "But for our purposes, which are very limited — namely, to consider the possible postponement of the election — it is possible. We wouldn't need to meet before, perhaps, eight o'clock this evening, and under the circumstances I'm sure the airlines and the Air Force could be prevailed upon to provide transportation. Moreover, we wouldn't need to get everyone here — even when we assemble under normal circumstances every member is not present. And as you know, a simple majority constitutes a quorum in both the Senate and the House."

"I suppose it's possible . . . " Travis said grudgingly, "but good God, Chauncey, would it be *right*? If we aren't able to reach some of our members in time, and as a consequence they're deprived of their vote, they may well dispute the legality of any legislation passed and we could be in an incredible mess in the courts. And," he added sardonically, "I can think of some who would like nothing better than that kind of fight."

Senator Howe's voice was unhappy as he replied: "You may be right."

The Congressman went on. "Look at the problem more specifically. Take the representatives from Hawaii. Let's say we were able to reach them and that they were to set out for Washington within the hour — which is pretty damned optimistic. It's now past three o'clock and the flying time from Honolulu is about ten hours. They couldn't possibly make it. I doubt very much that we could even get all of our people in from Alaska."

"I'm afraid I must agree."

Ethan's mind had been questing about as the others talked. "Gentlemen," he said, "are you prepared to entertain an unorthodox suggestion?"

"Anything."

"Then let me begin with a question: Does the Constitution require that Congress *must* convene in Washington?"

Senator Howe hesitated for only a second. "Let me see now
. . . . The matter is dealt with in Section Five. I'm certain there is no
inflexible requirement that we assemble in the capital. Just a moment and I'll double-check."

"While he's doing that," Travis said, "what's in your mind?"

"You're going to have to bear with me," Ethan said. "I warned
you it was a wild idea. It comes down to what is meant by the word
'assembled.' " Suppose each member of both Houses was to go to
a television station in his home state. Suppose further that you and
Senator Howe were to take your places in the House as you would
for a joint session. And suppose that one or all of the television
networks in the country were to tie it all together in a vast closed-
circuit. . . . "

"I'm beginning to follow you," Travis said.

"Now, if the various members of both Houses can see you and
hear you, and if they can speak to questions raised and hear each
other in the debate, are they not in every significant sense of the
word 'assembled?' "

"Fascinating," said Travis.

"If I'm not incorrect," Ethan continued, "the dictionary meaning of the word assemble is 'to gather together.' I don't think it
necessarily connotes that that gathering together be in one enclosed
space. And surely the *intent* of the provision is that members of the
Congress be able to communicate with each other."

Senator Howe broke in. "I've been listening while checking
here," he said. "It's an intriguing possibility. As to the question you
raised a minute ago: there is no doubt that the locale need not be
Washington. Let me read you Article Four, Section Five: 'Neither
House, during the sessions of Congress, shall without the consent
of the other adjourn for more than three days, nor to any other
place than that in which the two Houses shall be sitting.' The
implication is quite clear: Congress *may* adjourn to some other
place, but it must have the consent of both Houses to do so."

"Then my suggestion may be feasible?" Ethan said.

"I don't see why not. The purists may take issue with us but it's
my view that we're acting within the provisions of the Constitution.
And surely, when we've assembled — using the word as it might

properly be employed in this electronic age — either House has the authority, if it chooses to exercise it, to repudiate our meeting."

"Then we're agreed?" Ethan asked.

"I'll go along," Travis said. "What the hell, men, the situation is hardly a normal one. Seems to me it calls for some good old-fashioned Yankee ingenuity."

"*Yankee* ingenuity . . . ?" Senator Howe said.

"Uh. . . . Oh, sorry!"

"If we have consensus then," Ethan said, laughing, "I'm going to go off the line. Things to do here. Will you gentlemen follow through in contacting your people and getting them . . . " he laughed, "*assembled*? If we can help you, get in touch. Please leave word with Jim Rankin as to when you'll be arriving in Washington, and talk over with him, too, the timing in breaking the story to the press."

Near the television mobile units in Times Square, a scuffle, muffled cries and a sound of ripping cloth. A man broke past the police barricade and began to run toward the truck. In the struggle to restrain him, his jacket had been pulled off and a torn strip of shirt fluttered below his waist, exposing most of his back. His hair was disheveled and flowed behind him as he ran — fleetly but near to stumbling with every stride — arms outstretched toward the truck.

There were involuntary screams from among the crowd when they first saw the man — a moving figure in the abandoned openness that had come to seem permanent. Then there was a mass intake of breath and a sudden silence in which the man's shrill voice could be heard.

"I'll save him," he screamed. "I'll save him . . . God has told me to!"

He ran on.

From the crowd, a voice, "Stop him for Christ's sake!"

The man was not twenty feet from the truck when there was the sharp crack of a rifle shot. Within the same second there were a dozen shots. The man's body arched forward with the grace of a ballet dancer, collapsed bonelessly to the pavement and slid forward, face down, to lie inert. From beneath the body blood seeped, spread, and following the contours of the concrete, flowed to a sewer grating.

A sound of sobbing from the crowd, and of a man retching.

After a few minutes, two men in Red Cross uniforms, carrying a stretcher, walked tentatively into the open space beyond the barricades. So cautious was their progress that it took them more than a minute to reach the dead man. They placed the stretcher on the pavement, lifted the limp body onto it, put a blanket over and secured it with straps.

As they walked back toward the crowd their pace slowly accelerated until it became a run.

Ethan stopped his pacing and stood, shoulders bowed, in the center of the room. In effect, he thought, I may be the entire electorate. I and I alone may decide who will be President of the United States.

The Vice-President had borrowed Jaz Osterwald's White House office, and while other members of the Cabinet were lunching at the buffet Jim Rankin had laid on, Ethan had taken a sandwich and a cup of coffee and moved apart in an attempt to settle in his mind the course he would take if the Cabinet ended the debate equally divided. There were only three options, he knew that: to declare a conflict of interest and abstain; to go counter to his convictions and his own best interests and vote to pay the ransom; or to do as his conscience urged and vote no — with all the fearful consequences that might follow on that action.

Ethan was a disciplined man with an ordered mind, and as was his practice when confronted with a complex problem, had begun by setting out on a sheet of paper a series of what he regarded as the essential questions. It had been his experience that, if he did so and dealt with each question separately — each almost in isolation from the others — he was better able to penetrate to the heart of a problem. Now, as he paced the office, the sheet of paper with the questions printed in bold capitals lay in clear view on top of the desk beside the curdled coffee and the sandwich.

(1) HOW WILL JIM AND ARNIE VOTE?

He was almost certain that Jim Hilliard would oppose paying the ransom. Ethan recalled how, back in the spring of '73, the Secretary of State — then a senior civil servant — had participated in the indirect, once-removed negotiations with Cuba through

194

which an understanding was reached that the Castro government would no longer offer sanctuary to aircraft hijackers. Ethan recalled a think-piece in *Newsweek* magazine at the time in which Hilliard had been quoted and in which he had been unequivocal in his rejection of any concessions being made.

He could not, however, begin to speculate on which side of the issue Arnie Gustafson would come down. The Secretary of the Interior was a very direct man, earthy in language and sinewed of mind, but with a surprising strain of sentimentality. Ethan shook his head: He had never had either the opportunity or the inclination to get close to Gustafson, and it was impossible to hazard a reliable forecast as to what his position would be.

(2) WHAT WILL RESULT IF THE RANSOM IS PAID?

First, what will the kidnappers do? They'll simply board the plane and fly off with the loot; not much question about that. There would undoubtedly be a way to get at them when the whole sorry affair was over, perhaps even to recover the gold, but that was a matter for the CIA and for another day. More important at the moment: Would they fulfill their part of the bargain and telephone the instructions needed to set Adam free? Almost certainly, yes. They had nothing to gain by not doing so, and much to lose. So, the crisis would pass and the nation would return to relative normalcy.

(3) WHAT WILL BE THE POLITICAL RAMIFICATIONS IF THE RANSOM IS PAID?

Unpredictable. There could be little doubt that every American's initial reaction would be an enormous sense of relief in the knowledge that the President was safe. Few would be concerned about the payment of the fifty million dollars; first, because to most it was an inconceivable sum of money, and second, because government expenditures at every level had so accelerated in recent years that fifty million dollars was relatively inconsequential. Ethan had no doubt that it would be politically advantageous: The elation the electorate would feel with Adam safe could only be beneficial in tomorrow's elections.

But there would undoubtedly be an adverse delayed reaction, and that could be important if the election were postponed. Once emotions had subsided, the fact that two people, a man and a woman — communists at that! — had held a gun to the head of the United States government, had extorted fifty million dollars and had then been helped to escape, would be criticized, and vigorously, in the media and by eminent and influential people. Nor had Ethan any doubt that the issue would exacerbate and intensify for months, possibly for long enough to affect adversely the Presidential election two years off. He realized that if he were a candidate, he would be particularly vulnerable because of his central role. Certainly if he voted for the ransom his credibility would suffer.

There was a further worrisome possibility: that other criminals, having observed the success of the kidnappers, would abduct others in public life. It would almost certainly follow, just as other kidnappings had followed the Patricia Hearst abduction. And the ransom having been paid, the government would have set a precedent that would be awkward, if not impossible, to abandon.

(4) WHAT WILL BE THE EFFECT ON ME PERSONALLY IF THE RANSOM IS PAID?

In one word — disastrous. Ethan had reviewed his own situation the night before, puzzling over it until the early-morning hours. With Adam freed he would probably be forced to resign. For all that his intentions were not dishonorable, it would be difficult to justify his failure to repay the loan Joe Springlass had made him or, at least, to have had it formalized in a document. And having failed to do that, as Adam had pointed out, there was no other way to view the money but as a gift: income that should have been declared and taxed. And because the money had been used to pay off debts incurred in a political campaign, his failure to account for it under the so-called "Disclosure Law" was illegal. He could understand how Adam, with all the good will in the world, would feel required to ask for his resignation. The resignation, he knew, would end his political career and undoubtedly injure his law practice. Nor did he feel any assurance that the reason for his resignation could be kept covered: Some burrowing reporter would eventually discover the facts no matter how plausibly his retirement might be presented in the formal announcement. "Blue ruin!" he said half aloud.

There was a line bisecting the paper on the desk, and beneath it another series of questions. The first read: WHAT WILL HAPPEN IF THE RANSOM IS NOT PAID?

First, inescapably, there was the possibility — indeed, the probability — that Adam would be killed. He ran through the sequence of events that would follow a negative decision by the Cabinet. Presumably Gerry Regan, in the company of an FBI agent, would go to Moreno and notify him that he was under arrest. (Ethan had no thoughts on how the problem of the accomplice might be handled, and begged the question for the moment.) Undoubtedly promises would be made to the kidnapper that, if Adam were released unharmed, this would be borne in mind by the government in prosecuting the case. The question was: Would Moreno cooperate? Based on what Gerry Regan had told him on the telephone earlier, it seemed unlikely. "The guy's a certifiable nut," Regan had said, "a real fanatic."

There was, however, another option. Suppose the example of the Canadian government was followed. In October, 1970, members of a French-Canadian revolutionary group, the *Front de Libération du Québec,* had kidnapped the then resident British Trade Commissioner. In return for his release the Canadian government had granted the kidnappers and their families a safe-conduct to Cuba. There had been few adverse political repercussions; indeed, the Liberal government of Pierre Trudeau had been generally hailed for its action. Why couldn't the same pattern be followed here, Ethan asked himself. Weren't the situations analogous? If the kidnappers realized there was no chance of the ransom being paid but that they would be given a safe-conduct if they freed the President, surely they would agree to that. . . .

He suddenly stopped pacing and slammed a fist into his palm. "Damn! Damn! Damn!" he said. They *couldn't* follow the Canadian precedent. He'd forgotten that Moreno was also a murderer — he'd killed that teenager in Macy's. The government couldn't assist a murderer to escape without debasing justice. Damn! — the murder in Macy's made the parallel invalid.

Moreover, facing charges of murder and kidnapping, Moreno would undoubtedly realize that he had nothing to lose and refuse to cooperate unless his demands were met. Ethan suddenly remembered Moreno's statement to Regan that if the President were killed it would not be his, Moreno's, responsibility but the responsibility of those who refused to do what was necessary to save his life.

It was clear then that if Moreno would not cooperate — and the longer Ethan considered it the more it seemed reasonable to conclude that he wouldn't — three possibilities obtained: Adam would be killed when the explosives detonated at midnight, or killed during an unsuccessful attempt to enter the booby-trapped truck, or he would be freed through the fortuitous circumventing of the triggering mechanisms.

He had put the question directly to Regan earlier: "If you have

to go into the truck, what are your chances of getting in safely?"
He recalled the Secret Service man's long silence and his subdued
reply: "The odds are no better than fifty-fifty." And there was a
further complication: If in trying to penetrate the truck's defenses
a mistake was made, not only would Adam be killed but, in all
probability, so would everyone working on the rescue attempt.

Involuntarily, he began to examine his own interests. At first he
tried to thrust the thought away, but his mind would not be restrained and went questing among the possibilities. He found himself examining again and again the fact that, if the ransom were not
paid and Adam died, he would be President and the mistake he had
made in the matter of the Springlass loan would be erased.

He was suddenly impatient with himself: Why was he permitting his personal involvement to color his consideration of the
question? And why was he feeling guilt? Shouldn't he simply act
on his convictions — wasn't that his duty? Each member of the
Cabinet was going to vote as *his* conscience dictated; was his right
to do the same less because his responsibility was greater? He must
shake the idea that, if as a result of the Cabinet's collective decision
Adam were killed, the blame — if blame was the right word —
would be uniquely his. Nonsense! Each member of the Cabinet
knew now what the others were going to do, and if in the event
of a tie his vote happened to be decisive, it would be no more than
a matter of timing. But still. . . .

He stopped pacing, shook his head vigorously and said aloud,
"C'mon, Ethan, let's have an end to this nonsense!" Start from the
beginning again: What is the question before the Cabinet? Very
simple: It is, shall the ransom be paid? And where did he stand on
that? No need to hesitate; he was unalterably opposed. No concessions to extortionists; he had always preached that and practiced it,
and he couldn't change now.

But in the event of a tie his vote would still be decisive, and in
some tomorrow it might be argued that he had served his own
self-interest; worse, he might come to argue it to himself. Well, he
would resolve that right now. He would record his vote and seal
it in an envelope, and if a tie did eventuate, he would hand the
envelope to one of the members of the Cabinet and have him open
it.

He went to the desk, took a sheet of typing paper and wrote,

"I am opposed to meeting the ransom demands of President Scott's kidnappers." He read it, tore it up and wrote, "I am opposed to meeting the ransom demands of President Scott's or any other kidnappers." He signed his name, folded the paper, placed it in an envelope and was putting it in his jacket pocket when there was a tapping on the door. He opened it. It was Arnie Gustafson.

"Sorry to interrupt you, Ethan. Got in a bit early and just wanted you to know I'd arrived."

"Thank you, Arnie, glad you're here," he said, holding the door only partly open, not inviting him in.

"It's a son of a bitch, huh?"

"Yes, it is."

"Don't let it get you down though. We'll work 'er out."

"I hope so."

Arnie placed a hand on Ethan's as it rested on the doorknob. "If it comes down to it," he said earnestly, "you can chop the ransom money off my budget. We'll make do somehow."

"Thanks, Arnie. I appreciate that, but I'm sure it won't come to that."

Gustafson made as though to leave. "Just wanted you to know," he said. "Won't keep you any longer. See you at three."

Ethan closed the door and turned back into the room. Well, that tore it! — Arnie was for paying the ransom. The scenario was now clear: The Cabinet was deadlocked and the deciding vote would fall to him.

Across the width of the great oval table in the Cabinet room, the Vice-President of the United States faced Herbert Morris, Director of the Secret Service. At his left sat Chester Harrison, Secretary of the Treasury, his elbows on the table and his chin resting on the interlaced fingers of his hands. If Herbert Morris was ill at ease there was nothing to betray it, whereas Ethan was leaning forward, his face flushed.

"The loss of the plane is not important," he said. "What is important is that your people ordered the gold offloaded. Did you know it was being done?"

"I did," Morris replied.

"Was it your idea?"

"No. It was Mr. Regan's."

"Did you approve it?"

"I did."

"But surely you were aware the Cabinet had ordered the gold shipped to New York City. Mr. Harrison informed you of that, did he not?"

"He did."

"Then I would like an explanation as to why you took it on yourself deliberately to countermand an order by the Cabinet."

Morris's face was inscrutable: "I am prepared to accept full responsibility for what was done."

"Of course you're responsible," Ethan said testily, "but that was not my question: I asked you for an explanation."

"Mr. Vice-President," Morris replied, "the people we are dealing with are criminals. They have performed an overt criminal act. As a man whose entire life has been spent in law enforcement, I cannot countenance permitting them to do so with impunity. The plane was crashed to gain time, time during which . . ."

Ethan broke in, his voice icy. "Thank you, Mr. Morris, that will be all. The Cabinet meets in this room in a few minutes; I'll inform them as to the reason for your action. You should know that we have again ordered the gold shipped to Kennedy airport. It will arrive there by five this afternoon." He turned to Chet. "In the meantime, I believe Mr. Harrison has something to say to you."

The Secretary of the Treasury's voice was flat and without emphasis. "Mr. Morris," he said, "you are relieved of all further responsibility for the President's safety and for the operation of the Service. Will you please prepare your resignation and forward it to me."

A group of approximately seventy-five — mostly men, but including some women — was assembled in near-darkness in the National Theater. They were plainclothes men and women, drawn from the Secret Service, the Federal Bureau of Investigation and the New York Police Department. They watched and made notes as photograph after photograph of Linda Rodriguez was flashed on the screen. Some of the pictures were in color, most were in monochrome. So great was the magnification that all were grainy in texture and some were out of focus. The only sound in the theater was an occasional cough, a muted clicking from the projection room and the distant, almost inaudible hum of the air-conditioning system.

The lights went up and Gerry Regan strode on stage, a thin stick in his hand. A spotlight pinpointed and then bloomed to cover him but he waved it off. He stepped to a microphone.

"Now," he said, "you know what she looks like. As I explained, she's the female member of the team. You may have noticed in the photos that showed her to the waist that she had her hands in the pockets of her suit. The reason is simple: In one of her hands she's holding the remote-control device I described earlier."

He looked toward the projection booth. "Slide, please."

A crudely drawn representation of the west side of Times Square between 43rd and 44th streets was thrown onto the screen. It swam about erratically until the operator maneuvered it down to stage level. Gerry called out, "Hold it there," and approached the screen.

"This isn't much of a drawing," he said, "but it'll help explain your assignment. This 'x' here . . . " — he used the stick as a pointer — "indicates the Rodriguez woman's position. As you can see, she's standing against the marble facing immediately to the south of the entrance to the Paramount building. What I want you to do is to surround her, cut her off, isolate her. And I want it done in such a way that she won't be aware of it. You're all dressed in street clothes, and if you carry out the assignment properly, she'll never realize who you are or what you're up to.

"Let me give you a few suggestions," he continued. "First, never look directly at her. Second, never stay in one place more than a few minutes . . . move around, change position. Do it skillfully and she'll never know she has been completely isolated.

"The police have been instructed to bar any additional members of the general public from entering the area. Those there now will be left there, of course, so the crowd around her should thin out a bit and you should be able to operate without much difficulty."

He held up something invisible in the semi-darkness. "Know what this is?" he asked. "It's a pin. When I was a kid we called it a common pin; some people call it a straight pin. When you leave the theater you'll each be given one. It's your identification. If you're wearing a jacket or a suit, insert it in the lapel on the edge of the notch so that only the head is visible. If you're wearing a shirt or blouse, insert it in the front edge of the collar. In this way you can recognize each other." He smiled. "It's a trick I got from the Mounties up in Canada."

He peered out at the audience. "Questions?"

There were none. "Okay then, off you go." Suddenly his voice was heavy with seriousness. "Listen to me, all of you. Nobody, and I mean *nobody*, is to make a move against her without specific instructions from me. No exceptions. Is that crystal clear . . . ? Okay then, good luck."

At exactly three o'clock the Cabinet reconvened. Ethan quickly called the meeting to order and informed his colleagues of the firing of the Director of the Secret Service. He had hardly begun an explanation of the status of the debate on whether or not to pay the ransom when Arnie Gustafson interrupted.

"Excuse me, Mr. Chairman," he said. "No need for that. I don't need a rundown. As far as I'm concerned it's a simple matter of saving Adam's life."

Fifteen minutes later, a slightly disheveled and somewhat breathless Jim Hilliard arrived. "Have you taken a vote?" he asked.

"Not yet. We thought we'd wait for you."

Jim Walker broke in. "Mr. Chairman . . . "

"Jim."

"I hope I'm not out of line," he said, "but the rest of us have had the advantage of an extended discussion of the question. Jim and Arnie haven't. I think it only fair that before we move to a vote they be informed — and I don't think I'm telling anything out of school — that when we adjourned this morning's session we were evenly divided: four opposed to paying the ransom, four in favor. I shan't specify who was for what. Let me add one more thing: Just before you joined us, Jim, Arnie expressed himself as being in favor. Now, with that background, I think you're pretty well in the picture. Anything further you'd like to know?"

The Secretary of State turned to Ethan. "Mr. Chairman," he said, "have you stated your position?"

"No. As Chairman it seemed . . . "

Hilliard stopped him with an upraised hand. He was silent for a moment, massaging his chin.

"Gentlemen, and of course the estimable Miss Cown," he began, "no speech. If you debated the matter at great length this morning and ended in an impasse, I'm sure the last thing you want to hear is another speech." He paused. "Believe me, I dislike compounding the problem, but flying back this morning I had ample time to think my way through this quite incredible dilemma and I've made up my mind. I am bound to say — despite the affection and respect I feel for my friend and mentor, Adam Scott — that I simply can't bring myself to put the United States of America in the position of knuckling under to a gang of extortionists."

There was a sputter of disgust from Henrietta Cown.

A silence began to settle on the room. One by one the nine men and one woman around the oval table turned to look at Ethan. As the silence settled in, the clatter of a distant typewriter became audible.

"Do I hear a motion?" Ethan said.

Henrietta Cown said, "I move that the United States government accede to the conditions specified by the kidnappers for the release unharmed of President Scott; namely, the payment of a ransom of fifty million dollars in gold and the granting of a safe-conduct to a destination of their choice."

"Second," said Arnie Gustafson.

Ethan tapped lightly with the gavel. "You have heard the motion," he said. "Are you ready for the question?"

A number of voices murmured, "Question."

"All in favor so indicate by the usual sign."

Hands were raised and lowered.

"Five," Ethan said. "Opposed, same sign."

Hands were raised and lowered.

"Five," Ethan said.

There was the smallest suggestion of tremulousness in his voice as he continued. "The vote on the motion being five in favor and five opposed, it is incumbent on the Chair to cast a tie-breaking vote." He reached into his breast pocket and withdrew the sealed envelope. "The Chair would ask . . . "

He could not do it!

He had settled in his mind during the lunch break that to capitulate to the kidnappers was immoral, that it would surely lead to other crimes and that the nation would be dishonored in yielding. He had accepted the fact that the issue would devolve on him alone and that his decision would profoundly affect the future of the nation; in effect, determining who would be President. To take on the office of the Presidency would be to assume a terrifying burden; he knew how great a burden but was prepared to bear it if he had to. But now the moment of truth had come and his resolve faltered. Suddenly overarching every other consideration — even those affecting his own future — was the realization that if he voted against the motion and the President died, he would move into the White House past the mangled and bloody body of Adam Scott. And that he could not do.

He cleared his throat. "The Chair votes in favor of the motion. I declare the motion carried."

Henrietta Cown put a handkerchief to her eyes and sobbed. Herb Thurlow rose from his chair and walked slowly from the room. Ethan Roberts returned the envelope to his pocket.

Chapter Seventeen

L inda's body was trembling. Fifteen minutes had passed since the deranged man had run toward the truck and she had not yet recovered from the terror that had at that moment immobilized her. She felt her stomach heave and the bitter taste of vomit was in her throat. The terror had resulted from the fact that she did not know precisely how Moreno had booby-trapped the truck (Phillipe Gomez had ordered her to remain ignorant of the means used so that, if captured, she could not divulge it) and feared that the madman would trigger the explosion and kill not only the President and hundreds of others, but her as well. She was committed to *El Mano Verde* and to its goals, but not at the cost of blood. And now there were two dead: the boy in Macy's and the sad, sick man whose blood was still a shining stain on the pavement.

The murder of the boy had left her shaken. She had learned of it in a news bulletin on the lights on the Allied Chemical building and had read the details in the newspaper. Under the headline KIDNAP MURDER, the *Daily News* had a front-page picture of the dead teenager — out of focus and half obscured by a hand flung out in an attempt to block the camera's lens — and the image was imprinted on her memory: the head twisted to one side, the mouth slack and agape, the eyes rolled up in the sockets. . . . How could Roberto have done it? — deliberately break a man's neck, kill another human with his bare hands! She shuddered convulsively, remembering those hands on her.

She had fallen in love with him on their first day at the boot camp in the mountains. They had been assigned the task of finding a location from which a water supply could be drawn from a stream that tumbled past the campsite a quarter of a mile away. The day was sensual, fragrant with the scent of pine and wildflowers. The sun was a copper disc in a space-blue sky and the stream seemed almost to frolic in celebration of the loveliness of its surroundings. Off came their boots and into the water they waded, gasping at the cold and laughing giddily. As they climbed from the stream, Moreno put an arm about her and his fingertips touched the side of her breast. On the bank he drew her to him. The perfection of the day and the excitement throbbing in them at the prospect of their common adventure carried them to a sudden coupling on the hard ground and then to an hour-long idyl of touching and loving in the deep fragrant grasses of the clearing.

That night, as he had said he would, Moreno came silently to her tent, hissed the zipper of her sleeping bag and slid his hard, naked body in beside hers. When he was gone, she lay awake until dawn lightened the canvas above her, knowing she was in love.

During their early weeks in the United States the relationship was everything she had ever hoped for. Roberto was kind, patient, thoughtful. He was an accomplished lover, as considerate of her needs as his own, gentle usually, but animal at times. They made love every night of their first two months together. Sometimes he would take her in the daytime on the floor or against the wall, or having borne her in his arms to the bedroom, clothes strewn about, atop the bedspread. But as The Day drew nearer his passion diminished. He grew increasingly preoccupied, restless, taut. In their lovemaking, when she held him close after he was spent, even then he was not wholly hers. She was not able as before to drain away his tensions, to ease the tumult in him.

In the final few weeks they had quarreled, and in their quarrels Moreno was often cruel, untroubled by the breach and apparently indifferent to the need to repair it. And there were intimations of a terrible violence yeasting in him and erupting inexplicably, sometimes unprovoked. There were moments when she feared him. She had consoled herself with the belief that it was because of his absorption in the assignment, but realized now — leaning against the marble facing of the building, despairing — that for all the closeness they had felt, she had not known him at all.

"But Mr. Vice-President, you can't *do* this to me!"

"Gerry, I understand how you feel. . . . "

"But, sir, I've found a way to disarm the woman. We've come up with the equipment: special stuff from the research people at the Pentagon. We can knock out her transmitter. No risk. *Guaranteed!* I mean it. . . . "

"Gerry, listen to me, please? I'm sympathetic to what you feel — it goes against my grain as much as it does yours — but the Cabinet has made a decision and you will abide by it."

"But, sir. . . . "

"Gerry, I want to be sure I'm understood, so listen carefully. The decision has been made. You may not agree with it but you must obey it. If you don't feel you can, you must say so now and step aside."

"Yes, sir."

"So that there can be no misunderstanding, let me repeat myself: You will do nothing to the Rodriguez woman. You will not touch or interfere with her person in any way. Is that understood?"

"Yes."

"And do you agree to it?"

"Yes, sir."

"Very well then. Now, for your information, I have prepared a letter of safe-conduct. It's being forwarded to you by courier and you should have it within the hour. I shall announce the Cabinet's decision on national television at five. Will you personally see to it that the kidnappers have been notified of our decision before that time?"

"Yes, sir."

"I believe that's all for now . . . unless you have something?"

"No, sir."

"Very good. Keep in touch with us here. Good-by."

"Good-by."

Regan put down the phone and stood looking at it for a moment. He walked slowly across the office and in a sudden surge of frustration smashed a fist against the door. The panel cracked. He seemed unaware of the pain. After a moment he opened the door.

"Is Maggie still here?" he asked. His secretary nodded. "And the baby?" She nodded again.

"Get them in here."

With Regan in his office was an attractive woman of about thirty. She was wearing a gray pantsuit and had a baby in her arms. Gerry was pacing about her, acting out his words, concluding a series of instructions.

"Now, Maggie, let's go over it again. You work your way through the crowd and make as though you're going to walk right past her. Then you pretend to stumble . . . to twist your ankle, to sprain it. You're in pain . . . terrible pain. Before she realizes what's happening, you push the baby at her and say something like, 'Here! My baby . . . ! Take my baby!' Make it look like you're going to drop the baby, or faint. . . . Understand?"

She nodded.

"Do you think you can do it?"

"I think so."

"We had a psychologist in earlier — a Doctor Olsen. Among other things, she said there was a chance we might be able to get at this Rodriguez woman through her maternal urge. What I'm hoping is that, before she has time to think, before she can realize what's happening, instinctively she'll reach for the baby. When she does, we grab her."

Regan was circling Maggie as he talked, inspecting her.

"Something wrong?"

"No. Just want to be sure there's nothing to give you away, that you don't look like a cop."

"A cop on maternity leave," she smiled.

"Anyway, you look fine. Away you go." As she reached the door he said, "Maggie. . . . "

"Yes?"

"Remember now, we take no chances. *None*. If it doesn't work, just keep on going."

"I understand," she said, and left.

Regan turned, crossed to the window and looked down on the Square. "Jim," he said, "flick the lights twice and then leave them off."

McCurdy, who had been standing to one side watching, operated the light switch and then joined Gerry at the window. The sun would set at 4:50, but already it was growing dark and evening was swiftly descending through lowering skies. There was silence in the room.

McCurdy said, "You're taking a big chance, Ger."

"What the hell do you expect me to do: twiddle my thumbs?"

"I only mean, you've had orders. Look what happened to the Old Man."

"I've got orders not to *touch* her. I'm not going to."

"You're through if they find out."

Gerry raised a hand. "Hold it . . . ! There she is."

Through the window he could see Maggie moving through the crowd. It was slow progress. Without looking away, he put out a hand. "Binoculars," he said.

Twisting and edging her way, Maggie had now reached 44th Street. Holding the baby within the shield of her arms, she walked to the rear of the crowd where passage was easier. Gerry studied her and then swung the binoculars to the left to focus on Linda. He was struck by the fatigue evident on her face and in her posture as she leaned back against the building. Around her, Gerry recognized some of his agents. His practiced eye picked out others in the area who were plainclothes men and women.

Maggie entered his field of vision. "Please God," he whispered.

Maggie, looking straight ahead, approached Linda as though to pass. As she drew abreast, she stumbled and almost fell. Gerry sucked in a breath; for a moment he had thought she was actually going down. He could see her clearly: bent over, face contorted with pain, looking up at Linda in entreaty. He saw her hold out the baby, saw her lips moving, and saw the agents on either side gather themselves.

It seemed to Gerry Regan that all motion stopped, frozen as in a film. Linda, startled, looked at the baby and then at Maggie, hesitated, and turned away.

Regan spun around and hurled the binoculars across the room.

On the rooftop of 1500 Broadway, a Marine helicopter settled slowly, and after hovering inches above the pebbled surface, touched down. Jim McCurdy, crouched against the blast of the rotors, ran across the roof to the aircraft as the pilot switched off the motor and opened the door.

"Mr. McCurdy?"

"I'm McCurdy."

"Not the easiest place to get into," the pilot grinned. "How many floors are we?"

"Thirty-three."

"Do you have a departure time yet?"

"As close as we can figure, around 5:30. Start up your motor at about 5:20. I don't want any delay after we bring them up."

"Will do."

"Some idiot could take a shot at you."

"Yeah. . . . Right."

"You've been briefed on your destination?"

"Yes, sir. Kennedy. They said the tower would radio instructions on exactly where to sit down as I make my approach."

"Right. See you in half an hour then," McCurdy said. He ran across the roof to a housing leading to the stairs and ducked inside as the rotors whistled to a stop.

LITTLE ROCK, ARKANSAS, NOV. 6 (AP) - THE NUDE AND MUTILATED BODY OF 18 YEAR OLD ROBERTA JEAN KING, AN EMPLOYEE OF THE LITTLE ROCK, ARKANSAS, CENTRAL POST OFFICE, WAS DISCOVERED THIS AFTERNOON IN A DITCH ON A SIDEROAD APPROXIMATELY TEN MILES FROM THE CITY LIMITS. THE BODY, THE THROAT CUT AND OTHERWISE MUTI-LATED, HAD EVIDENTLY BEEN THROWN FROM A CAR TRAV-ELING AT HIGH SPEED. IT WAS DISCOVERED BY A GROUP OF TEENAGE CHILDREN RETURNING FROM A SCHOOL BASKET-BALL GAME. LITTLE ROCK POLICE CHIEF, WILLIE JERMYN, SAID THE WORD "EQUALITY" WAS SCRAWLED ON THE DEAD GIRL'S STOMACH WITH LIPSTICK. CHIEF JERMYN TOLD RE-PORTERS THAT THE MURDER WAS PROBABLY THE WORK OF A SMALL TERRORIST BLACK GROUP, THE ATTICANS, WHO HAD KIDNAPPED THE GIRL EARLIER TODAY, DEMANDING A RANSOM AND A SAFE-CONDUCT IDENTICAL TO THAT BEING ASKED FOR THE RELEASE OF PRESIDENT SCOTT. . . .

An idea had been forming in Gerry Regan's mind and he was refining it as he passed from the National Theater lobby to the foyer of the adjoining office building at 1500 Broadway, flashed his identity card at a police officer and took an elevator to the eighth floor.

Moreno was quartered in a suite of offices normally occupied by Draper Theatrical Enterprises. The hall outside was clotted with policemen, reporters, photographers and television cameramen. The air was fetid with cigarette smoke and sweat. As he emerged from the elevator there was a surge toward him and a storm of flashbulbs almost blinded him. He was suddenly imprisoned in the moiling turbulence of a mob of newsmen.

"I have nothing for you," he shouted. "Nothing."

"Has the Cabinet made a decision?"

"I said, nothing."

"There's a rumor the President's ill. Is it true?"

"It is *not* true."

"We hear the Cabinet's going to pay."

"I can't help what you hear."

"Do you deny it?"

"I neither deny it nor confirm it."

"C'mon, Regan . . . give us *something*."

"I don't have anything for you. When I do you'll get it. Not before."

"Is it true your boss has been fired?"

Gerry was suddenly out of patience. "Will you get the hell out of my way," he shouted.

He shouldered through to the door leading to the Draper offices and slipped inside. Moreno had been moved to these quarters shortly after Regan had been told of the Cabinet's decision. Guarded by a platoon of infantry in full battle dress, the kidnapper had been brought in through the rear entrance with such speed and efficiency that only a few people in the crowd on 43rd Street realized what was happening.

Draper Theatrical Enterprises occupied a reception room and three offices. A half dozen policemen and a single Secret Service agent were seated in the reception room. As Gerry entered they leaped to their feet.

"Relax," he said. "Where is he?"

The agent pointed to a door bearing a nameplate reading ROBINSON DRAPER — PRESIDENT. "In there," he said.

Regan turned the handle and walked into the office. Jim McGillvray was with Moreno, who was standing with one foot on a window sill, leaning against the sash, looking down into the street. Gerry gave an almost imperceptible jerk of his head and McGill-

211

vray left the room. Moreno had turned as he heard Regan enter. As the door closed behind McGillvray, he said with a touch of mockery in his voice, "Mr. Regan, I believe."

Gerry did not respond. He stood in the center of the office, looking about His face was impassive but his mind was racing, examining the repercussions of the plan he had been contemplating for the past half-hour. It was, he knew, unprofessional and perhaps stupid, but he was finding it irresistible. He put a hand in his jacket pocket and pulled out a pack of cigarettes, shaking one free. Moreno, smiling, stepped forward, flicked his thumb on a lighter and offered the flame. Gerry disregarded it, struck one of a tattered book of matches and lit the cigarette.

"Roberto Moreno," he said, exhaling the smoke in the kidnapper's face, "I have been instructed by the Vice-President to inform you that the government of the United States has agreed to pay you and your accomplice the sum of fifty million dollars in gold and give you a safe-conduct to a destination of your choice."

Moreno broke into a smile. The smile expanded swiftly into an explosive, exultant laugh. "Hah . . . !" he said, slapping his hands together and almost springing into the air.

"A United States Marine helicopter has been laid on to transport you to Kennedy airport at precisely 5:30 this afternoon. It has already landed and is now on the roof of this building. A safe-conduct, signed by the Vice-President, will be delivered to you here within the next few minutes." He paused. "How do you plan to contact your partner?"

"When I have the safe-conduct in my hand, I'll give one of your men a code-word and tell him where my partner is. He can bring her here." The smile was ear to ear. "Surprised you, didn't we?" he chuckled gleefully. "Didn't know it was a woman . . . right?"

"We've known it was a woman for hours."

"The hell you have."

"Her name is Linda Rodriguez," Gerry said, simulating a bored recital of familiar facts. "She was born in Oaxaca, Mexico. She's thirty-one. She is at this minute positioned on the west side of Times Square next to the entrance to the Paramount building. Both of you are members of a revolutionary group known as *El Mano Verde* . . . ."

Moreno's smile faded. "You got that from the goddamn CIA," he snarled. "Fat lot of good it did you!"

"I'm not here to argue. . . . "

"And you had me figured as a fool," Moreno broke in.

"A fool?"

"This morning. In your car. Remember?" he sneered. "Who's the fool *now*?" The voice was taunting, the smile on the face was tight, the scar at the corner of the mouth was livid and hate was smoldering behind the eyes.

The plan that had been forming in Gerry's mind was now complete — each move, each action. Yes, he said to himself, the time is right.

He hooked a hard left to Moreno's face. All the frustration and anger of the day was in the blow. The skin of his knuckles transmitted a sensation of flesh mashing and of gristle cracking, and he felt joy. He took a half-step forward, and throwing the punch from his hip, rammed his right fist six inches into Moreno's stomach. A gust of air and spittle exploded from Moreno's mouth over his face, and Gerry exulted in it. Then, as Moreno bent forward, doubling over, he met the descending face with the bone and muscle of a rising thigh. Moreno pitched back to the floor and lay there, conscious but unmoving. Slowly, he struggled to his elbows, rubbed his face with his hand, drew it away bloody, looked at it stupidly and began to get up. He raised his eyes to Regan and sank back onto an elbow, shaking his head.

Gerry looked down at him, his face impassive. "You know," he said softly, "it's been a bad day. And that was one small pleasure I just couldn't deny myself."

He turned and left the room. It was not until the following morning that he realized he had broken a bone in his hand.

From the helicopter as it swept in from the northwest, the Pan World Airways 747-B looked like an enormous bird surrounded by its chicks and poised in a nest of light. As the copter began its descent, it could be seen that the light emanated from a circle of portable floodlights, that the nestlings were a cluster of service vehicles and that the perimeter was formed by two hundred Marines in battle dress.

Some fifty yards to the east, other Marines encircled a smaller, darker area at the center of which stood a ramp-signalman holding aloft two shielded flashlights, rotating them in small circles. The helicopter swooped in, and with the precise movements of a huge hummingbird, dropped to within inches of the ground, hovered for a moment and settled on the grass. A tumbling doughnut of dust and debris raced outward.

McCurdy threw open the cabin door, latched it, climbed down and extended a hand to Linda. She was followed by Moreno. Bent beneath the blast beating down from the rotors, they ran from the helicopter toward the jet. As they went, the Marines — flowing with the viscosity of a magnified amoeba — moved with them, bulging toward the larger circle and rupturing to form a laneway through which they passed.

As they emerged into the brilliant light bathing the 747, Moreno's battered face could be seen: his eyeballs were scarcely visible through puffed and purple slits, his nose was formless and a livid welt drew his swollen mouth to one side.

At the foot of the mobile stairs leading to the cabin, the trio halted and Moreno turned to McCurdy. "Your gun," he said.

McCurdy shook his head.

"The gun, dammit!"

"What for?"

"I want to be goddamn sure the pilot of this thing does what he's told."

McCurdy hesitated, considered, reached into his jacket, withdrew a Colt .32 from his shoulder holster and passed it to Moreno. Moreno checked to see that it was loaded, engaged the safety catch and slipped it into the inside pocket of his jacket. Then, without a word, he turned, followed Linda up the stairs and ducked into the cabin. McCurdy nodded, the cabin door was swung shut and secured and the stairs were wheeled away. As the motors began to raise their scream, the Marines parted to form two lines, and on the double, moved off. The great aircraft wheeled and lumbered away. McCurdy watched, barely masking the anger that had reddened his face and compressed his mouth into a thin line.

The plane reached the end of the runway, turned slowly, paused trembling, mounted its tumult and accelerated down the runway. He watched the shining metal bird lift off and, lights winking, move up and away in a shallow climbing turn, suddenly to disappear as it thrust into the overcast.

He stood for a moment in the gathering silence staring at the spot where the plane had disappeared. Then he said, "Goddamn son of a bitch!"

Juan Rivera, Supervisor of Ground Maintenance at JFK for Pan World Airways, seemed in exceptionally high spirits as he climbed into his jeep, rammed it into gear and scooted back to the terminal; particularly for a man who only two hours earlier had raised every kind of hell when ordered to service the aircraft and supervise the transfer of the fifty million dollars in gold bars from the Army plane to the giant 747-B.

He had his reasons. Rivera was a Cuban expatriate, the once prospering owner of a tool and die factory in Havana. The three principal fingers missing from his left hand were a memento of his escape from a Cuban prison; they had been crushed between a concrete dock and the launch that had ferried him and a half dozen other refugees to Florida just before dawn on a foggy February morning in 1962.

For all his remonstrance, he had seen to it that the 747-B was readied, had supervised the stowing of the gold, had done an external inspection walk with the Captain and then, his face mirroring his resentment, had stood beneath a wing watching the positioning of the troops in preparation for the arrival of the kidnappers. Ten minutes before the helicopter swept in from the northwest, he had decided to make another circle of the great jet — had even walked the wings — tinkering, checking. And when finally the plane was gone and the excitement had subsided and the Marines had marched off, he had walked slowly to his jeep.

As he went, the single remaining finger of his left hand was rubbing rhythmically on the base of the thumb, and a small mirthless smile was flickering at the corners of his mouth.

Part Three

Chapter Eighteen

The rain had begun at six o'clock, almost coincident with the departure of the kidnappers' plane. Heralded by erratic shudderings of light and grumblings of sound, it slashed in from the northwest to tumble over the tops of buildings and race through the canyons of the streets. The downpour drove into Times Square and swiftly hustled all but the hardy into shop and subway entrances. When, fifteen minutes later, the olive-green troop carriers rumbled into the Square and disgorged their helmeted and raincaped troops, only a few hundred onlookers remained, huddled in every available haven. Sodden and subdued, they offered little resistance to the soldiers as they chanted their litany, "Clear the Square. Everybody out," and shuffled off. After the last few eccentrics had been flushed from their places of hiding, the soldiers formed a misshapen circle roughly one hundred yards in diameter around the armored truck, and at a command, stood shoulder to shoulder at parade rest.

Times Square was almost unrecognizable. The only movement in the semi-darkness was the frantic scurrying of the rain as it fled the gusting wind, and the ghostly movement of the reader-lights as they slid solemnly across the faces of the building:

KIDNAPPERS' PLANE NOW APPROACHING GULF OF MEXICO
. . . . . NO ANNOUNCEMENT YET OF DESTINATION . . . . .
PRESIDENT SCOTT REPORTED IN GOOD SPIRITS AND OPTI-
MISTIC ABOUT RELEASE . . . . . CONGRESS MEETING IN HIS-
TORIC TELEVISION SESSION TO DISCUSS ELECTION POST-
PONEMENT . . . . . TIMES SQUARE EVACUATED BY TROOPS BUT

TELEVISION CAMERAS WILL REMAIN . . . . . HERBERT THUR-
LOW, MINISTER OF AGRICULTURE, RESIGNS CABINET . . . . .
SAYS, "I'LL MAKE MY REASONS CLEAR AFTER PRESIDENT
SCOTT IS RELEASED . . . . . "

The line of soldiers parted and an arc-acetylene welding truck
entered the Square. It was the first of a complex variety of vehicles
to cluster about the armored truck. Within the next ten minutes,
two ambulances were parked nearby, air compressors were towed
into position and a fire department pumper wheeled in close and
snaked hoses across the streets to nearby hydrants. The duplicate
of the kidnappers' truck rumbled north from 43rd Street and pulled
up a dozen yards from the other. Army generators soon fed elec-
tricity into the ordered tangle of heavy-duty rubberized cables
reaching out to a dozen portable floodlights, each focused on the
armored truck.

Gerry Regan walked around the truck to stand on tiptoe by the
door on the driver's side.

"Mr. President," he shouted. When there was no response, he
called out again, "President Scott . . . ?"

Peering through the window, he could see the President's face,
pale in the light of the giant floods. His lips were moving but the
sound was enclosed in the truck and overpowered by the ambient
chaos and Gerry could catch nothing of what he said. He held up
a hand, his fingers forming the familiar V-for-Victory signal, and
the President returned it, smiling.

He saw Ziggy Mayer nearby and beckoned to him. "Ziggy,"
he said, "I'll need a large pad of paper and a marking pencil.
Something like an artist's drawing pad if you can find one. If not,
anything large enough for me to print messages on and show them
to the President."

"Done," Ziggy said, and hastened off.

One of the Army engineers touched his arm. "Telephone, sir."

The Signal Corps had set up a field-telephone system some fifty
feet away. He walked over and took the telephone held out to him.

"Regan here," he shouted.

A distant, almost inaudible voice rasped in his ear. He plugged
his other ear with a forefinger. "Louder," he shouted.

"Gerry. . . . It's Ethan Roberts."

"Yes, Mr. Vice-President."

"Please bring me up-to-date on what's happening."

"Yes, sir. We've cleared the public out and we're setting up everything we might need. Just in case we don't hear from Moreno and company. . . . "

"There'll be no attempt to enter the truck in the meantime?"

"No, sir. It's just insurance."

"If you need me, I'll be here at the White House. When you go off the line I'll have Jim Rankin fill in your people as to the fastest way to reach me."

"Very good, sir. Any word from the plane?"

"Nothing since fifteen minutes after they were airborne. Our people assume Moreno has done something to incapacitate the transmitting apparatus. We do know they're heading out over the Gulf of Mexico at the moment — we've been tracking them with radar."

"Yes, sir."

"Actually, the airline people thought the kidnappers might tamper with the radio, so they've hidden an auxiliary system, an extra transmitter, aboard. They can use it in an emergency."

The 747-B was four hours and ten minutes out of Kennedy when Captain Liam O'Connor left the flight deck and descended the spiral staircase to the first-class cabin where Moreno and Linda were sitting, drinks in hand, talking.

"I wonder, Mr. Moreno, if you'd mind coming with me to the flight deck?" the Captain said.

"Why?"

"We have a problem."

"Tell me here."

"I'd prefer that you talk to the Flight Engineer and look at one of his instruments."

"What's wrong with it?"

"There's nothing wrong with it, but it indicates that we're losing fuel, and that poses a problem."

"What kind of a problem?"

"Not a serious one — that is, not as far as the safety of the aircraft is concerned — but it means we're going to have to land."

Moreno had his feet on the armrest of the seat in front. He sat up quickly, spilling some of his drink. "What are you trying to pull?" he said, anger in his voice.

Captain O'Connor sighed heavily. "Believe me, Mr. Moreno, I'm not trying to pull anything. It's a simple fact . . . we're losing fuel."

Moreno got to his feet, and as the Captain turned, followed him up the stairs with Linda behind. The flight deck, forward of the lounge, housed the Captain, the First Officer and the Flight Engineer. A hundred illuminated instruments glowed in the semi-darkness. Seated before an instrument panel making notes was a ruddy-complexioned, bearded man of about thirty.

"Mr. Moreno," the Captain said, "this is Flight Engineer Donald Burns."

Burns had a heavy brogue and was given to succinct speech. He wasted no time in greetings. "We've sprung a leak," he said, "and we've got to land. That's all there's to it."

"Where's this instrument you wanted me to see?" Moreno said brusquely.

Burns pointed to the fuel gauge on the panel before him. It was calibrated to measure in thousands the pounds of fuel in the tanks, and ranged from 310 to zero. At its center was a digital readout counter that measured fuel consumed. The pointer indicated 44,-000 pounds and the digital readout showed the amount of fuel consumed at close to 85,000 pounds.

"So, what's it mean?" Moreno said.

"It means we've got to land."

Moreno looked at him balefully, holding him with his eyes. Burns looked back, unblinking. "Who do you think you're kidding?" Moreno said, his voice heavy with menace.

Burns could see anger gathering behind the kidnapper's eyes. "If you'll listen to me, sir," he said politely, "I'll explain. We measure fuel in pounds rather than in gallons. The capacity of this aircraft is 310 thousand pounds. That corresponds to 42 thousand gallons. We had that amount aboard when we departed Kennedy. At an airspeed of just short of six hundred miles an hour, we burn approximately 20 thousand pounds, or three thousand gallons, an hour . . . that's an average of three thousand, it varies for a lot of reasons. . . ."

"Get to the point."

"Well, I run a routine fuel check every hour. Standard procedure. When I checked two hours ago I found that fuel reserves were away down. We're not fighting a headwind, all four engines were operating normally, the digital readout showed consumption normal, so the only conclusion I could come to was that we were losing fuel. I informed Captain O'Connor. . . . "

" . . . And I told him to monitor it and make another check in half an hour. Same problem. No question about it, we're losing fuel."

"Losing it how?"

"I don't know."

"What do you mean, you don't know? Aren't you in charge of this goddamn plane?"

"Yes, I am. But the fuel tanks in this aircraft run from the wingtips to the fuselage and I haven't been able to get a visual on it. Believe me, we've looked."

"You're trying to tell me a plane like this can spring a leak? What kind of a fool do you take me for?"

"I'm sorry, Mr. Moreno, I don't have an explanation. The tanks have an inner and outer lining and should be leakproof. The only possibility I can come up with is that, in the excitement at Kennedy, the maintenance people left off a refueling cap and the fuel is being sucked out. . . . "

Moreno stood motionless, his mind racing. "Where are we right now?"

Captain O'Connor turned to the First Officer. "Bill," he said, "give me an INS. . . . "

"To hell with the technical stuff! *Where?*"

"Okay, our position?"

After a moment the First Officer said, "Over the Gulf of Mexico at 52 thousand feet, approximately four hundred miles east of Guatemala City."

"Turn around. Go back to the States."

"I'm sorry, sir," Burns said, "we can't. We're an hour and a half out of Miami and we haven't any more than . . . " he checked the fuel gauge, "about five thousand gallons."

"That's enough. You said you only use three thousands gallons an hour."

"True, sir, but I estimate we're losing fuel at close to a hundred gallons a minute. That means we've got to land in, at most, half an hour."

"Land where?"

"Our best option is Guatemala City. Failing that, San Salvador."

Moreno's mind reacted swiftly. Within seconds he had appraised the entire Caribbean area as though a map had been spread out in his brain. And in those seconds a panic was born and began swiftly to burgeon. Nowhere within half an hour's flying time was there a country whose government did not have an extradition treaty with Washington. A landing anywhere in the region would lead to his and Linda's arrest and to their deportation to the United States.

All right — they would land at Guatemala City. He would demand that the jet be refueled and released. He would use the stewardesses as hostages and kill them one by one unless his demands were met.

But . . . even if the Guatemalans accepted his conditions, could he reach his destination before midnight? He looked at his watch. 10:20. By the time the plane landed and contact was made with the terminal it would be at least 10:50. By the time an official authorized the refueling, it would be past eleven. And, inevitably, there would be delays: delays while the authorities considered their response, while they checked with the CIA and the CIA with Washington. If only he hadn't ripped out the 747's radio he could talk to the tower and have clearance arranged before they landed. . . .

It struck him like a hammer blow to the skull: *there wasn't enough time*! The explosives would detonate at midnight, and with the President dead their edge was gone. Even if the Guatemalans did permit him to refuel, the Americans could put fighter planes in the air and head them off.

Moreno felt his brain swell in his skull. Pain. Dizziness. A fluttering in his eyeballs and a surge of nausea. Then, as suddenly, the pressure broke and he was calm and the picture all came clear. They were trying to trick him — and he'd almost fallen for it! They *had* to try something, so they'd rigged the fuel gauge to show the reserves low, or they'd lied to him about the reading. Yes, it was a trick . . . a goddamn *Yanqui* son-of-a-bitch trick!

In a voice so low Captain O'Connor could barely hear him, he said, "You'll keep going."

"I'm sorry, Mr. Moreno, I can't do that."

Moreno reached into his jacket and pulled out the gun Jim McCurdy had given him. "You'll do what I say," he said quietly, "or I'll kill you."

Captain O'Connor swallowed hard. "Mr. Moreno," he said, "if I do, this aircraft will crash. When it does, I'll be killed and so will you, and so will everyone aboard. If you kill me now it makes very little difference." He turned to the First Officer. "Bill, set a course for Guatemala City."

Moreno was staring at O'Connor but his eyes were unfocused. He seemed not to be breathing. For an interminable moment he stood motionless, then, without any change of expression, he pulled the trigger. O'Connor gasped, put his hands to his stomach and crumpled. Moreno turned, slowly, mechanically, swinging the gun in an arc toward Burns. Linda cried, "Roberto!" and leaped on his back, clutching at his arms. The gun fired, the bullet punching through the floor and lodging in a seat in the cabin below. Burns scrambled from the chair and hurled his weight against Moreno. The three of them fell to the floor, threshing about. There was another shot and the struggling subsided. Burns lurched erect. Linda, sobbing, strained to pull her right arm from beneath the dead weight of Moreno's body. A welling, scarlet stain was spreading with astonishing speed on his shirt front.

Gerry Regan stood beside the armored truck, arm upraised. The cacophony of noise from the more than a dozen pieces of equipment encircling the truck diminished until the only sound was the humming of generators. Gently he placed a foot on the running board and raised himself until he could look inside. In the glare of the floodlights the President's ghostly face was clearly visible.

"Sir . . . ?"

Adam Scott called out, "I can hear you."

"We've had some bad news. The kidnapper is dead. We're going to have to try to get you out."

"I understand."

"There'll be some risk. We'll have to cut a hole through the wall."

The President nodded.

"Can you reach the gunport nearest you?"

"Yes."

"Open it, please."

Adam pressed a small spring and turned it one hundred and eighty degrees. A circle of steel plate the size of a silver dollar pushed out and down and clear.

"I'm going to direct a hose through the gunport onto the opposite wall, to cool it while we cut. You're going to be pretty uncomfortable. . . . "

"Do what you have to do."

Gerry stepped down and swung his right arm in a wide circle. There was an immediate surge of sound and activity. Motors roared. Men moved to their tasks.

A powerful light directed at Gerry's face was flashing on and off. He walked to the field telephone unit. "It's the Vice-President, sir," a corporal said.

"Regan here."

"Gerry, it's Ethan Roberts. Tell me what your plan is."

"Yes, sir. We're going into the truck through the wall opposite the President. We'll cut an oval-shaped hole — an oval rather than a rectangle because it has a shorter circumference. To keep the heat down, we've rigged an underwater acetylene torch and we'll flood water on the cut as it's being made. At the same time, we'll direct water onto the inside of the wall through a gunport. Trouble is, the wall has a layer of batting sandwiched between two sheets of steel and the torch can't cut through all of them simultaneously . . . so we'll have to do it twice. Once we're through we'll send in a man with a pair of metal cutters, snip the chain on the handcuffs and take the President out."

"How do you rate your chances?"

"Same as before, sir . . . we make it or we don't."

"Yes. . . . What's being done to protect those workmen and soldiers I see on the television?"

"There's nothing we *can* do. We need them. We've cleared out everybody who's not essential."

"And after you get the President out?"

"We've got the Army Ordnance Corps' best bomb-disposal man standing by." He glanced up at the reader-lights and frowned. "If there's nothing else, sir, I'll go off the line. We've got exactly thirty-seven minutes."

On the television screen, Robertson Kirk is giving a detailed explanation of the armored truck's defenses. He is working in a set that includes blown-up photographs of Times Square, a life-size mockup of an armored truck and a table on which there are a number of objects.

"The kidnappers have planned carefully and well, and to this point have frustrated any attempts to rescue the President. They have made it virtually impossible to get into the truck without endangering Mr. Scott's life . . . that is, of course, without instructions which, it now seems, will not be coming.

"Let me show you with this mockup of the truck how nearly impregnable it is. As you can see, the two front doors and the one at the rear are locked with electrically operated bolts, with the wires from those bolts leading, presumably, to this wooden box in which the explosives are stored. Unfortunately, because the wiring is hidden behind a plywood inner lining, there is no way of knowing exactly where it is."

He crossed to the table and picked up an object and the camera cut to a close-up of his hand.

"I have here a heat detector, the kind of device normally used in fire-alarm systems. One very much like it is mounted on the ceiling of the truck with wires leading from it to the explosives. Let me demonstrate just how sensitive it is. If I take this cigarette lighter and hold it a couple of feet below . . . . Nothing. But watch now as I move it closer . . . . There! — it set off the buzzer here on the table. These detectors are so sensitive that they can be activated by as little as a five-degree rise in temperature within twenty seconds.

"Now . . . . This is a vibration sensor. There's one like it mounted, probably glued, to the ceiling of the truck. Normally, devices like this are used in burglar-alarm systems. I've set this one so that it will take a considerable impact to trigger it. For instance, if I place it on the table and then strike the table with this hammer — like so — nothing happens. But if I deal it a heavy blow . . . . There!

"Now, let me make a small adjustment with this screwdriver. This time I'll merely tap the table with a knuckle . . . . And there she goes.

"Therein lies the problem facing the President's would-be rescuers. To get into the truck and get the President out you must take certain risks. Open a door and you break a circuit and detonate the explosives. Cut through a wall and you confront two problems: The heat from the

acetylene torch may set off the heat detector, or you may inadvertently sever a wire and activate the blasting cap. Try to go in through the windshield by breaking the glass and you may trigger the vibration sensor.

"And all the while, a timing device is ticking away, set to go off at midnight."

He looked off-camera, reached out and brought into the picture a piece of wire copy.

"Here's a bulletin just in: The Associated Press in Washington reports that the Congress, meeting in an unprecedented joint session on closed-circuit television, has just voted to postpone tomorrow's Congressional elections for two months."

The armored truck presented an eerie sight. Starkly illumined by a circle of floodlights, it sat on shivering reflections at the center of a shining expanse of water. As the workmen went about their tasks, grotesque shadows leaped and cavorted on its walls. A fire hose, the nozzle removed, gushed a soft flow of water onto the roof and sent it cascading down the sides. A slender hose poured its stream through the open gunport. A third was flooding the steaming, sputtering flame of the acetylene torch as it slowly traced a knurled gouge in the steel wall. Water splashed against the welder and every few seconds a helper wiped his mask clear. The storm had peaked and the thunder was almost constant, each clap seeming to smash against the walls of the truck.

The welder stopped, stepped back and tilted up his mask. His assistant took a crowbar from a loop in his coveralls, inserted it in the cut and pried the metal outward. Again a touch of flame to metal and a rough oval of steel plate fell away revealing a matching white area, scorched at the edges. The welder removed a glove and seized a fistful of the batting; but before he could tear it away, Gerry Regan, who had been standing at his elbow, grasped his arm.

"Hold it," he said.

He bent forward, directed a flashlight onto the area and peered closely, probing gently with his fingers, pulling away tufts of the cotton. Satisfied, he stepped back.

"Just wanted to be sure there were no wires."

The welder tore away the batting and adjusted the flame of his torch. Regan turned to McCurdy who had drawn near. "Moment of truth coming up," he said. "If there are any wires there, they'll be between the inner steel plate and the plywood."

The welder leaned forward, lowered his mask and began to cut.

ETHAN T. ROBERTS,
VICE-PRESIDENT,
THE UNITED STATES OF AMERICA.
THE WHITE HOUSE.
WASHINGTON D.C.

DISREGARD NON USE OF NORMAL DIPLOMATIC CHANNELS BY REASON OF EXTREME URGENCY THIS COMMUNICATION. PAN WORLD AIRCRAFT, U.S. REGISTRATION N-53854, EX J.F. KENNEDY AIRPORT, NYC, MADE EMERGENCY LANDING GUATEMALA CITY 9:54 PM (CST). ROBERTO SALDIVAR MORENO AND CAPTAIN LIAM STRUTHERS O'CONNOR DEAD ON ARRIVAL OF GUNSHOT WOUNDS. LINDA RODRIGUEZ HOSPITALIZED. EXTREME SHOCK. MEMBERS OF CREW SAFE AND WELL. GOLD BULLION INTACT ABOARD AIRCRAFT. SHIPMENT SEALED BY CUSTOMS. AIRCRAFT UNDER PROTECTION GUATEMALA ARMY UNIT. ADVISE SOONEST RE: DISPOSITION AIRCRAFT AND GOLD. ALSO RE: BODIES MORENO AND O'-CONNOR. DO YOU DESIRE JUSTICE DEPARTMENT HERE EXTRADITE RODRIGUEZ?

GENERAL ROBERTO MORALES,
VICE-PRESIDENT,
THE REPUBLIC OF GUATEMALA

When the water first spurted and then began to stream through the gunport, Adam had scuttled from it to the end of his tether. But the flow scattered off the wall and in minutes he was drenched. If one of Regan's objectives was to keep down the temperature within the truck, he was doing a hell of a job! Adam picked up the blanket which earlier he had draped over the back of the driver's seat, shrugged it about his shoulders and crouched, sitting on his heels, his back against the wall.

He studied the wooden box in the corner. Water was splashing on the top and running down the sides. The floor of the truck was covered to a depth of half an inch. He wondered if the water might short the mechanism and render it inoperative . . . or perhaps activate it. He felt an urge to move away as far as possible but knew that was pointless: in the first millisecond, confined by the walls of the truck, the explosion would disintegrate him.

Unaccountably there was the sound of a slight impact from beneath the truck. It was a gentle tap, but in his heightened imagination Adam felt it transferred from the wall to his spine. The accumulated fatigue of the past six weeks and the mounting tension of the day suddenly dissolved his composure, and near-panic enveloped him. He stood up, banging his head on the ceiling, and then fell back against the wall as his knees buckled. The tide of panic flowed, flooding into his belly, dizzying his brain. He shook his head vigorously, driving it back, willing it away.

After a minute he looked at his watch. Half an hour to go. He could hear the hissing of the acetylene torch as it gnawed at the steel plate, and he pondered the circumstance that had put his life in the hands of a man he had never met, a man who, scorning the danger to his own life, was striving blindly through the steel toward him.

"Steady, friend," he whispered. "Steady."

Chapter Nineteen

T he tap on the metal that had been transferred
to Adam Scott's spine had been caused by Gerry Regan who had
crawled beneath the armored truck to scout its underside in the
small hope of chancing upon something, *anything,* that might make
access possible.

Disregarding the water cascading from above and flooding the
pavement — "What the hell, I can't get any wetter!" — he had
squirmed under the truck on the side away from the welder and was
now lying on his back. He poked the beam of his flashlight through
the rusted welter of driveshaft, connecting rods, beams and braces,
searching for he did not know what — a crevice, a crack, some
minuscule point at which this impregnable steel box might be vulnerable.

The underside of the floor was visible but seemed unassailable
despite a half dozen spots from which water wiggled, sluiced or
dripped. Pushing with his heels, he "walked" his shoulders to the
front of the truck. Now the engine, caked with dust-laden grease,
loomed darkly above him and the smell of coolant was sharp in his
nostrils. He played the flashlight beam about, craning his neck,
shifting. As the light swept across the firewall his brow drew down
in a frown of concentration. He reached up and tapped it lightly
with a knuckle, then suddenly flipped onto his stomach and slith-
ered from beneath the truck.

Scrambling to his feet, smeared with filth, he sprinted to the
other truck. Zucker was on the far side, shielding against a possible
explosion. Gerry seized him by the upper arms and thrust his face
close.

"The fire wall!" he shouted. "The fire wall between the engine and the cab — is it armored?"

Zucker concentrated, his brow knit.

"Yes or no, dammit!"

"No, it isn't. You don't need armor there. The motor would stop any bullet . . . "

Gerry dragged him to the front of the truck and flung up the hood. "What would I have to do to get the motor out of there?"

"You mean, take it right out . . . ?"

"I want to go in through the fire wall."

"Oh . . . . Right. Of course! Six cuts with a torch will do it. See that bracing member there between the front wheels? Take it out first, then cut those four brackets by which the motor is bolted to the frame, and the engine and driveshaft will fall away."

"How long would it take?"

"With two men cutting . . . ? Eight, ten minutes at most."

Gerry peered into the engine cavity. "There *still* wouldn't be enough room for a man to go in through the fire wall."

"There would be if you hoisted the front of the truck."

"*Right!*"

He was gone, splashing through the rainwater to where Ziggy Mayer and Jim McCurdy were standing.

"Ziggy . . . I need a tow truck with a crane. Fast! Jim, get me the Vice-President." He gave him a shove in the direction of the telephone equipment that sent McCurdy to his hands and knees, then he turned and ran to the welder. "Hold it!" he shouted, seizing the man by the arm.

The welder straightened up and in an automatic reflex adjusted the flame. "What's the problem?"

"Just stand by."

He was gone again, racing to the telephone, grabbing it as it was held out to him.

"Sir, Gerry Regan here."

"What's the trouble?"

"No trouble. I've just learned there's no armor-plate between the engine and the cab. I want to change the plan and go in through the fire wall. I'm almost certain there won't be any wiring there."

"But how can you possibly . . . ?"

"Excuse me, sir, there's no time to explain. Do I have your permission?"

"Well now, hold on a minute, Gerry. What's the risk?"

"I don't know. But I *do* know that what we're doing now is pure guesswork. She could blow any second."

"Is there enough time?"

"I think so."

"Couldn't you follow *both* paths?"

"No, sir. That would double the risk."

"But . . . ."

"Sir . . . .The way we're going, everybody could get killed. This way, if I see we aren't going to make it by midnight, we can clear everybody out."

"Everybody but the President."

"Yes, sir. I'm afraid so, sir."

"Stay on the line. I'll have to check with the Cabinet. They're right here."

Regan covered the mouthpiece of the telephone. "Clear the area in front of the truck," he shouted. "Lights, cables, everything! Jim, move the Command car. Park her over there at 43rd facing south. We may have to get out of here in a hell of a hurry."

He turned to a soldier standing nearby. "Sergeant."

"Sir?"

"Get me some mattresses."

"Mattresses, sir?"

"Mattresses. A half dozen of them."

"But where would I get mattresses, sir?"

"I don't give a damn where you get them. Break into the Castro Convertible store over there. Steal them from a hotel . . . but get them! *On the double,* sergeant!"

He was pacing at the limit of the telephone wire, writhing with tension. Finally, he could endure it no longer and shouted into the telephone, "*For Christ's sake, sir. Will you tell them to get off the pot!*"

He paused listening, his face flaming. "Sorry, sir. Yes, sir. Thank you, sir."

He tossed the telephone to a soldier and ran toward the truck, his eyes fixed on the traversing lights. They read 11:36.

The digits changed to 11:41 as a tow truck came hustling into the Square preceded by a New York Police Department cruiser, light flashing, siren whooping. Regan took one look and struck his forehead in despair.

"Too small," he groaned.

As he spoke, a second truck entered. Except for its color and the lettering on the door panel, it was identical to the first. Regan's initial look of dismay suddenly changed. "Back them both in," he shouted. "Team 'em!"

As the trucks maneuvered into position, there was a deep-throated roar and a third truck raced toward them. In flamboyant script on both sides was the legend *Starvin' Marvin's 24-Hour Towing Service.* In the driver's seat was Ziggy Mayer, steering with one hand while encircling the neck of a man in coveralls with his right arm. "He didn't want to come," he explained to Regan.

Released, Marvin wandered about, wailing that his truck — his brand-new truck — was being stolen, announcing that if it was damaged he was going to sue, and demanding to be told who was in charge. One of the soldiers pointed to Regan and he approached him nattering his complaint. As Marvin's chant grew more insistent — "My new truck . . . ! Who's gonna pay? Tell me, who's gonna pay?" — Regan suddenly let out a growl, grabbed him by the seat of the coveralls and the scruff of the neck, and propelled him close to the armored truck.

"Who's gonna pay?" he snarled, stabbing a forefinger at the pale face of the President visible within the truck. "*He's* gonna pay!"

Suddenly silent, Marvin turned and shuffled away.

The tow truck's engine roared. McCurdy threw a lever. Gears began to rotate and a drum to revolve. A steel cable stretched, creaked, grew taut and quivered, and the front end of the armored truck began to lift. Slowly the body rose above the wheels and then, to Regan's horror, stopped, while the front end of the tow truck began to lift. McCurdy threw the lever to neutral.

"She's too heavy," he shouted.

"Bring in the others."

"Too dicey. We'd never be able to coordinate them."

A ragged circle of workmen had emerged from behind their equipment and were watching. Gerry waved them in. "All of you," he shouted. "On the front of the tow truck. Weigh her down."

The men swarmed over the truck, sprawling across the hood,

standing on the front bumper, climbing on top of each other. The front of the tow truck sagged.

McCurdy threw the lever and gunned the engine. Inch by inch the front of the armored truck rose. As the wheels cleared the pavement, it rolled forward. Gerry leaped between the two vehicles, cushioning the impact as they moved together.

"Block the rear wheels," McCurdy roared.

Others leaped in to help hold the trucks apart and a distant voice shouted, "Okay. She's blocked."

McCurdy put the tow truck in gear, inched forward until the two vehicles were clear and set the brake. Once again the crane began to hoist. Slowly, the front wheels rose above the pavement. Out of the corner of his mouth Regan murmured to no one in particular: "Drop her now, and we'll all be playing *Hail to the Chief* on harps!"

Two welders, their shoes removed, cautiously mounted the running boards of the armored truck, draped themselves on the fenders and paused to light and adjust the oxygen flow to their torches.

All was ready. Earlier the welders had burned a hole in the floor of the truck to drain out the water and had cut the cross brace between the front wheels. The mattresses had been heaped beneath and a half dozen soldiers were ranged along each side of the truck, grasping the body and frame, holding it steady. The engine hood had been raised and when the men reached down into the motor cavity, it appeared that they were being swallowed by some enormous crocodilian creature.

Coordinating their movements, the welders plunged waist-deep. In seconds, a sputtering white light flared as their torches ate through the rear engine brackets. Molten metal dripped to a mattress and a fireman played water on it. The welders surfaced, squirmed forward and again leaned down into the engine cavity. Over the hum of the generators a muffled countdown could be heard: "Five . . . four . . . three . . . two . . . one . . . *now!*" and the shuddering light of the torches flared again.

There was a grinding screech of tortured metal and the motor and driveshaft plummeted to the mattresses. The weight gone, the truck reared, fighting the restraining hands like an unbroken bronco. One of the welders slid into the cavity where the motor had been and began a cut in the fire wall. The torch gouged through the thin steel as a sculpting tool through clay. In minutes, a roughly rectangular hole had been opened into the interior of the truck.

As the welder stepped back, struggling to keep his footing on the greasy surface of the motor, Jim McCurdy swung down in front of him, inserted his arms and then his shoulders through the opening and wriggled through. A pair of heavy-duty metal cutters was passed to him.

For agonizing seconds there was no sound from within the truck and no sign of movement other than the intimations of activity communicated to the men holding the truck steady. Then a pair of stockinged feet appeared at the hole and the President of the United States was hauled unceremoniously into sight.

In a wild scramble, everyone piled into the two smaller tow trucks and they roared off to the perimeter of the square. Police and soldiers raised a small cheer as the trucks skidded to a stop and the President, dirty, unshaved and disheveled, climbed down. Hands outstretched, he walked toward Gerry Regan as he leaped from the other tow truck.

"Gerry," he said, "I don't know how I can begin to . . . ."

Regan grasped him by an upper arm and propelled him to the Command car. He jerked the door open, gave him a shove, slammed the door and slapped the roof with his palm. Tires spun and the limousine sped away.

Regan arched his back, squinting, trying to decipher the lights almost directly above him. As he looked, they changed to read 11:58. He seized a bullhorn from a police officer.

"Everybody take cover!" he bellowed. "Let's get the hell out of here!"

At the center of Times Square, the armored truck stood alone like a dying animal frozen on film — its jaws agape, rearing, its entrails on the sodden mattresses. The only sound was the rush of wind and the muffled hum of generators from the abandoned television mobile units, their cameras locked in focus on the truck. The only movement was a ruffling of the surface of the pools of water on the pavement and the solemn procession of the numerals 11:59 across the face of the Allied Chemical building.

They changed to 12:00. Thirty-seven seconds later the armored truck disintegrated. Around the world, millions of television screens went blank. The following day, pieces of the truck were found as far as half a mile away.

Chapter Twenty

The President, in sport shirt, jacket and slacks, and showing no evidence of the previous day's ordeal, paused in the sunlight at the foot of the ramp leading to Air Force One. Joan had already climbed the stairs and disappeared into the cabin. Jim Rankin and the others who had come to see him off had withdrawn, as had the photographers and the press, and Adam and Ethan Roberts found themselves alone.

Adam reached out and took the Vice-President's hand and shook it warmly. "From all I hear," he said, "you did a hell of a job yesterday."

Ethan shrugged. "It was a rough day all around."

"Yes, but especially for you, and I want you to know that I'm grateful."

"Thank you."

There was an uneasy silence. Adam broke it. "I suppose I should say a word about our conversation Sunday afternoon. I gave it a lot of thought yesterday." He gave a short laugh. "I had the time."

Ethan smiled thinly. "I guess so."

Adam drew a deep breath, almost a sigh. "Tell you the truth, I don't know what to do. It's a sticky problem."

Ethan reached into his jacket pocket and took out a sealed envelope. "Let me make it easier for you," he said, offering it.

"What is it?"

"My resignation."

Adam made no move to take it. "Is that the same envelope you took to the Cabinet meeting yesterday?"

Ethan flushed. "How do you know about that?"

"Jim Walker told me this morning. He said that when it was your turn to vote, you took out an envelope and then put it away again. Was it your resignation?"

"No. I had recorded my vote in advance."

"But changed your mind."

The Vice-President gave a slight nod of his head as though to dismiss the subject.

"You had intended to vote Nay?"

"Yes."

"But you didn't . . . or couldn't."

Ethan made no response and for a long moment Adam studied his face. "I've been thinking about that ever since Jim told me about it, and I have a question for you: Was what you did, voting against your conscience — in effect, voting for mercy rather than justice — was it an act of weakness or of strength?"

Ethan looked at him directly. "I've been thinking about it, too, Mr. President, and to tell you the truth I'm not sure."

Adam sighed. "Neither am I." He took the envelope and put it in his pocket. "And I suppose the decision *I've* got to make is of the same kind. If it's all right with you, I'd like to think it over for a few days."

Ethan nodded and the two men shook hands.

Adam turned, began to mount the stairs and then looked back. "And will you do something for me?" he said. "You think about it, too."

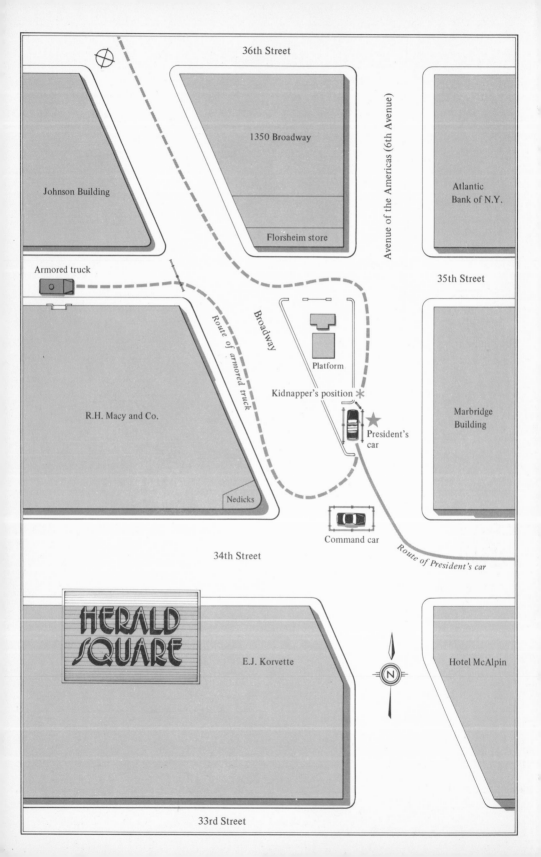